# PRAISE FOR MATTHEW FARRELL

## *Tell Me the Truth*

"The one obvious, immediate truth in this tale of lies upon lies is that Matthew Farrell has crafted a hard-charging, twisty police procedural that literally hits home."

—Lee Goldberg, #1 *New York Times* bestselling author

"Police investigator Susan Adler has her work cut out for her in this exciting suspense novel where everyone is suspect and their deep, dark secrets only complicate matters. This twisty, fast-paced read kept me guessing until the very end!"

—T. R. Ragan, *USA Today* bestselling author

"I won't lie. You will love *Tell Me the Truth*, the audaciously talented Matthew Farrell's latest Adler and Dwyer thriller. Smart. Engaging. Compulsively readable. It's the kind of book that defies you to set it aside."

—Gregg Olsen, #1 *Wall Street Journal* bestselling author

"*Tell Me the Truth* is a fast-paced, well-written thriller. Just when you think you have a handle on what happened, Farrell pulls the rug right out from under you, sending the investigation in a completely different direction. It is a riveting, nonstop thrill ride. Filled with scandalous secrets and lies as well as countless twists and turns, this book will keep you up all night. Farrell is a master storyteller. Don't miss any of his titles!"

—Lisa Regan, *USA Today* and *Wall Street Journal* bestselling author

"Matthew Farrell is an excellent writer with the power to captivate his audience. This is a surprising and intense novel that keeps you guessing until the very end."

—Caroline Mitchell, Amazon Charts bestselling author

## *Don't Ever Forget*

"Farrell keeps you turning the pages."

—*Kirkus Reviews*

"The intricate plot takes many twists and turns. Farrell knows how to keep the pages turning."

—*Publishers Weekly*

"Farrell has done it again! A crime thriller that grabs you from page one. Engrossing, haunting, and compelling, *Don't Ever Forget* is his best yet."

—Liv Constantine, international bestselling author of *The Last Mrs. Parrish*

"Matthew Farrell has done it again. A tense and twisty thriller, *Don't Ever Forget* grabs you by the throat from the first page and does not let go. The result is an edge-of-your-seat, up-all-night read that packs a final punch you won't soon forget. Fantastic!"

—Danielle Girard, *USA Today* bestselling author

"Take a deep breath now, because once you start, you won't get another chance. *Don't Ever Forget* is a twisty, pulse-pounding read from a writer who has quickly established himself as a can't-miss master of thrills."

—Brad Parks, international bestselling author of *Interference*

"Fans of fast-paced thrillers will be engrossed in this propulsive page-turner that expertly delves into memory, crimes of the past, and terrors that haunt us our whole lives."

—Vanessa Lillie, bestselling author of *Little Voices*

"Matthew Farrell's delicious new thriller is definitive crime fiction: propulsive, compulsive, unputdownable, and, oh yes, unforgettable. Get it now."

—Bryan Gruley, author of *Bleak Harbor*

"Matthew Farrell does it again. He's intricately woven together a diabolical and propulsive story of deception with betrayal and madness. *Don't Ever Forget* is engrossing, jarring, and unpredictable. It kept me on my toes as I journeyed with investigator Susan Adler through a wild maze, stopping at nothing to find the truth. An absolutely thrilling adventure."

—A. F. Brady, author of *The Blind* and *Once a Liar*

## *I Know Everything*

"An exciting police procedural . . . The high-energy narrative swerves into surprising and terrifying territory before slamming into its truly chilling finale. Farrell takes the reader down some dark and twisting paths."

—*Publishers Weekly*

"This sinister novel is perfect for suspense junkies who love *Dirty John*."

—Women.com

"Matthew Farrell's skill as a storyteller is evident from the first pages of this novel. He draws readers in, assures them the story will be a typical murder mystery following the usual pattern, then tears up the outline and throws it away."

—New York Journal of Books

"*I Know Everything* takes off like a shot, *with* a shot, and the pulse-pounding pace never lets up. Fans of John Sandford and Lawrence Block will flock to Matthew Farrell!"

—Wendy Corsi Staub, *New York Times* bestselling author

"Dark and constantly surprising, this is a must-read for fans of twisted, intelligent thrillers."

—Mark Edwards, bestselling author of *The Magpies*

"A page-turner from beginning to end. Take a deep breath and hang on—this relentless thriller will keep you guessing until the very last masterful twist."

—Jennifer Hillier, author of *Jar of Hearts*

"Seriously haunting."

—Betches

## *What Have You Done*

"A young crime writer with real talent is a joy to discover, and Matthew Farrell proves he's the real deal in his terrific debut, *What Have You Done*. He explores the dark side of family bonds in this raw, gripping page-turner, with suspense from start to finish. You won't be able to put it down."

—Lisa Scottoline, *New York Times* bestselling author

"A must-read thriller! Intense, suspenseful, and fast paced—I was on the edge of my seat."

—Robert Dugoni, *New York Times* bestselling author

"One hell of a debut thriller. With breakneck pacing and a twisting plot, *What Have You Done* will keep you guessing until its stunning end."

—Eric Rickstad, *New York Times* bestselling author

# TELL ME THE TRUTH

# OTHER TITLES BY MATTHEW FARRELL

*Don't Ever Forget*

*I Know Everything*

*What Have You Done*

# TELL ME THE TRUTH

MATTHEW FARRELL

Published by Thomas & Mercer, Seattle

www.apub.com



ISBN-13: 9781542022613
ISBN-10: 1542022614

Cover design by Micaela Alcaino

Printed in the United States of America

*For Angelo and Marie:*

*Thanks for taking this journey with me. It's been quite a ride.*

# 1

The moment Noel Moore stepped through the front door and put his bags down, the hairs on the back of his neck stood up. It was a couple of hours past midnight, so the house was supposed to be quiet, but on top of that stillness was an unease that told him things were not as he'd left them.

The bottom floor was a maze of interconnecting rooms full of furniture and fixtures that his wife, Mindy, had picked out with their interior designer. He stepped around overstuffed couches and wingback chairs as he wove through the formal living room, then the dining room, the family room, and the kitchen. Nothing seemed out of place in the darkness. Everything appeared as it should have been.

He was conscious of each step he took up the grand staircase and along the hall toward the suite he and Mindy shared. His movements were muffled by the runner that stretched from one end of the second floor to the other. He opened the double doors and crept in.

The room offered only shadowy outlines of things he knew were there. A dresser. A nightstand. Mindy's vanity, tucked in the alcove just outside the sleeping area. Their bed sat in the center of the room, its four oak pillars stretching toward the ceiling. The covers were pushed back. The bed was empty.

Noel craned his neck to listen for something that might tell him where his wife was. The en suite bathroom was dark, but he crossed the room and poked his head in anyway.

"Mindy?" he whispered.

No response.

Noel left the suite and walked down the hall to his son's bedroom. He was familiar with the outlines in this room too. Charlie's oversized drafting desk, which sat under his window. The indoor basketball hoop he'd begged for leading up to his thirteenth birthday. The beanbag chair always leaning against the closet door that wouldn't stay shut. The bed. His boy.

Charlie was a belly sleeper. He was on his stomach with his face peeking out from under the top sheet. His arms were out in front of him like he was flying. Noel could hear him breathing as he slept peacefully. Everything was fine here.

He retreated from Charlie's bedroom and made his way down to the last door at the end of the hall. He turned the knob and pushed into his daughter's room. Jenny had used a night-light since she was three years old, so there was no need to decipher the outlines of anything. In the glow of the small bulb, he could see her dresser, her writing desk, and the wicker swing chair that Noel had masterfully hung from a beam in the ceiling. He could see the antique dollhouse they'd put together one Christmas Eve, probably ten years ago. But most of all, he could see Jenny's empty bed.

"Mindy?"

Movement flashed in Noel's periphery, and he stepped toward the bedroom window. He caught the distant beam of a flashlight bouncing through the woods at the back of the house. As soon as he began to track it, the flashlight went out. Noel pressed his hands against the glass, watching for a few minutes, waiting for the flashlight to come back on, almost willing it to do so. But the area within the thick brush and tall trees remained as black as the night.

He left the room, hurried through the hall, and descended the stairs before barreling out the back patio door, which had been left unlocked. The night was cool for August, but he felt hot as he ran through the yard and into the woods that surrounded the house.

"Mindy?"

As soon as he reached the edge of the yard, he realized he'd forgotten to grab a flashlight himself. Luckily, the moon was full and sat in a cloudless sky, enabling him to navigate through the low-hanging branches of elms and maples. He fought through the thorn bushes that scratched his ankles and shins and dodged the cluster of birch trees just past the old fort Charlie and his friends had built a few summers ago.

"Hello?" he whispered. "Mindy? Who's back here?"

The clearing was just ahead. Noel knew this was where the neighborhood kids met to drink and smoke and hang out. Over the years he'd found piles of discarded beer cans, empty bottles of liquor, and countless cigarette butts, which had been the evidence his wife had needed to get a confession from their then-fourteen-year-old daughter after they'd caught her hiking back to the house at dawn.

Noel stopped running and held his breath to listen. There was no noise. No voices. No whispered laughter. Nothing. He crept toward the clearing, then suddenly heard the crunch of fallen leaves.

"Who's there?" he called. "Answer me."

The footsteps continued toward him.

Noel pushed past the last set of berry bushes. "Whoever is there, I want—"

He stopped as he saw his wife stumbling out of the clearing, catching herself before falling to the ground. She regained her balance and stood, looking at him, her eyes wide with terror. She opened her mouth to speak, but only a low groan emanated from the back of her throat.

Time slowed—then stopped. With the help of the moonlight, Noel could see every detail: The blood on Mindy's face. On her arms. The stains soaked through the T-shirt she always wore to bed. The blood dripping from her fingertips like she'd dipped her hands in paint. He saw the knife she was holding, too, its steel blade trembling in her grip.

"Mindy," Noel choked out. "What happened?"

She tumbled against him, and as soon as her face hit his chest, she began sobbing and screaming, and all he could do was hold her tight to muffle the screams until he could find out what was going on.

He knew they had to stay quiet.

It was important not to wake the neighbors.

# 2

Sobbing in the distance. Short, quick breaths full of pain and sorrow. Someone was calling his mother's name.

*"Mindy. Mindy, talk to me. Honey, please. Tell me what happened."*

It was his father. Even in the realm between consciousness and sleep, Charlie knew that was his father's voice.

*"Mindy. Mindy. Wake up. Hello. Can you hear me?"*

Charlie opened his eyes. The light from the hallway outlined his bedroom door. Quiet finger snapping and subdued claps came from his parents' room next door.

*"Mindy."*

He sat up, listening. His father sounded scared. He was whispering, but it was the tone of his voice that told Charlie something wasn't right.

He flipped the covers off, then stopped when he heard footsteps leave his parents' bedroom, shuffle down the hall, and enter the hallway bathroom. His mom and dad had their own giant bathroom, so he wasn't sure why they were using the one he and Jenny shared. Maybe his mom was sick and needed medicine out of the cabinet behind the mirror? That's where they kept all their meds along with Jenny's gross girl stuff.

The linen closet next to the shower opened, then shut. The footsteps walked back out into the hall and disappeared into his parents' suite.

Charlie climbed out of bed and opened his door. The six sconces lining the hallway were all on, and from where he stood he could see that his parents' bedroom lights were on too. Everything on the second floor looked like it was seven o'clock at night instead of two o'clock in the morning. He was surprised Jenny hadn't woken up with all the noise, but her bedroom was at the far end of the hall, and she was usually a pretty deep sleeper. He'd have to tell her about this—whatever this was—in the morning.

The wool runner in the hall scratched his feet as Charlie inched toward his parents' room. Maybe he could help. He'd taken a first aid class last year and knew a thing or two about treating a fever or a cough. Better still—if his mother was contagious, he might catch something that would keep him home from school for a few days. He'd take anything but the stomach bug. He couldn't handle puking. That was a nonstarter.

Charlie pushed on the bedroom's double doors and stood on the threshold. He stared for about three seconds—three seconds before his father shouted his name, leaped off the bed, and shoved him back out into the hall—but in those three seconds, Charlie saw more than he ever wanted to.

There was blood. So much blood.

On the hardwood floor. On the oversized area rug under the bed. There was spatter on his father's dresser and across the wall closest to his mother's vanity. He could hear the water running in the tub in the en suite bath, which drew his attention to the pile of towels stacked right outside the bathroom door, all of them stained red.

"Get back to bed!" his father's voice thundered, low and growling and full of panic.

As Charlie backed away, he stumbled and lost his balance, falling and hitting the back of his head against the hallway wall. Tears immediately welled in his eyes. He scrambled to his feet. "I was coming to help you. I heard you calling for Mom, and I thought she was sick. I was trying to help."

"I don't need your help. Get in your room! Get in there and don't come out until your alarm goes off for camp. You understand?"

"What's going on?"

"In your room! Go!"

He'd never seen his father like this before. The rage in his voice and the panic in his eyes scared Charlie. He ran to his room, slammed the door closed, and dove into bed. His mind looped the scene over and over again as he tried to make sense of what he'd seen in his parents' bedroom. The blood. His mother looking all dazed and out of it. Why was she covered in blood? What was happening? And where was Jenny? How could she be sleeping through all that noise?

The bedroom door opened, and Charlie pulled the covers up over his head. He shut his eyes tight and bit his bottom lip as footsteps approached and pulled the comforter back down. His father stood over him.

"I'm sorry I yelled," he said. His voice was back to normal now. Calm. Measured. "I didn't mean it."

"Is Mom okay?"

"Mom's fine. Just stay here and let me figure out what's going on. Don't try and think about it, and don't make me answer any questions right now. Forget what you saw. Just stay here and let me take care of it. Deal?"

Charlie could see dried blood on his father's hands and forearms. A few stains on his shirt.

"Deal."

"I'll see you in the morning. We can talk then."

Charlie watched his father leave the bedroom until the door was shut and only the halo from the hallway lights remained.

# 3

Susan Adler pushed the shopping cart down the aisle, searching for inspiration among the multicolored balloons, streamers, party hats, and place settings at her disposal. She was determined to make the twins' birthday party a special one. It had been a long year, one of wicked anniversaries since the Bad Man came into their lives and nightmares became the norm. It had been one of tears and night terrors and uncertainty and the sensation of never really, truly being safe. But as the year had progressed, it had also become one of healing and smiles and playdates and laughter as her twins—especially her son, Tim—had started to get past what had happened the day her work followed her home and had almost taken her family away. She, too, had wondered if she would ever get past it.

Today, though, the question was, What kind of party could she throw for two seven-year-olds whose tastes had begun to diverge? Casey was getting into Barbie, and Tim liked trucks. Casey loved dance and soccer. Tim enjoyed video games and basketball. She tried to think of a theme they could do together but was coming up empty. The store was full of too many choices. It was overwhelming.

"Can I help you find something?"

She turned around to find a middle-aged man standing next to her. His thin frame was overtaken by the large red smock he was wearing. His name tag said DENNIS - MANAGER.

"You can," she said. "I'm throwing my twins a seven-year-old birthday party in a couple of weeks. It's their first party with friends from school, so I thought I'd do a little recon to see what was available."

"Okay," Dennis replied. "Let's start with the basics. What's your theme?"

"That's what I'm struggling with. They're a boy and a girl, so I'm trying to think of something that both kids would like."

They started walking down the aisle as Dennis explained the different themes that were available. Susan followed along, listening, until her phone rang. She held up a finger and checked the caller ID. It was the Cortlandt barracks.

"I have to take this," she said.

"Sure," Dennis replied, waiting.

Susan accepted the call and put the phone up to her ear. "This is Adler."

"It's Triston."

Sergeant Mel Triston was the duty commander for the day shift and had been her temporary partner on her last case. He was one of the good ones, and on the cusp of a well-earned retirement.

"Yeah, Mel. What's up?"

"Barracks up in Lewisboro called. Their investigator is tied up with a hit and run, and they need assistance. You're next on the board."

"What do we have?"

"A homicide. Eighteen-year-old girl. Her mother found her in the woods behind their house this morning. Stabbed. The dad called it in. Lewisboro PD needs an investigator to assist. That's you."

"Okay. Text me the address and have Liam meet me at the scene."

"Ten-four."

Susan disconnected the call and placed her phone back in her bag. "Sorry about that. I'm with the state police, and I just got an assignment."

"No worries," Dennis said. "We'll be here when you're ready. You're off to more exciting things now."

"Let's hope not too exciting," Susan replied. "I have a party to plan."

# 4

"Charlie!"

The morning sun poured through Charlie's windows. Another beautiful summer day. He sat up in bed and snatched his phone from his nightstand to turn off the alarm and check his Instagram account. Last night's post had gotten an insane amount of likes, which made him smile. Then he frowned and began scrolling through, making sure his streams were still active. That was important.

"Charlie! Come down here!"

He froze when he heard his father's voice. Everything from the night before came rushing back.

The whispers that had woken him.

His mother's distant, vacant stare.

His father's panicked rage.

The blood.

Charlie dropped his phone on his nightstand, hopped out of bed, and hurried to his door.

"Buddy! You up?"

The second floor was still. Empty. Charlie made his way down the hall and turned into the bathroom. The linen closet was shut, and everything appeared as it should have. No mess. He took a second to use the toilet, then tiptoed toward his parents' room.

The double doors to his mom and dad's suite were open. Charlie poked his head around the corner, and his mouth dropped. He couldn't believe what he was seeing. The same warm sunlight that had been streaming in through his bedroom windows illuminated his parents' room, making the entire space glow. The room itself was immaculate. The sheets and comforter had been changed. The blood that had been on the dresser and spattered on the wall was gone. The area rug that had been under the bed had disappeared, and the hardwood floor was spotless. The space smelled fresh, like vanilla or cookies.

He walked farther inside and glanced toward the bathroom. There were no bloody towels piled next to the door. The bathroom was gleaming. The bedroom looked like it always looked.

Had he been having a nightmare?

Charlie reached behind him and felt the lump on the back of his head from when he'd slammed it against the hallway wall. Sure, it was possible he could've gotten the bump some other way while he was sleeping, but it had seemed so real. It had to have happened. He wasn't crazy.

The house was unnervingly quiet. On any other morning, his father would be yelling goodbyes, worried that he would miss his train into the city. His mother would be shouting for him to come down and eat before his camp bus came, and Jenny would be either complaining she had nothing to wear or fighting with their mother about something stupid like using too much gas during the week or spending too much money instead of saving it for school. The noise and chaos would continue as they scarfed their breakfasts and ran out of the house so he could catch the camp bus and Jen could meet up with her friends. There was none of that this morning, and that scared him the most.

"Charlie!"

"I'm coming!"

Charlie left his parents' bedroom and walked down to the end of the hall where Jenny's room was. He opened without knocking, hoping to catch his sister doing her hair so she would yell at him and he would give her the finger and things would be normal again. Instead, he found the room empty. Bed unmade. Book bag still in the corner next to the vanity. No Jen.

Charlie ran downstairs and into the kitchen. That room was also empty when it shouldn't have been. He saw his father sitting on the couch in the family room.

"Hey, Dad."

His father looked at him as he approached. His eyes were glassy, like he'd been crying, but Charlie had never known his father to cry. Not even when they watched *ET* or *This Is Us*. He was a man of steel. Why would he be crying now?

"What's wrong?"

Charlie hadn't seen his mother on the love seat until he was all the way in the room. She was looking out the sliding glass doors toward the backyard and surrounding woods. She had that vacant look again, sitting completely still, legs together, back straight, unmoving. Just staring. She was clean too. No blood on her hands or arms or face like he'd seen last night. She wasn't in the oversized T-shirt she always wore to sleep in and instead had on a blue silk nightgown that went all the way down to her ankles. Her hair was clean and pulled back in a ponytail.

"Come here," his father said.

Charlie walked toward his father. The specks of blood that had been on his hands and forearms the night before weren't there.

"What's going on?" he asked. "Where's Jen?"

A single tear broke free and slipped down his father's cheek. "Something's happened," he said in a choked whisper. "The police are on the way. They're going to want to talk to you. Don't be afraid. Everything's going to be okay."

"What happened?" He looked between his mother and father as panic started setting in. "Tell me. Where's Jen? She's not in her room. Where is she?"

"They're going to ask you if you saw anything last night. They're going to want to know if you woke up at any point during the night.

Like, maybe to go to the bathroom, or they might ask if a noise woke you. Something like that."

"Okay."

"What are you going to tell them?"

Charlie opened his mouth to answer, then stopped. He stared at his father, who was locked in on him. He could feel the tension and sadness and overwhelming weight of grief between them. The room was suffocating.

"I'm going to tell them I was sleeping," he whispered more to himself than his father. "I never woke up until you called me this morning. And I never heard anything."

His father did his best to smile as another tear broke loose. "That's good," he said. "That's my boy. Now, come sit."

# 5

The Moore residence was on the east side of Lewisboro, just off Elmwood Road, on Hillcrest Court. The beautiful cul-de-sac was tucked away from the main roads and held four other houses on its meticulously manicured swath of land, a mixture of high-end residential living and untamed forest. Each house was slightly different, but the overall aesthetic screamed serious wealth and success.

Liam Dwyer sat in his car, looking up at the multitiered modern-day colonial with angled roofs and three separate brick chimneys. His breath came in short bursts as his stomach tied itself in knots. This was the first time he'd be walking onto an active crime scene since he'd been a forensics specialist in Philadelphia three years earlier. The memory of the Kerri Miller case was still as fresh in his mind as it was the day he entered the Tiger Hotel and found himself accused of murder. He'd almost died in the process of proving his innocence, but in the end, the people responsible were caught and his life was given back to him. He'd met Susan when she was bringing her son to a child psychologist in Philadelphia who happened to be on the same floor where his doctor was. They'd struck up a friendship, and after he'd assisted on an investigation involving a series of cold cases and a missing elderly man, she'd offered him a temporary position as a consultant with the New York State Police. Before he could change his mind, he agreed, packed his bags, moved into the hotel the department had rented for him in White Plains, and was now about to embark on his first case after several months of vetting and training. He was still, and always would be, a forensic scientist. But today he was learning to be an investigator as well. He stared at his hands gripping the steering wheel and laughed at his nervousness. He'd been the new guy before. He could do it again.

Susan waved and walked toward his car. She was wearing a pair of black slacks and a white blouse, her shield sitting on her belt, her side-arm snug in her shoulder holster. Her hair was pulled back in a ponytail, and there was a professional aura of determination that he'd noticed she always put on when she was working. She looked good, but that was nothing new. It didn't matter if Susan was working a case or hanging out in the waiting room at the psych unit in Jefferson Hospital. Liam could feel his heart flutter just a bit as she approached.

"Glad you could make it," she said.

Liam opened the car door and climbed out. The morning sun was halfway up the sky now, and the summer heat was already taking hold. He smiled and tapped his leather bag as he slung it over his shoulder. "Wouldn't miss my first case. As soon as Mel called, I was on the road. I didn't realize the state police assisted where a town already has a police department."

"The Lewisboro PD only has twelve officers," Susan replied. "We help cover their jurisdiction, and when cases pop up, we typically are the ones who have investigators to spare. We also have access to forensics and county medical examiners, so it works out. This is the first time I've been assigned here, though." She looked him up and down. "Nervous?"

"Excited."

"Good. Let go see what we got."

He followed her toward the giant house. Wraparound porch. Three-car garage. Wood siding with copper gutters lining the edge of each overhang. He figured the taxes alone must be forty or fifty thousand a year, and the team of landscapers needed to maintain the grounds probably cost as much as the cleaning crew that was needed for the interior. That plus the utilities it took to keep the place running, and the total sum was undoubtedly more money than he'd ever make in a year. But that was life in communities like these. They had them outside of Philly too. It was a life he'd never know and really never cared to.

They walked under the barrier tape that blocked off the road in front of the house and stretched to both sides of the property. Three Lewisboro police cruisers, one state police cruiser, and an ambulance were parked in the driveway. A forensics van was next to where Susan and Liam had parked. It was oddly quiet. No shouts of instruction or sirens or radios crackling.

They followed a stone path around back, and when they turned the corner, they came upon the scene. More tape stretched into the yard and cut off the neighbors on both sides. Police officers and state troopers walked in and out of the woods and milled about the in-ground pool area and back patio. A woman in uniform broke away and approached them.

"You state police?" she asked.

Susan nodded. "I'm Susan Adler. Investigator out of the Cortlandt barracks. This is Liam Dwyer. He's a consultant for our troop and a crime scene expert."

The woman was all business. Red hair in a tight bun, green steely eyes, forties, fit. She was pretty without any makeup and looked them up and down before extending her hand. "Christine Dunes. I'm the sergeant in charge."

They all shook.

"Thanks for coming," Dunes said as she followed their gazes across the property. "We don't see a lot of homicides in Lewisboro."

"Happy to help in any way we can," Susan replied.

"What're we looking at?" Liam asked.

"Jennifer Moore. Eighteen. Found by her mother this morning in a clearing about a hundred yards back there. The father called it in. Stabbed in the chest and stomach area. We cordoned off the scene. The ground is still a little muddy from the rain we've been having, so there could be footprints. We stayed away as best we could until forensics came. We didn't want to disrupt anything you guys might be able to find."

"I appreciate the forethought," Susan said.

Dunes nodded. "Not a problem."

Susan put on her latex gloves and motioned them both toward the woods. "Okay, let's have a look."

---

Jennifer Moore had been a beautiful girl. She had an athletic frame, thin but toned. Her hair was long and curly. Dirty blonde. Her lips, full. Now there was just the slaughter.

Her body was lying faceup. Eyes closed. Arms out to their sides. Left leg bent and folded under the right. She was dressed in a plain white T-shirt and a pair of pink mesh shorts. She'd been wearing flip-flops, but her feet were bare now, the flops themselves off to the edge of the kill site. Her entire torso was covered in blood, down to the tops of her hips and the sides of her stomach. There were two deep cuts in her chest that looked to be about four inches long. Blood had splashed up onto her face. It was a mess.

"This is how the mom found her," Dunes explained.

Liam looked at the scene before him as flashes of the Tiger Hotel popped into his mind. Kerri's body hanging from the orange extension cord. The blood pooled at her feet. The smell of the place. It came back in a wave so strong it almost knocked him off his feet.

"You okay?"

He looked away and saw Susan staring at him. The concern on her face said all it needed to. He quickly gathered himself.

"I'm fine," Liam said. He cleared his throat, shut his eyes for a moment, then took in the scene again, his breath steady and slow. There were disturbances around the body. Trampled bushes. Snapped branches. "Did the mother touch anything?"

"Not sure," Dunes replied.

"What did she say?"

"Nothing. She's in shock. Hasn't said much other than mumbling." Dunes moved out of the way as one of the forensic guys began snapping pictures. "We've been getting all the information from the husband, and he said she came in the house screaming to call 911, then went into shock. She's almost catatonic."

"Catatonic?" Susan turned and looked at the sergeant. "Is that a real thing?"

"Google said it is. Had to look it up myself."

John Chu, the state police's lead forensic specialist, was huddled over the body, placing soil samples into a plastic container. He stood up when he saw them. "Hey, Susan. Liam."

Liam waved. "Find anything?"

"Not really. Stabbed three times. Two in the chest, one in the stomach. Not sure which one killed her or if it was just the blood loss. We'll know more when we get her back to the ME for a full examination and autopsy."

"Any defensive wounds?" Susan asked.

"None that I can see out here, but we'll check again once we get her cleaned up. We're also going to take samples of all this brush that has been broken or stepped on, and we'll scan the area once the body is moved to see if we can find anything that might've been discarded."

"You're going to find more than you want," Dunes chimed in. "This clearing here is where kids come to drink and hang out. They don't bring trash bags with them."

Chu nodded. "It's okay. We'll do what we do."

"Anything else at this point?" Susan asked.

"No," Chu replied. "After I'm done here, I have to take samples from the family. I'll call you later and give you my summary."

"Sounds good."

Susan, Liam, and Sergeant Dunes broke away from the body and began retracing their steps back through the woods toward the house, following the same path the officers had made. Liam felt himself calming. Even after three years away from the job, old habits began to percolate, and an analytical mind that had lain dormant for too long started to awaken.

"No defensive wounds tells me she never saw the attack coming," he said. "If someone was coming at you with a knife, you'd throw your hands up instinctively."

"Agreed," Susan replied. "It was dark. She could've been down before she even knew what was happening."

"How popular is that spot for kids?" Liam asked.

Dunes hopped over a fallen birch. "It's not like the entire high school has bonfires there, but it's a pretty regular spot for the kids who live out this way. Especially in the summer. This area is on the outskirts of town, so it's kind of like a satellite hangout."

"How many would you say come by on a regular basis?"

"Fifteen? Twenty?"

"You think you can get me names?" Susan asked.

"I can certainly try."

They walked in silence until they got back to the yard. Liam could see a cluster of people standing on the other side of the police tape, taking pictures and videos with their phones. They hadn't been there when he arrived, which meant word was beginning to spread. A full-blown police response was unusual in sleepy, affluent places like this, and the neighbors would want to know what was going on. The press would be next.

A young girl at the edge of the cluster caught his eye, and Liam stopped. She looked to be around the same age as Jennifer and was visibly upset. Even from where he stood, Liam could see the mascara running down the girl's cheeks as she hopped up and down, pleading with one of the officers to be let in. Her body language told him she knew the Moores or Jennifer specifically. No one else in the street was reacting with such passion.

He motioned to get Susan's attention. "You see that girl there?" he asked, pointing.

She nodded.

"We should find out who she is. I think she could be a family member or friend of the family. She's really carrying on."

"I'll get an officer on it."

They made their way toward Sergeant Dunes, who was waiting on the stone patio that led into the house.

"You ready?" Dunes asked.

"I am," Susan replied as she took one last look around the yard. "Liam?"

Liam nodded. "Yup. Let's go meet Mom and Dad."

# 6

Charlie was sitting on the couch in the formal living room. His father was seated on one of the two overstuffed armchairs next to the fireplace. His mother sat in the other one. No one spoke. Police officers came in and out of the house, sometimes asking his father something about locks on the doors or where the alarm pads were located, but most of the time just passing by without saying anything.

Jen was dead. Her body was in the woods in the back. His father had told him what happened earlier and explained how things would go. So far, he'd been right. The police had arrived. Then more police. Then the crime scene guys, who were like scientists. A few questions from the officers who first came. A few more from the lady sergeant. Charlie had given his answers as best he could, hoping they couldn't tell he was lying. He didn't talk about waking up the night before and seeing the blood and the panic and carnage overtaking his parents' bedroom. And he definitely didn't mention the other thing. The thing even his parents weren't aware of. The thing that made his stomach hurt and the tears come, even when he thought there were no more tears to cry.

Throughout all of it, his father's instructions echoed in the back of his mind.

*Don't talk about it.*

*Forget what you saw.*

*They're going to want to know if you woke up at any point during the night.*

*I'm going to tell them I was sleeping,* Charlie had replied.

*That's good. That's my boy.*

But why didn't his mother move? She still had that same vacant stare she'd had the night before when he walked into their bedroom, but she seemed to have gotten worse. She just sat in the chair, head leaning to the side, looking straight ahead, a quilt draped over her legs. It was the middle of the summer. Why did she need a blanket when it was ninety degrees out?

Sergeant Dunes, who'd questioned them earlier, walked into the living room with a man and a woman behind her. Charlie's father rose from his seat.

"Mr. Moore, this is Investigator Adler of the New York State Police and their crime scene consultant, Liam Dwyer. The state police will be assisting us in this investigation, and Investigator Adler wanted to walk through everything with you."

His father nodded, chewing incessantly on his thumbnail. "Of course."

Investigator Adler sat on the couch with Charlie while the man remained standing. Charlie could feel himself stiffen, certain they'd discovered he'd been lying, and now they would arrest him and force him to confess to what he saw the night before. And what he'd *done*.

His father sat back down on the chair as Investigator Adler took out a notepad from her bag. She smiled at Charlie before turning her attention to his parents.

"Before we get started," she began, "I just wanted to let you know how sorry I am for your loss."

His father nodded again, chewing on his nail, his knee bouncing up and down. "Thank you."

"I'm going to have to ask you some questions. Some of them might be difficult to answer or could touch a nerve, but they're important or I wouldn't be asking them. We need to know everything so we can start putting the pieces of this puzzle together."

"Okay."

"I'm sure I'll be asking things you've already covered. Just bear with me while we go through them again. I need to hear directly from you."

"I understand."

Sergeant Dunes was called out into the hallway by one of the officers.

Investigator Adler opened her pad and leaned forward. "Tell me about what happened this morning."

His father brushed his hair back and let out a sigh. His hands were shaking, his eyes glassy with tears. "I was away for three days visiting a client in Florida. I got in this morning about two and went to sleep. Mindy and I woke up, came down for breakfast, and the kids weren't around. It wasn't unusual for Charlie not to be up yet. The camp bus is later than his school bus. But we usually see Jen, so when she wasn't downstairs, I went to check on her in her room. She wasn't there, either, so we figured she went for a run. She does that sometimes. There's a jogging trail that you can pick up in the woods, and it eventually connects you to a walking path. Mindy went out to see if she could spot her coming in because they had planned to go shopping for school. She was leaving for Duke in two weeks. Next thing I know, Mindy comes back in the house screaming for me to call 911 and that Jen was dead."

"Did you go out and see for yourself?"

"Yes. I called 911 and then ran to the woods. I was only there for a few seconds, though. As soon as I saw the blood . . . I . . . I turned back and waited for the police to arrive. I couldn't stay."

"Jennifer had a white T-shirt and pink shorts on," the investigator said. "We also found flip-flops at the scene. I don't think she went jogging."

Charlie's father shook his head. "No. That's what she sleeps in."

"Did you check on the kids before you went to sleep?"

"No. It was late. I just crashed."

"So you're not sure if Jennifer was in bed or already gone when you got home."

"No, I'm not sure."

"Any idea why she'd leave the house at night like that?"

"No idea."

More notes.

"Who were you seeing in Florida?"

"Uriah Sitchel. He's a client. My partner and I run a boutique investment firm for high–net worth investors. Uriah's been with us for a while now. He lives on Sanibel Island."

"And he can vouch you were there."

"Of course. I have receipts from my plane ticket too."

"What's your partner's name?"

"Arthur Breen."

"Name of your firm?"

"Phoenix Capital. Nothing big. Artie and I are the managing partners, and we have a small staff of admin, compliance, and a few young kids out of college."

The investigator stopped writing. "Had Jennifer been fighting with anyone recently?" she asked. "Any enemies? Boys she broke up with? A current boyfriend? Online bullying? Anything like that?"

"Not that I know of."

"Would your wife know?"

They all turned to look at his mother, who remained in the overstuffed chair, looking out toward the yard and the woods, her eyes seeing nothing.

"Honey," his father said as he reached over and touched Charlie's mother. "Mindy, can you answer the investigator's question?"

His mother closed her eyes and shook her head as more tears slipped down her cheeks.

"She's been like this since she came back. I guess it's shock? I don't know what to do."

"It's okay," the investigator replied. "Does Jennifer have a job?"

"No. It was her last summer before college, so we said it was okay for her to relax. She's a good kid. I have no idea who could've done this."

His voice trailed off, and Charlie saw tears well in his father's eyes. He quickly wiped them away, his leg still bouncing. Charlie wanted so badly to rush across the room and hug his father and tell him everything was going to be okay. He wanted to apologize for what he did and try and explain that he didn't mean for any of this to happen, but instead, he sat on the couch, a coward whose secrets would stay with him because he was too chicken to fess up and face the consequences.

"I'm going to need a list of Jennifer's friends, and we need to find out if she had a boyfriend," the investigator said.

"I'll do my best."

The man who had come in with Investigator Adler peeled away from the living room and walked down the hall, where he disappeared with another officer.

"I understand the place in the woods where you found Jennifer is a hangout spot for the kids around here," Investigator Adler continued. "Sneak some beers? Smoke a joint? That kind of thing?"

"Yes," his father replied. "That's my understanding."

"Does Jennifer hang out there too?"

"I'm not sure. I work a lot, so I'm not around as much. My wife would know."

"Is sneaking out of the house something you can see Jennifer doing?"

"Not really. There's no need to sneak around. She was pretty open with us. Jen was an honors student. Number eight in her class. She went out and had fun and went to parties with her friends like all kids her age do, but there was no need to sneak out. She'd usually just tell us where she was going."

"Except for last night?"

His father shrugged. "I don't know what to make of that."

"Any kids in the neighborhood that you can think of who might have a certain intensity to them? Anger issues? Compulsion issues? Things like that."

"I have no idea."

The investigator turned to Charlie and smiled. All he saw were the jaws of a predator, ready to pounce on its weak and cornered prey.

"You must be Charlie."

He nodded and felt his stomach clench.

"I'm sure this is all a bit much for you. Overwhelming, right?"

He nodded again.

"I'm sorry for that. We won't be here much longer." She swung her body toward him so they were facing each other. "Did you hear anything last night or early this morning? Did you hear your sister walking around? Anything that wasn't normal?"

Charlie looked at his father, who was staring back at him. His father's words echoed in his head again.

*They're going to want to know if you woke up at any point during the night.*

*I'm going to tell them I was sleeping.*

*That's good. That's my boy.*

"No, I didn't hear anything." Charlie's voice shook as he spoke, and he wondered if the investigator could tell he was lying. "When I came down this morning, my dad told me what happened and that Jenny died. Then all the police came."

"And you didn't hear anything unusual last night or early this morning?"

"No."

"Any idea what your sister might've been doing in the woods?"

Before Charlie could answer, the front door slammed open, and there was some kind of commotion involving the officers who'd been stationed in the foyer. Voices were raised, then ceased, followed by footsteps that quickly clicked down the hall to the living room.

"Everyone stop what you're doing *right now*."

The woman standing there was tall, thin, blonde, and looked to be somewhere around his mom's age. Her skin was smooth and tan, and her blue eyes fixed on the investigator. Charlie held his breath as the mood in the room suddenly tensed up.

"Can I help you?" the investigator asked.

"You're damn right you can. I'm Charlotte Walsh, a partner at Agnew, Polaris, and Walsh, and Mr. Moore's attorney."

"I see. Well, we were—"

"I don't care what you were doing," Charlotte Walsh snapped. "We're done here." She pointed a finger at Charlie's father. "Noel, don't say another word to these people."

His father held out his hands. "It's okay. We were going over what happened."

"It's definitely *not* okay. You don't say anything else." She looked back toward the investigator. "Why are you in the house? The crime scene is outside."

"The crime scene is where we determine it is," Investigator Adler replied. "And we need to retrace the victim's steps before she went outside. Mr. Moore gave us consent."

It was clear the attorney wanted to say something else, but instead, she turned back to Charlie's father. "You didn't have to give consent. They have no right to be in here if you don't want them inside."

"It's okay. We need to find out what happened."

"Then I suggest you let them do their job and you stay quiet. These people will take your words and twist them to make you look guilty, and no client of mine is going down that road."

The man who'd come in with Investigator Adler reentered the living room. "Susan, can I see you for a sec?" he asked.

Investigator Adler got up from the couch.

"Yes, good. Go," Charlotte Walsh barked. "I suggest you wrap this up quickly and leave. Any further access to these grounds will require a warrant. We're done here."

Charlie stared at the scene and couldn't believe what he was seeing. The attorney had come in and stopped the police cold. It was like they were powerless against her. He looked at his father and noticed his leg had stopped shaking.

Investigator Adler started to leave, but she stopped when she reached the hall. "Mr. Moore, I'd like to see your daughter's bedroom, if that's okay. I could get a warrant if that's what you want, but with time being of the essence and all, I suggest you allow us to conclude our initial investigation."

"No deal," the lawyer lady replied. "Get me a warrant or get out."

His father looked at the lawyer. "It's okay, Charlotte. We need to find out what happened."

"They can find out what happened *outside* where the crime scene is."

His father looked back at the investigator and shrugged. Investigator Adler nodded and disappeared down the hall with the man she'd come in with. As soon as they were gone, Charlotte Walsh rushed into the living room and knelt down in front of Charlie's father, whispering her condolences and rubbing his hand. His father listened as she spoke, nodding his understanding, breaking down for a moment, then going over what he'd already told them. When they were done, the attorney stood up and went over to his mother, where she knelt down with the same whispers of instruction and sympathy. His mother gave no reaction except the tears that slipped down her face. That was the best she could offer.

Charlie looked on, helpless and scared, as his father leaned back in his chair, stared up at the ceiling, and exhaled a deep breath that was shaky and full of hurt. He began to cry, and it was at that moment that Charlie knew all of it—the police, the crime scene, the sorrow that had swept over the house like a remorseless tidal wave—was his fault, his doing. But it was also his secret.

A secret he knew he had to keep as if his life depended on it.

# 7

The inside of the house was even more impressive than the grounds. Coffered ceilings, built-in bookcases, handcrafted wainscoting. Liam led Susan into a grand foyer with mahogany walls and marble floors. A lavish sweeping staircase was the room's centerpiece.

"Who's the woman?" he asked, nodding back toward the living room.

"Charlotte Walsh. Partner at Agnew, Polaris, and Walsh. They're a prestigious firm that specializes in criminal defense for wealthy clients and white-collar crimes. Very influential in political circles, which is always a pain in the ass for us. They have offices on Manhattan and in Miami, Chicago, and Los Angeles. They're good, which means getting anything from the Moore family will be close to impossible from this point on."

"Not sure why she's taking such an aggressive approach. We have no suspects, and we're not pointing fingers. She's trying to shut us down before we can even figure out what happened."

"She's on the offensive," Susan replied. "That's what the good lawyers do. Shut it down before we have a chance to draw any conclusions. Happens all the time. She'll instruct the Moores not to talk to us unless we charge them with a crime, so we'll need to conduct this investigation knowing we get zero input from them."

Liam stopped next to one of the two hand-carved banisters. "I want to go over something with you in case I misunderstood."

"Okay."

"The report the responding officers took said Mrs. Moore went out the back door near the family room to look for Jennifer."

"Right."

"And she came back in the same door."

"Correct."

"And no one touched the body."

"That's what the report says."

Liam pointed to a small area on the base of the banister. "While you were in there, I was poking around down here and came across this."

Susan bent down and took her phone out, then turned on the flashlight app.

"It's blood," Liam explained. "Two drops. Dry, but unmistakably blood."

"Any idea how old?"

"Looks to be consistent with last night or early this morning. There's still a bit of tackiness to it."

"So if no one touched anything outside, why would there be blood in the house?"

"Exactly."

"Did we get a picture?"

"Yeah, I had one of the techs take a shot of it."

"You see anything else?"

"No. That was it."

"Okay." Susan stood back up. "I'll have John grab a sample, and we'll see if we can get a match to Jennifer. In the meantime, let's go see her bedroom."

"I thought the lawyer said no access."

Susan crinkled her face. "Did she? I don't recall hearing that."

They walked up to the top of the stairs and turned left. The door at the end of the hall was open. Liam followed Susan inside. It was a typical teenage girl's room. The color on the walls was a more mature teal instead of the pink you'd expect from someone younger. The bed, dresser, nightstand, and writing desk were all white with matching details in the woods and the same glass hardware. It had clearly been a set, and an expensive one, judging from the quality of the craftsmanship. A wicker chair hung from the ceiling with a purple cushion and blue pillow tucked inside. Cute. An antique dollhouse sat in the corner, the last remnants of Jennifer Moore as a child.

The bed was unmade, the blankets and sheet flipped back. Liam remained in the doorway while Susan slowly walked around the room. There were a couple of notebooks on the desk from the school year that had just ended and a small pile of office supplies, still wrapped, waiting to be transported to her new college in a few weeks. Such a tragedy.

"You see a phone?" Susan asked.

"No," Liam replied. He pointed to the desk. "Charger is right there, but no phone."

"Remind me to check with John. She might've had it with her at the scene."

Susan opened the closet door and walked in. Liam watched as she dug through the clothes that were hanging on the multitiered racks and checked the shoe shelves that took up an entire back wall. He felt like this was something he should've been doing, and he'd done so in the past as part of a crime scene unit, but he was wary of getting in the way, so he stayed put. She looked under Jennifer's bed and inside each of the desk drawers. Nothing out of the ordinary.

"Anything strike you as odd?" she asked.

"All looks normal to me. It's a kid's room."

"I agree. Let's go."

They made their way back toward the top landing. When they reached a bedroom with closed double doors, Susan stopped and peeked in.

"You're really pushing the envelope on not hearing the lawyer demand a warrant, huh?" Liam said.

"Hold on."

"What is it?"

He walked up behind her as she opened the doors farther.

"You see the line around the bed? The sun faded the hardwood floors, except for the darker area around the bed. The sun didn't have a chance to fade that."

"They had a rug there."

"A rug that looks like it might've recently been removed."

"How recently?"

"That's the question."

They slipped into the room and started looking around. Nothing else was out of the ordinary. Bed was made. Things were neat. Main bathroom was clean.

"You smell that bleach?" Susan asked.

Liam put his hand over his mouth and nose. "Oh yeah. And some stronger vanilla scent trying to cover it up."

"I might have to get that warrant after all. Bleach cleans blood. I don't like that."

"I don't see anything else that stands out."

"Okay. Let's go."

They snuck back down to the first floor and returned to the living room. A woman and a priest were sitting on the couch Susan had just been sitting on. She was in her fifties, blonde, attractive—Liam could see the resemblance to Mindy and Jennifer. Her eyes were red from crying, and she was hugging Charlie against her. The priest looked a little younger, dark hair, dark eyes, charming smile. Charlotte stood in the center of the living room, arms folded across her chest, watching everyone. When she saw Liam and Susan, she pointed to the woman.

"This is Sidney Krittle. She's Mrs. Moore's sister. And this is Father McCall. He's the family's priest. They just arrived."

Susan waved. "Nice to meet both of you."

"Are you done?" Charlotte asked.

Susan nodded and put her notepad back in her bag. "Yes, I think that's all I have for now. Our forensic tech is going to need to swab everyone's cheek and take fingerprints so we can eliminate prints and DNA. Mr. and Mrs. Moore, we're also going to need the shoes you were wearing when you went out into the woods so we can match the treads."

Noel looked at his attorney. "That okay?"

Charlotte nodded. "The police don't need a warrant to collect DNA, and they'll have to eliminate your shoe treads from the scene. It is what it is."

"This is going to be an active crime scene for the next day or so," Susan continued. "We'll get the warrant Ms. Walsh has requested, and then we'll be inside the house and out back. I suggest you find a hotel or somewhere to stay because you can't be here. I'll let you know when we're done."

Sidney Krittle started crying again as she rubbed Charlie's hair. "Please find who did this," she said. "Please. Whatever it takes."

Liam listened as Susan said something reassuring. He thought about the blood on the banister, and the missing carpet in the bedroom, and the faint smell of bleach in the main bath.

Between the story the family was telling and the clues that had been left inside the house, something wasn't right. This case had layers. All the tough ones did.

# 8

Susan and Liam left through the front of the house. As soon as they pulled the door closed, Susan could hear her name being called.

"Investigator Adler! Investigator Adler! Over here!"

A woman was approaching, late twenties, dark hair and dark eyes. A little too much makeup, but it was done with precision, like it was supposed to be too much. A white blouse peeked out of a dark-blue pantsuit. Undoubtedly a reporter. Word had officially gotten out.

The woman scurried across the expansive driveway and stopped at the footpath. "My name is Donna Starr," she said. "Channel twelve news. Can I ask you a few questions?"

"You're inside a police barricade," Susan replied. "You have to get back across the street."

"Can you confirm that Jennifer Moore's body was found in the woods behind her house this morning?"

"I have no comment. This is an open investigation."

Susan walked past the reporter, and she stepped in front of Liam.

"We have reports that the victim was stabbed several times. We understand the mother found her and is now in such a state of shock that she herself is unresponsive."

Liam put up his hands. "I have no comment either."

"We're leading with this story in an hour. This is your chance to correct any information I've been given that might've been wrong."

Susan climbed into her car and shut the door. She watched as Liam did the same. It was amazing how much information Donna Starr had gotten in such a short period of time. Susan wasn't sure how many of the uniformed officers knew the details of what was going on, but it wasn't uncommon for someone to leak something to the press for a quick fifteen minutes of fame or for a favor that could be called in later. This was the type of case that could spin out of control in the hands of the media, and with a high-priced attorney representing the family, it would be even more important to keep a lid on things until they knew what they were dealing with.

Sometimes that was easier said than done.

---

By early afternoon, Jennifer Moore's body had been removed from the scene and transferred to the medical examiner's office. The crowd that had been no more than a few neighbors curious to see what was going on had grown to almost fifty people. The onlookers took up both sides of the street, forcing the Lewisboro Police Department to call in extra officers to patrol the perimeter. Once the Moores and all official personnel were cleared out, a patrol car was left behind to babysit the area. The police tape remained stretched in front of the house, in the backyard, and farther into the woods. No one was allowed anywhere near the scene.

Susan and Liam walked onto the investigator's unit at the Cortlandt barracks and crossed the floor. Susan put her bag down on her desk and watched as Liam slid into her former partner's chair. Normally when someone sat in that seat, she felt a pit in her stomach and instantly flashed back to Tommy Corolla and the harm he'd done to her family. But there was none of that baggage with her new partner. In fact, it somehow felt right looking at Liam across from her.

"You good?" Susan asked, looking at Liam, smiling. "First case with me and all."

"I'm great," Liam replied. "It's nice to be back working on something. After the James Darville case, I was anxious to jump back in on a more regular basis. Plus, I was never really on this side of the investigation. It's different from forensics. Should be interesting."

"Good. And now you can assist me in briefing Crosby. Come on."

Susan took her notepad and Liam grabbed his bag. They walked to the other end of the unit and into Crosby's office.

Senior Investigator Jasper Crosby was sitting behind his desk talking on the phone when they entered. He motioned for them to sit, and they did. Crosby's large frame took up most of the office. He was a former college football player and a well-respected supervisor. He was also Susan's mentor and one of her best friends.

Crosby hung up the phone and sighed, rubbing his bald head. "We got the go-ahead on Getty Square."

"For the drug raid?" Susan said. "That's great."

"That was the mayor of Yonkers. He wants a photo op and press conference if we make the bust. It's bad mojo putting the cart before the horse like that, and I don't like it. I told him I'd call him when it was over." Crosby shuffled through a small stack of folders, coming away with one that was close to the bottom. "Give me the quick and dirty on the Lewisboro scene."

Susan opened her notepad. "We'll be running lead and working out of their local police headquarters. The barracks over there has no extra room."

"Okay."

"Our vic is eighteen-year-old Jennifer Moore. Found in the woods by her mother this morning. Stabbed in the chest and stomach. We were in the middle of interviewing the father and son when counsel showed up and ordered the family to stop cooperating."

"Who was it?"

"Charlotte Walsh. Agnew, Polaris, and Walsh."

"Big money."

"He looks like he has it."

"Continue."

"Mr. Moore had been visiting a client of his in Florida for the past three days and arrived early this morning. We're tracking down the client for confirmation, but we were given his flight info and ticket receipts. Flight seven-two-five, if you can believe that."

Crosby smiled. "My old shield number when I was on patrol."

"Yup."

"At least you won't have to look it up when you're filing the report. What else?"

"We took swabs, and they packed up for a few nights away from home," Susan said. "We're waiting on a warrant that should come any minute now; then we need John Chu's team to finish sweeping the interior of the house. Charlotte Walsh stopped us in the middle of that. But he's done with the yard and woods in the back where the body was found. We dispatched officers who went door-to-door, stretching out three blocks in all directions. No one saw anything."

"House big?"

"Enormous."

"Alarm system?"

"Yes, but was apparently never set or was deactivated by the victim when she went outside. Mr. Moore can't remember if he shut off the alarm or not when he got home from his trip."

"Cameras?"

"None."

Crosby made a few notes in his folder, then leaned back in his chair and slid his hand over his mustache. "How was Mom and Dad?" he asked. "Calm? Distraught? Freaked out?"

"The dad was pretty calm," Susan said. "Probably in shock. The mom was almost completely unresponsive. An ambulance took her to Putnam Hospital Center for treatment." She glanced at Liam. "Liam and I snuck upstairs before the attorney kicked us all out. Something's not right."

"Talk to me."

"First, Liam found a droplet of blood in the main hallway, and according to Mr. Moore, no one touched anything at the scene in the woods, so why would blood be in the house? Then, when we went upstairs, we noticed a section on Mr. and Mrs. Moore's bedroom floor that wasn't faded from the sun like the rest of it. That unfaded section matched what you would think would be an area rug. But no one found a rug on the premises or in any of the vehicles. It could've been removed years prior and has nothing to do with the case, but it's something I'd like to look into. We could also smell bleach in and around the main bath. The place was spotless, like it had just been cleaned."

"Do we have a TOD?"

"Nothing official. John said sometime early morning. Maybe one or two."

"And when was 911 called?"

"A little after eight."

Crosby sat up in his seat. "Plenty of time to roll a rug and remove it from the property. Clean up, but miss the spot in the hall."

"So you're thinking this could be an inside job?" Susan asked. "A family thing?"

"No necessarily," Crosby replied. "But I don't like the fact that you found blood inside the house, and I don't like that you could smell bleach in the main bath. Not with a rug possibly being removed. Too much to be a coincidence. Keep an eye on it."

Susan and Liam got up from their seats.

"That's the plan," Susan said.

"Next steps?"

"Just the warrant so John's team can get into the house and we can make this bedroom thing official. After that I've got Mr. Moore's partner on my list. Arthur Breen. I want to see what he might know. And there was this girl on scene this morning. Liam noticed her. I had one of the uniforms get me her name and number. Anja York. Supposedly a good friend of the victim's. We'll follow up with her as well."

Crosby's phone began to ring. He snatched the receiver off the base and pointed to both of them. "Play everything cool. We don't know what's what yet, and with the lawyer involved, we don't want any missteps. Work the case. Go where it leads you."

"We will."

"Okay, get out of here. I have a heroin bust to coordinate, and this mayor is putting on the bad mojo every chance he gets."

# 9

The hotel room at the Holiday Inn in Mount Kisco was nice, but tiny. Two beds, a small round table, a desk with a few drawers in it, a dresser with a TV on it, and a bathroom. That was it. They could have afforded a much nicer and roomier place, like the suites they got on vacation in the tropics, but when the police offered to put them up, Charlie's dad simply nodded in agreement, and here they were.

The lone survivors.

The EMTs had taken his mother to the hospital so she could get some rest. At least, that's what they told Charlie. Aunt Sidney and Father McCall had followed the ambulance. Before she left, Aunt Sidney gave him a wet kiss on his forehead and promised him that everything was going to be all right. As she was rubbing his chin, he saw her bottom lip start to quiver, and then she burst into tears, falling into Father McCall's embrace. It was all very dramatic. Charlie had no idea what he was supposed to say and knew he couldn't tell her anything about what happened the night before, so he didn't say anything.

The TV was on in the background, and Charlie and his father both sat at the table nibbling on Chinese food neither of them wanted. The reporter who was outside the house all day was on the screen, live from the corner where Charlie caught the bus each morning during the school year. He could see a few of their neighbors in the background, watching her recount what had happened as Jennifer's school picture from her yearbook suddenly popped up.

*". . . was only weeks away from leaving for Duke University and the promise of the next chapter of her life that lay ahead."*

"How'd they get that picture?" Charlie asked.

"I don't know," his father replied. "The yearbook is probably online. Or maybe one of the neighbors gave it to them."

Charlie rolled a piece of broccoli across his plate, flipping it onto the chicken he would normally be devouring. His father was doing the same with his lo mein.

"I'm not hungry," he said as he pushed his plate away.

His father looked at him. "Me either." He dropped his fork and tried on a smile. "I wanted to tell you how good you did today. I was proud of you."

"I told them I was sleeping."

"I know. And I'm guessing you have some questions you've been wanting to ask. It's okay now. You can ask me."

Charlie looked down at his plate, unsure if the invitation was legit or if it would unleash another panicked rage like he'd encountered the night before.

"I won't get mad," his father said, sensing his trepidation. "Seriously. I know you want to ask me things. Go ahead."

"Okay. Why did you tell the police that Mom found Jenny this morning? I saw you guys last night. I saw what Mom looked like. I saw all the blood."

His father leaned forward in his chair and gently placed his elbows on the table. "I know what you saw, and that's fine. There's no undoing it now. But that needs to be a secret. A very important family secret. You can't tell anyone what you saw. Not even Aunt Sidney or Grandma or Pop-Pop or anyone. This needs to be between you, me, and Mom. That's it. You think you're old enough to handle that?"

"Yeah."

"Good."

"But what did I see?" Charlie asked. "What was going on in your room?"

"A mistake," his father replied. "That's all it was. Just a mistake that I needed to clean up."

"Is that why the rug in the bedroom is gone, and the towels are gone, and the bathroom is, like, superclean?"

"Yes."

"And that's why you lied to the police."

"Yes." His father slid his plate to the side and leaned even closer toward him. Their eyes locked. "If I told the police what happened last night or if you told the police what you saw, they would break this family up. I know that sounds crazy, but it's true. They'd blame us for what happened to your sister, and me or your mom could be taken away. You'd have to leave our house and your school and your friends. I don't want that to happen. I want us to be together. Understand?"

Charlie nodded. "Yeah, I get it."

"I knew you would."

"Can I ask you something else?"

"Sure."

"Did Mom kill Jenny?"

Without warning, his father slammed his hand down on the table, shaking the cartons of food and plastic utensils. A bottle of beer toppled over. What had been a gentle man only seconds before had suddenly transformed into a snarling beast. He stared at Charlie, his nostrils flaring, his eyes filling with tears, breaths coming deep and ragged.

"I never want to hear that question come out of your mouth again. Do you understand me?"

Charlie wanted to stop, but the words seemed to fall out of his mouth. "It's just that I've seen them fight," he continued. "And it's not like normal people having an argument. They used to fight so bad. Yelling and screaming so loud. They used to hit each other. Did you know that?"

"Enough."

"I don't think they liked each other very much."

"Enough!"

The room was silent but for the reporter rambling on in the background.

"You said you wouldn't get mad," Charlie whispered under his breath.

Charlie's father wiped his eyes and got up from the table. "No more questions," he said. "Clean up that mess and put everything outside the door. The hotel staff will take it for us."

Charlie nodded and watched as his father crossed the tiny room and fell onto his bed. Charlie took the containers from the table and tossed them into the larger bag the delivery guy had brought everything in. When he was done, he placed the bag outside in the hall and closed the door.

He could keep a secret. That wouldn't be a problem. He could keep all of them. No one had to know about last night. No one had to know about his mother being covered in blood and his father helping her get cleaned up. And no one had to know about the fights Jen and his mother used to have. The ones that turned violent. The ones where things were thrown and punishments were handed down. He could keep all those secrets.

And he could keep his secret too.

Of that, there was no doubt.

# 10

Susan stopped in the foyer of her house and let the door close behind her. She'd been thinking about the case since she left the barracks, but as she followed the mountain roads of Route 9 that led her home, she began to think about the family that had been affected by Jennifer Moore's murder and how those lives had been changed forever in the blink of an eye. A mother and father suddenly had no daughter. A brother had no sister. As she looked at the spot on the floor where the Bad Man had died nearly two years ago, she couldn't help but think how close she'd come to her own life having been changed irreparably. A mother without children. A daughter without a mother.

She dropped her bag on the bench in the foyer and made her way toward the kitchen. She'd been lucky. The kids were healthy. Her mother too. Her son still usually walked around the house to avoid stepping across the spot on the floor, and he was still seeing Dr. Radcliffe in Philadelphia, but the visits were down to once every three weeks now, and on occasion, Tim sometimes ran over the spot in the foyer without thinking, which showed real progress. The first anniversary of the incident had come and gone, and once Tim knew he could get through it, he began to come out of his shell a bit. Not all the way out, but he was getting there. Baby steps. That's all she could ask for.

She walked into the same kitchen she'd walked into for the last eight years. First as a married woman, then as a new mother, and now as a single mom, divorced, her own mother living with them full time. This hadn't been the life she'd thought she'd end up with, but at the same time, she had no regrets. She was happy, and it had been a while since she was able to say that with a full heart. She'd even found Liam within the chaos of what the Bad Man had left in his wake, and that was something positive.

She could feel the spark between them, thought maybe he felt it, too, but she was reluctant to make that first move. Too much hung in the balance. They'd both been through so much—the Bad Man, her divorce from Eric, what Liam had been through with his ex—and were damaged because of it. She had her family to think about as well as herself. But still, his presence always made her feel better. And maybe one day . . .

"Mommy!"

"Hi, Mommy!"

Casey and Tim were sitting on one side of the kitchen table. Her mother, Beatrice, was sitting on the other. They were working on a jumbo jigsaw puzzle that looked to be about 20 percent complete. The blond tops of the twins' heads were so identical it was hard to tell who was who until they looked up and she saw their round faces, green eyes, and faces full of freckles. They looked like they were getting older each day, and it killed Susan to admit it. With Casey's hair pulled back, Susan could see the hint of the woman her little girl would one day be, and she noticed how Tim's thin lips and square chin always made him look so serious, until he smiled and her baby boy returned.

"Hey, guys! You know, we're going to need this table to eat on one of these days."

The twins jumped off their chairs and came over with hugs and kisses.

"Mommy, this puzzle is five gazillion pieces, and we're going to do it all!" Casey exclaimed. "It's got puppies on it. Black ones and brown ones and white ones too! Can we get a puppy? Can we? For our birthday?"

Before Susan could answer, Tim interrupted.

"It's five hundred pieces, not five gazillion. Gazillion isn't even a real number." He looked at his sister and shook his head, and all Susan saw was his father. "And we can't have a puppy because it'll chase the chickens, and that's not fair. The chickens were here first."

"The puppy doesn't have to go out in the yard where the chickens are."

"Then how're we going to play with it and give it exercise?"

"We can walk it. And we can train it not to chase the chickens. We can train it. We can!"

Susan held up her hands to stop the debate before it got heated. She couldn't deal with an argument at that moment and just wanted to relax for a second. Maybe sip at a glass of wine.

"No puppies," she said. "Maybe some other time."

"But—"

"Maybe some other time."

The twins moped back to their chairs but were soon reabsorbed in working to find pieces that would fit into the part of the puzzle that was already complete.

"How was your day?" Beatrice asked, placing a piece that looked like it was going to be one of the dogs' noses. Her upper arm jiggled a little as she pushed the piece into place. She looked up at her daughter. As always, her round face swallowed her eyes when she smiled, and her jet-black hair somehow made her look younger than she was. "You look beat."

"I'm fine," Susan replied. She opened the pantry and retrieved a bottle of malbec she'd uncorked a few nights earlier. She poured herself a glass and took a nice first gulp. "New case. Just processing everything."

"Is it the one up county? The girl found in the woods?"

"Yeah."

"It's all over the news. I saw some state trooper cars there and was wondering if they got you involved."

"We have a barracks up there, but their investigator was occupied with another case, so we got the call."

"It's big news. NBC and CBS picked up the story from News Twelve."

"Great."

"You wanna join us? We could use some help finding more pieces for the yellow Lab. Might help you take your mind off of today."

"Yeah, Mommy! Help us!"

"You can have my seat."

"No, that's okay," Susan said. "You guys keep working, and I'll get dinner started."

"The steak's been marinating," Beatrice said. "Just preheat the oven, and we'll be good to go."

"Is Liam coming over?" Tim asked.

"No, honey. Liam's at the hotel. He has a lot of homework he needs to do for his training."

She took another sip of her wine, then started pulling pots and pans out of the cabinet next to the pantry. The twins had sensed Liam's kindness from the day they met him and always looked forward to seeing him when they took their trips to Philadelphia. Now that he was in New York, they asked about him coming to dinner almost every night. Their love for him was another reason she had to tread lightly around romantic aspirations. If she screwed up their friendship with an overture that wasn't reciprocated, it could jeopardize what he had with her kids. That was a bridge too far.

The kitchen filled with strategic conversations about yellow Labs and finding the eyes that matched the white poodle, but all Susan could think about was Jennifer Moore, who'd been slaughtered and left for dead in the woods behind her house.

In most of the homicide cases she'd worked over the years, the victims had been adults. She'd had a child homicide her first year as an investigator, and even though it had eventually been ruled accidental, it was still tough to work on. A father had left the screen out of his second-floor window and his son, still trying to master the art of walking, went right through the opening and fell. This case was different. Although Jennifer Moore was technically an adult at eighteen, she was a kid as far as Susan was concerned. Two weeks away from starting a new life in college. She couldn't help but look at her own kids and put herself in the shoes of Mindy and Noel Moore. Then she thought about the missing rug and the blood on the bottom of the stair banister and tried to imagine the unimaginable. It was too much.

"Any luck at the party store this morning?" Beatrice asked, breaking Susan from her thoughts.

Susan snapped back and turned the dial on the oven to set the temperature. "That place was huge. I was overwhelmed the second I walked in there."

"I could help you if you want."

"Yeah, I think I'll take you up on that. Maybe we'll go for a ride this weekend. I met the store manager, and he gave me some ideas. I'm leaning toward a petting zoo party."

Casey immediately dropped her puzzle piece and threw her hands up in the air. "Yes! A petting zoo party!"

"We can have animals come?" Tim asked.

"Yup," Susan replied. "And pony rides."

Now both kids jumped up and down in their seats.

"Petting zoo! Petting zoo! Petting zoo!"

Beatrice laughed. "I don't think you need my help anymore. I believe we're having a petting zoo party."

Susan laughed as well. "I think you're right."

And that was okay. Because she knew she'd only have her kids for a little while and then they'd be all grown up, and things like petting zoo parties and puzzles at the kitchen table would be nothing but memories. She'd come to realize over the past few years that every day was precious, and sometimes she didn't see that in the minute-to-minute responsibilities a single mother working full time had. She would let them have their petting zoo party, and in return they would give her a memory she'd cherish forever. Sounded like a fair trade. In fact, it sounded close to perfect.

# 11

Liam sat at the desk in his hotel room, poring over the crime scene photos John Chu had emailed over. In the background, a rerun of *Who Wants to Be a Millionaire?* was playing, with Regis Philbin's unmistakable voice whispering through the room, asking time and again, *"Is that your final answer?"*

His mind was churning. He hadn't been expecting such a rush from being at his first crime scene since Philadelphia and was excited to see the rust hadn't built up as he feared it might have. He'd been through a lot since his last job, and the fact that his skills and instincts were pretty much picking up where he'd left off was a welcome surprise. The leg he'd been shot in had grown stronger, and he'd shed the cane a few months earlier. Now it appeared he might be on the road to shedding the emotional scars left in the wake of all that had been destroyed in the process of clearing his name. Maybe there was a light at the end of his tunnel after all.

His cell phone rang, and he picked it up. It was Susan.

"Hey."

"Oh, damn. Did I wake you? You sound like you were sleeping."

Liam laughed and cleared his throat. "No chance. Too much adrenaline from today. Couldn't sleep if I tried. I was going over the crime scene pictures John sent over and also doing a little digging on Noel and Mindy Moore. Figured I'd get a jump start on things before tomorrow."

"I was doing the same thing," Susan replied. "*You* are supposed to be going over the stuff they gave you in class so you can pass your certification. You can't be a consultant without it."

Liam glanced at the small stack of papers and forms on the nightstand beside his bed. "That's all done. Besides, it's not like a test or anything. I just need to interview with the superintendent so he can get a feel for me and what I'll be doing here."

"And you think that'll be a walk in the park?"

"Do you know how charming I am? This will be a piece of cake."

Susan laughed. "I can't think of any more expressions to toss at you, so just tell me what you found."

Liam took the notes he'd made and pulled up the Phoenix Capital website. "From what I could find online, it looks like Mindy Moore is a stay-at-home mom and a volunteer with the high school. She's also part of the PTA and volunteers with the Guiding Eyes in Yorktown. She has a degree in accounting from Syracuse, which I'm assuming is where she met her husband because Noel has a finance degree from there. He graduated a year before she did."

He could hear Susan typing on her laptop.

"Her social media accounts are private. Can't see anything."

"Yeah, same with Noel. But I picked up some things on the school's Facebook page and the Guiding Eyes page, and Noel's LinkedIn account is public. I just started matching pieces from those."

"What's Noel's story?"

Liam flipped the pages in his notebook. "Looks like he and Arthur Breen both came up together at Lehman before the firm went bust in '08. Got laid off and ended up opening a boutique wealth management and investment firm—Phoenix Capital. They have one office on 46th and Madison on Manhattan, and it's just the two of them. The website is pretty sparse, so I did some digging through articles and networking newsletters. My guess is Uriah Sitchel isn't the only highflier they bank. They claim to have over two billion under management."

More typing from Susan's end. "I'm going to try and set up a meeting with Arthur Breen for tomorrow. We'll need to work around the family's sphere of people and see what we can find out before Charlotte Walsh squashes that too."

"Sounds good."

"Anything else?"

"No. I'll see you after my interview?"

"Yeah. I'm going to swing by Putnam Hospital on my way in and see how Mrs. Moore is doing."

"Okay. I'll see you tomorrow."

Liam hung up and leaned back in his seat for a moment, feeling the same sense of comfort and . . . peace . . . he always felt around Susan. She'd done so much for him since they met at Jefferson Hospital. He was certain there were feelings there that went beyond a good friendship, but he couldn't risk taking it to the next level and ruining what they already had if she wasn't interested. Susan was coming off a divorce, and what he was coming off of with his former wife was something catastrophically worse. The fact that he could still feel anything remotely close to affection was a miracle in itself. They just weren't ready. Maybe someday. Not yet.

Liam shook off his thoughts and moved his mouse over to his favorites. He left the Phoenix Capital website and clicked on Instagram. They already knew Jennifer's Instagram, Twitter, and TikTok accounts were private, and he doubted an attorney like Charlotte Walsh would ever let her clients give them access without a warrant. The boy, Charlie, also had an Instagram and TikTok, and they were private too. Neither of the kids was on Facebook. But he had another idea and hoped it might work.

Anja York.

It didn't take long for Liam to find Anja's profile. He recognized her face from seeing her at the Moore house earlier that morning. He clicked onto her Instagram page and exhaled a breath of relief when he saw that Anja's account was public.

It appeared Anja and Jennifer were indeed friends, but best friends would be a stretch. Judging from the pictures Anja was constantly posting, she was the kind of kid who was friendly with just about everyone. It took Liam almost twenty minutes to scroll through all the photos and short videos before he stopped, sat up, and nodded to himself in the otherwise empty hotel room. He enlarged the picture, then took out his phone and took a picture of the computer screen so he could email it to Susan for the file. It was a photograph of Anja and Jennifer in their prom dresses, standing in front of a full-length mirror, taking that once-in-a-lifetime-night pic, big smiles, bodies relaxed. It appeared they were in Noel and Mindy's bedroom.

It also appeared they were standing on a rather large area rug that took up most of the hardwood floor.

And the picture was only seven weeks old.

# 12

The second day of Jennifer Moore's murder investigation brought Susan to Putnam Hospital Center. She checked in with the front desk, took the elevator to the third-floor medical surgical unit, and found Mindy Moore sitting up in her hospital bed. The woman's eyes were closed, and a steady hum of a breath escaped from her slightly parted lips; the only other sound in the room was the heart monitor maintaining a steady rhythm. Mindy was sleeping.

Susan walked closer and studied what she could see. A single IV line led from Mindy's right arm to a bag hanging above her. Susan was no expert, but it looked to be saline. Just keeping her hydrated. There were no marks on her face or neck. Nothing on her arms. Her hands were fine, her fingernails cut very short. Strange for a woman of such means not to have a top-of-the-line manicure. Susan fished her phone out of her pocket and took a picture.

The hospital room door opened, and a middle-aged man walked in. He was tall, with thick glasses, a gray beard and mustache, and a tuft of hair on top of his head. He smiled warmly and extended his hand.

"The nurses told me you'd arrived. I'm Dr. Fields, Mrs. Moore's physician."

Susan dropped her phone back in her pocket and shook the man's hand. "Investigator Adler, state police. Thanks for meeting with me."

"Give me a second, and we can talk."

"Sure."

Dr. Fields made his way over to Mindy's bedside and checked both the monitor and the IV. He punched a few keys on the small tablet he was cradling and flipped through several screens with his finger. A few more commands, and he was done.

"How's she doing?" Susan asked. "In general."

"She's in good health, considering." He looked up from his tablet. "Let's talk in the hall."

Susan followed the doctor out of the room. He stopped when they reached a small alcove that overlooked a garden behind the hospital. It was just the two of them.

"When I saw on the news what happened to Jenny, I just couldn't believe it," Dr. Fields said, shaking his head. "I've been the family's primary care physician since Noel and Mindy moved here twenty years ago. Jenny was such an angel. Such a beautiful person."

Susan took out her notepad. "I know we have to tread lightly because of HIPAA, so I'll try and be as general as I can. But it's important for me to understand some things for the investigation."

"I'll do my best."

His response told her that Charlotte hadn't gotten to the medical staff yet to gag them. Perfect.

"Tell me about Mrs. Moore's state. How is she?"

Dr. Fields paused, deciding how much he could say. "She's suffering from shock. I would assume finding your child murdered in the woods behind your house could cause such a reaction. She's been pretty much unresponsive since she arrived."

"Has she been conscious?"

"On and off. She came in overloaded with Valium, so we had to counteract that a bit. Her sister told us that Noel had given her some Valium to keep her calm after she found Jenny in the woods. Apparently it was left over from a past prescription. I think he gave her too much. We're still giving her meds to keep her calm but watching the dosage very closely. She's been up for meals, although she hasn't eaten much."

Susan made a few notes. "What can you tell me about the family?" she asked.

"The family?"

"Are the Moores loving? Did they seem like a normal family? Anything I should know that might help the case?"

"They're terrific," Dr. Fields replied immediately. "Like I said before, I've known them for two decades. Loving family. Great kids. From what I could see, Noel and Mindy are the quintessential couple. Noel's self-made. Not many people can say that. Came from a working-class family. His mom was an elementary school teacher in Brooklyn, and his dad worked for the sanitation department. Mindy is a saint. Always volunteering or raising money for a cause she believes in. Active in her kids' lives. A wonderful woman. For Jenny to meet her end like that? It's unfathomable."

Susan listened to the doctor's description, and from what she'd seen, she had to agree with his assessment. The Moores seemed like decent people. So how did their daughter end up slaughtered in the woods behind their house?

"Last question," Susan said. "When Mindy was brought in here yesterday, was she bathed? Did anyone give her a bath or a shower or clip her nails or do her hair? Anything like that?"

Dr. Fields shrugged. "I have no idea. I wouldn't think so, but you'd have to ask the nursing supervisor. I'm not an attending physician here. They're granting me access because I'm Mindy's doctor and the family is known in the community. She was already in her hospital gown when I arrived yesterday."

"Okay, thanks." They shook again. "You call me when her condition improves."

"I will."

---

"Any news on Mrs. Moore's condition?"

Donna Starr sidled up to Susan as soon as she came out of the hospital's main entrance. She had her phone out, recording the conversation as they walked.

"Ms. Starr, I have no comment, and I'll continue to have no comment. We might have a press conference at some point, and I'll be sure you're on the invite list, but meeting me outside places during my investigation will only end up making our situation worse."

"Yeah, but this story is getting big," Donna said. She was talking fast. "I pulled up in front of the Moore house today to get some B roll, and news vans from all three of the majors were out there. I also heard CNN is asking around."

"That's good to know, thanks."

"All I'm saying is that you could use a friend on the inside. Someone local who knows how important our families and communities are here in Westchester. The majors will just want to exploit the murder-in-a-peaceful-suburb angle. I can give the viewers the real story. We could help each other out. I give you some info as I learn it, and you can be an unnamed source in some of my stories."

Susan shook her head. "Why do I get the feeling you've offered that same deal to more than just me?"

"This is our community. I need to protect it."

Susan reached her car and opened the door. "As I said, you'll get all the information you need if we decide to do a press conference. In the meantime, I'd ask that you leave the professionals involved in this case alone so they can do their jobs and we can find whoever is responsible for what happened to Jennifer Moore."

"Oh, that's good. Can I quote you on that?"

"Sure. Why not?"

Susan climbed into her car, and Donna immediately stepped between her and the door.

"Move away, please."

"Hold on. I got some information you might be able to use. Friend on the inside, remember?"

Susan sighed.

"Take this for what it's worth, but I have it on good authority that people like Mindy Moore, who are susceptible to such extreme cases of shock like what she's experiencing now, are sometimes prone to a type of catatonia called excited catatonia."

"Okay."

"With excited catatonia, the person appears wound up and can be restless and agitated. Sometimes even aggressive. They may not know they're being aggressive at the time, as they're in a kind of out-of-body state, but they can be very physical." Donna bent down, her voice almost a whisper. "What if Mindy Moore was suffering from excited catatonia and hurt Jennifer without realizing what she was doing?"

Susan started the engine and waited until the reporter finally backed away before shutting her door and driving away. Excited catatonia. She'd have to look into it.

# 13

Knowing she would be checking in on Mindy Moore at Putnam Hospital, Susan had made arrangements with Jennifer's friend Anja York to meet at the Mount Kisco Diner, which was a mile down the road. She arrived ten minutes early, and Anja was already there, waiting outside, sucking on a vape pen. The girl was shorter and a bit thicker than Jennifer, but there was no question she was gorgeous. Her black hair fell in waves to her chest. Her olive skin was even darker in the summer sun, and there wasn't a blemish to be found. She was dressed in a white tank top, jean shorts, and flip-flops, trying to look casual, but Susan could tell she'd put the outfit together with meticulous thought.

"You got here early," Susan said as she approached.

Anja took a drag of her vape and let the smoke float from her lips as she spoke. "I wasn't sure what traffic would be like on 117, and I didn't want to keep you waiting. It can get really backed up sometimes with the construction."

"You ready? Breakfast's on me."

"Lead the way."

Susan pointed to the vape pen. "Those things are worse than cigarettes."

"Only the black market ones. These are safe."

"They're literally killing people."

"Fake news."

They walked into a diner that was only half-full. The early-morning rush was gone, and the lunch crowd was still a couple of hours away.

Susan asked for privacy, and the man behind the counter walked them to a corner booth by the restrooms, away from everyone else. They each ordered a coffee as they skimmed the menu.

"I appreciate you seeing me," Susan began as she traced the pancake and waffle section with her finger. "I know you wanted to talk sooner, but we needed to take care of a few things with the investigation first."

"When Jen wasn't answering my texts or calls, I knew something was up." She sniffled. "But I never would've expected . . ."

Her voice trailed off, and she took a moment.

"She was my best friend."

"Really? I didn't get that impression from your Instagram account. Seems like you're friends with everyone."

Anja chuckled. "Nothing on social media is *real.* Jen and I were besties since kindergarten."

"I understand you went to the prom together."

"Yeah. We went stag just for laughs. Had a great time."

"I saw a picture of you and Jennifer in her mom's room. You guys were looking into the full-length mirror?"

"Sure. If you say so. We got dressed in her parents' room, so I guess that makes sense."

Susan pulled out her phone and showed the picture Liam had sent her. "This is the one I was talking about."

Anja glanced at it and nodded. "That's us."

"You guys do anything to mess up that rug? Spill anything or stain it that night?"

"No. Not me, anyway. I was always real careful when I was at Jen's house. That place is like a castle."

Susan put the phone back in her pocket and paused for a moment, watching Anja struggle with where to begin. The young girl looked down at the table.

"When I pulled up to the house and saw the police cars and all the people standing around and that yellow tape all over the place, I knew it was bad. I thought something happened to Mr. Moore. It didn't even occur to me that it could be Jen."

"Why would you think something could've happened to Mr. Moore?" Susan asked.

"I don't know. He's rich. He handles a lot of accounts for super-wealthy people. I've seen those movies where they have to launder money and get caught in a bad situation with, like, the mob or drug cartel people. Stuff like *Ozark* or *Breaking Bad* or something."

"Do you know about any of his clients?"

"No. I just thought it was bad when I saw all the commotion and figured something happened to him."

Susan closed the menu and dug into her bag. She pulled out her notepad, opened it, and made a few notes.

"Do you know what happened to Jennifer?"

"Yeah. She was stabbed and left for dead. It's all online."

"Can you think of anyone who could do something like that to her? You have to be really angry to hurt someone like that. Did Jennifer have any enemies or old boyfriends or people who might want to harm her like that?"

Anja wiped her eyes again and nodded immediately. "Oh yeah. I think it was Glenn. Had to be."

And just like that, Susan had a suspect.

"Who's Glenn?"

"Glenn Baker. He graduated John Jay in 2019. Too much of a loser to go to college. Works at the Mobil station on Route 35 in Cross River doing oil changes and tire rotations. He's an asshole in the best get-back-at-your-parents kind of way. Bad reputation. Zero ability to feel compassion for anyone else. Deals a little on the side too."

"Sounds like a special guy."

"Jen was crushing on him since we were in the sixth grade and he was in eighth. She finally got her hands on him last year. Or should I say, he finally noticed how hot she is, and he gave her the time of day.

They dated for about six months and then he got a little too possessive and put too much pressure on her, so she broke up with him. That's when he started stalking her."

Susan wrote in her notepad. "I got the impression that Jennifer was the kind of kid who might date the high school quarterback or the captain of the debate club. She doesn't strike me as the kind of person to be attracted to an auto mechanic. I'm not saying there's anything wrong with that. Hell, I'm putty in their hands if something goes wrong with my car. I'm just saying, this guy is older, sounds a bit gruff. Deals drugs. Not a match for a Duke-bound honors student."

Anja chuckled. "Let's just say Jen had a dark side that no one knew about except a handful of her closest friends. Her mom was a school nazi. Always on her about grades and appearances and how she should act to reflect properly on the family. It got better when Jen appeared to be shaping up, but a few years back, her relationship with her mom was rough. Constantly fighting. I'm talking knockdowns. Serious fights that ended in punishments that would've gotten her mom arrested if Jen ever said anything."

More notes.

"About two years ago, Jen started playing nice and got good grades. She started dressing better and joined a bunch of stuff at school to keep her mom off her back. She got super religious and joined her aunt's church in Yorktown and did a bunch of volunteering. It worked for the most part, but there were still way too many nights her mom would keep Jen home to study when we were all out having fun. I felt bad. But when Jen finally was allowed to go out, she took *full* advantage. No quarterback or debate captain could handle my girl when she was ready to party. Jen might've loved Jesus, but she also loved her tequila. Loved to chase a drop of acid with a joint. Loved her music. And *loved* to flirt." Anja paused and blew her nose. "And that's where Glenn comes into the picture. Hot guy, in a dirtbag kind of way. He was a loser. Rebel. Druggie. Jen's type of guy when Mommy wasn't around. But she was still a virgin, if you can believe that. She'd mess around, but for whatever reason, she drew a hard line when it came to sex. Didn't even like going down on a guy. I think she was scared to cross that bridge or used her religion as an excuse. Used to piss Glenn off, but she didn't care. She was the best."

The waitress came with the coffees and took their orders. Anja began to cry again and whimpered her way to a bacon-and-cheddar-omelet order while Susan chose a short stack of pancakes. She needed a break from all the eggs her family ate thanks to the chickens.

Susan waited until the waitress left. "You think that the fact Jennifer wouldn't have sex with Glenn caused some of the problems with them?"

"For sure," Anja replied. "That's what I meant when I said he was putting pressure on her. He was always trying to get her to do sexual things with him, and she wasn't into it. Sometimes I thought he'd, like, end up raping her or something. I mean, take no for an answer, right?"

"How was he stalking her?"

"He'd show up *everywhere*. Before school. After school. Follow her in her car. Always texting. Always calling. He even showed up at her National Honor Society ceremony and stood in the back so she could see him when she was up on stage. It was hard for Jen because she couldn't tell her parents what was happening. She got back together with him a few times just to stop the stalking, but things always got worse, and she'd break it off. Then the pattern would start again. And now she's gone."

Anja pulled more napkins from the dispenser and wiped the mascara that ran down her face. She looked just like she had out in front of the Moore house the day before. Distraught. Confused. Scared.

The food came, and the two of them began eating. Susan ran through the information she'd just learned and felt like she had a solid lead to follow up on. A jealous boyfriend. An ex-girlfriend weeks away from leaving to start a new life. An argument. A desperate attempt to hold on to someone he thought he was losing forever. And then it was over. One wrong move, and lives had changed. She'd seen it before, and there was no doubt she'd see it again. It could be a textbook crime of passion—but how would that explain what they'd found at the Moore house? The blood on the banister. The missing rug. The ultraclean bathroom.

"Jen was a sweet person," Anja said softly. "I don't want to give you the wrong impression. She was like a sister to me. She didn't deserve what happened to her, and there's no one on this planet who would want to hurt her like that. No one."

Susan picked up her mug of coffee. "Except Glenn Baker."

Anja sighed, then nodded. "Yeah, I guess. Except Glenn Baker."

# 14

Charlie sat on the edge of his bed, watching a cartoon he knew he'd seen before. The blue mouse and the orange squirrel and the white cat were all familiar to him. He just couldn't place the name. He hadn't bothered with it since he was in fourth grade, which to an eighth grader felt like a lifetime ago. But that morning he watched it, comforted by the memories and the feelings it brought him. Back when he was younger and things were happy and simple. All that had changed now. Nothing would ever be the same again.

His father was in the bathroom, the steam from the shower meandering out into the rest of the hotel room, reaching for him before evaporating into the cool air. It had been a strange night sleeping there. Charlie had spent much of it awake and staring up at the ceiling, thinking about his sister, who he still couldn't believe was dead, and his mother, who was in some hospital. His father had begun snoring around midnight, and that had kept up until Charlie finally dozed off at three. They'd both slept until the digital clock on the nightstand started buzzing at nine.

Three raps on the door pulled Charlie from the television. They were loud and quick, one after the other. He looked back and forth between the door and the bathroom.

"Get that, will ya?" his father called.

"Okay."

He hopped off the bed and walked across the room before peering through the peephole, his shoulders relaxing the moment he saw who it was.

Artie Breen, or Uncle Artie to the Moore children, stood in the doorway with coffee and juice in one hand and a bag of Dunkin' Donuts in the other. Artie was his father's best friend and partner from work. He was also Charlie's godfather. Artie seemed tall, and was bald and always in a good mood. Charlie loved it when he'd get him into wrestling submission moves, but there'd be none of that today. Everyone was too sad.

"Hi, Uncle Artie," Charlie said, stepping aside to let him in.

The smile that was always on Artie's face was gone, replaced instead by lips that were pressed together and eyes that were red from crying. "Hey, champ. How you holding up?"

"Good, I guess."

"I brought you and your dad some breakfast." He placed the bag down on the table and took two coffees and a juice out of the cardboard holder. "I'll be honest. I don't really know what to say. I loved Jen like she was my own kid. I can't believe any of this is happening."

"I know."

"I'm so sorry. I just—"

Tears filled Artie's eyes, and he turned away, wiping them with a handkerchief he had in his breast pocket.

"Hey, pal."

Charlie's father emerged from the bathroom with a towel wrapped around his waist. Artie turned back around, and they hugged, each man pulling the other closer. They both cried for a moment, then took a few deep breaths and let go. Charlie watched it as if he was still watching the show with the blue mouse and the orange squirrel and the white cat. It didn't seem real. The guilt he felt pressed on his shoulders. He opened his mouth to confess but stopped when his father broke the silence.

"Thanks for the breakfast," his father said.

Artie nodded. “Yeah, man. Anything. Anything you need. I’m a phone call away. Day or night. I’m here for you. You know that.”

Charlie took a breath and dug into the bag, pulling out a chocolate glazed, listening to the men talk as his father got dressed.

“I obviously won’t be to the office for a bit. There’s so much to do.”

“Don’t worry about any of that. I’ll cover your clients and calls. Take as much time as you need.” Artie wiped more tears. “How’s Mindy?”

“The same. I called this morning.”

“Have the police said anything?”

“No. They got a warrant so we had to leave the house overnight so they could finish their examination or investigation or whatever they call it.”

“But Jen was found outside. Why’d they need access inside the house?”

“They’re treating the house and the property as one big crime scene. Charlotte’s on it.”

“No leads?”

“Not yet.”

Charlie fished a straw out of the bag and opened his orange juice.

“Have you talked to Uriah?” his father asked.

Artie shook his head. “No.”

“Call him today. Let him know what happened and tell him you’ll be his contact for the time being. I don’t want the Hudson Tiers project to be affected by what happened. Everything has to stay on schedule.”

“Understood.”

His father stopped speaking and looked down to the floor. “You remember last week when I left you that voice mail and you were joking with me that you could hear Mindy and Jen arguing in the background?”

“Yeah, sure,” Artie replied. “You were giving me the account numbers we needed for the ACH payments so I could pass them on to Uriah’s GC for his subs.”

"Right. You still have that voice mail?"

"I think so."

His father took a step closer toward Uncle Artie and softened his voice. "When you get into the office, I need you to delete it."

"The message has the account numbers on it."

"Write the numbers down and delete the voice mail. I'm not sure what road these cops are going to go down, and I don't need recorded evidence of Jen and her mom fighting a few days before she's found dead."

"It was just an argument."

"What seems normal to some might seem abnormal to others. Got it?"

Artie exhaled through his nose and nodded. "I got it. No worries. As soon as I get in the office, I'll delete it. I'm heading there now."

"Thanks."

Artie stuffed his handkerchief back in his pocket. "You really think the cops would go down that road? With Mindy, I mean?"

"I have no idea what the police are going to do," his father replied. "I wish I did, but I don't."

# 15

After her meeting with Anja York at the diner, Susan made her way back to the Lewisboro police headquarters to do a little recon on Jennifer's ex-boyfriend before she stopped by to question him. She ran a background check and performed a rather intense Google search on the guy. It wasn't hard to find him.

Glenn Patrick Baker was born just three days after the towers fell in 2001. He was raised in Lewisboro and was homeschooled through his elementary years until he began attending the district's public middle school and then moved on to John Jay High. He graduated on time, but from what she could glean from social media and copies of the yearbook she found online, it looked like he got out of there by the skin of his teeth. He'd even been suspended twice for fighting.

His arrest record was littered with misdemeanors, but nothing too serious. His worst conviction was a B and E charge that came about when he and a friend broke into a house they thought was empty, but the owners were home. That mistake gave him thirty days in jail, but the rest of his arrests came with only fines, warnings, or community service. He was an annoyance but didn't appear to be dangerous, and if he really was a small-time dealer, there were no drug convictions to confirm it.

More digging online showed that Glenn never went to college, and it appeared that after a few jobs at the local ShopRite, a painting store, a landscaping business, and a hobby shop, he settled in at the Mobil station on Route 35. Wild side or not, Susan couldn't figure out how a girl like Jennifer Moore ended up with a guy like Glenn Baker.

By noon, Liam had returned from Hawthorne, successful in his interview and approved to serve as a consultant as far as the New York State Police was concerned. Susan ran through her busy morning, highlighting her meeting with Anja York, the fact that Anja had confirmed the rug was in Noel and Mindy Moore's bedroom, and her suspicion that Glenn Baker had been involved. She also recapped her visit with Mindy's doctor, her encounter with Donna Starr, and the theory about excited catatonia. They were back on the road a half hour later, searching for their newest suspect.

Susan turned right into the gas station and parked at the side of the building. Liam was holding a picture of Glenn on his lap, and Susan glanced at it as she pulled into a spot next to the shop. Glenn was a scrawny kid, pale, black hair that was long in the front and buzzed short in the back. He had a silver ring threaded through his pierced bottom lip and cheeks full of acne. A thin, patchy beard lined the very edge of his jawline and made his face look dirty. He was smirking in the picture, which was all Susan needed to know about the guy. He was the personification of a punk.

Susan and Liam got out of the car and walked toward a group of men who were in the garage bays working on three cars simultaneously. One car was on a lift and had all its tires missing. The second car was on the ground and looked like new tires had already been installed. The third car was on the lift with an oil pan underneath. None of the men spoke as they worked. Music played somewhere in the background.

Susan ducked into the first bay and stepped in front of the man working on the car with all the tires missing.

"Excuse me," she said.

The man looked her up and down. "Can I help you?"

"I'm looking for Glenn."

"Over there." He pointed toward the car that was on the ground. As soon as Susan looked in that direction, she saw Glenn Baker climbing out of the driver's seat.

"Glenn Baker!" she cried. "Can I have a word, please?"

Glenn froze as she approached. She pulled her shield from under her shirt so he could see it.

"Police!" someone yelled in the background.

The men began to step back.

Susan put her hand up. "State police," she said calmly. "I just need to ask you a few questions."

Glenn shook his head once, then dropped the wrench he was holding and lunged for the back of the shop. Before Susan could react, he was out the rear door and had disappeared along the side of the building. Susan ran through the back of the shop and jumped through the back door in time to see Glenn crossing the parking lot in a full sprint.

"Stop!"

The scrawny kid leaped over a rusted wrought iron fence without slowing down and ran into the woods that surrounded the gas station. Susan followed in pursuit, running as fast as she could, listening to leaves crunch underfoot and watching branches bend and snap as she focused on the kid running in front of her, trying to see if he had a weapon or anything she should be concerned about. The air was heavy, and it wasn't long before her breath grew short and her body began to overheat. She pushed herself, pumping her legs and watching her subject for any sudden moves.

Glenn wove in and out of the trees, jumping over bushes and fallen limbs and sliding down a small embankment on his butt. Every few feet he'd turn around to see if Susan was still chasing him.

On the west side of the tree line, her sedan flew by, down a dirt road that was supposed to lead to a residential section of Cross River. Susan watched as Liam maneuvered the car to the edge of the woods and slid to a stop, kicking up dust that swallowed everything around it. Footsteps on the gravel turned into steps on the underbrush as Liam closed in on Glenn from the opposite side. Susan kept pushing herself forward, focused on the kid, who stopped for a moment, then disappeared.

He was gone.

Susan took a moment to catch her breath in the heavy, thick air. She ran to where Glenn had stopped and saw that he was lying on the ground, wheezing and coughing. Liam was on top of him.

"I think I knocked the wind out of him," Liam said as he climbed to his feet and took a step back. "Not the fall you wanna take when you're not expecting it."

"Nice tackle," Susan said as she snapped her holster closed. "You play football?"

"In high school. Long time ago."

"Remember when you used to need a cane?"

Liam smiled. "My physical therapist is no joke."

She bent down next to the kid. "Just breathe, Glenn. Slow. In and out. You're fine."

Glenn did as he was told and got his breathing under control.

Liam folded his arms across his chest. "So, should we interview him while he's down or take him to the station?"

"I thought we could talk here, but he's making it harder on himself than it needs to be." Susan stood back up and wiped her hands. "Why'd you run?"

"I don't know," Glenn wheezed. Dirt and leaves clung to his nappy beard. "I got scared. Someone yelled *cops*, and I bolted."

"I wasn't trying to hide the fact that I was police. It wasn't an ambush. As soon as I saw you, I took out my shield so you could see it. We just wanted to talk. What're you scared of?"

Liam pointed toward the ground next to the kid. "Maybe he was scared we'd find the bag of pills that just fell out of his pocket."

Susan nodded. "Maybe. Or maybe he's afraid we're here to arrest him for the murder of Jennifer Moore."

Glenn sat up quickly and tucked his knees against his chest. His wiped his face and shook his head. "Yo, I didn't do that! I just heard about it last night. I loved her, man. I would never hurt her."

"Yeah, you look real broken up about it."

"I am! What do you know? Just because I ain't crying don't mean I ain't hurt."

"Still, we need to talk."

"Okay. So, talk."

"Tell me about Jennifer."

"What do you wanna know?"

"How long have you two been together?"

Glenn thought for a moment. "About half her senior year. Six months? Something like that."

"First half of the school year or second?"

"First. We knew each other from when I was in school, but we officially met at a bonfire in September. Broke up around Saint Patrick's Day. But I can't lie—we've been on again, off again the whole time."

Susan took out her phone and placed it on the ground. "You mind if I record this? Don't want to forget anything."

"I don't care. It's cool."

"So why'd you break up?"

"Because she was a Jesus-freak tease," Glenn hissed. "She'd play the game real good. Get me all hot, then when it was time to pull the trigger, she'd turn into the Virgin Mary, and I'd end up with nothing. I did everything I could to try and get her to understand that it was more than just sex for me, but it didn't matter. Anytime I tried to touch her and take it to the next level, she shut me out, talking about how she's saving herself because that's what God would want. After a while I realized I wasn't getting anywhere and had to bail. Figured she was using me to party, but sometimes you gotta pay to play. You know what I mean?"

"You're a hell of a guy."

"Yo, I didn't care that she was a virgin or that she was religious. I didn't even call her out on her hypocrisy of using drugs and drinking to destroy her body while trying to save it from sex. All that shit was cool. I would've waited for whenever she was ready. But the thing that got me was that she'd initiate everything and then just shut down and freak out like she was panicking or something. She was deranged when it came to sex and messing around. I never understood that."

"So how does a nice girl from a rich family end up with a guy like you?"

Glenn laughed. "Man, I asked myself that same questions more times than you can count. She liked to party, and she had a dark side. I guess I was her devil to offset her god."

Anja had said something similar.

"Tell me about her dark side."

"Jen was a trip. Her mom was a hard-ass, so she had to act like she was a good girl and an honor roll genius, but when she was on her own, Jen let loose. She was into all kinds of drugs. Pot, coke, LSD, painkillers. Didn't matter. She drank too. Whatever she could get. Her mom had this tracer app and was always checking in to see where she was, so I always had to meet her somewhere that didn't seem suspicious. She told me once that she'd piss in a jar before she went out and hide it in the bathroom because sometimes her mom would make her take a drug test when she got home."

"Are you serious?"

"Why would I lie?"

"I'm not saying you're lying," Susan said. "But maybe you weren't seeing the whole picture in the moment. What if Jennifer didn't love you? What if she loved the drugs you were dealing and she loved that you're the kind of guy her mom would hate, but you didn't come to terms with that until now? You realized she was using you. So maybe that got you mad. Like, mad enough to kill her."

"I told you I had nothing to do with that!"

"Where were you two nights ago?"

Glenn rubbed his side where Liam had tackled him. "Home. Sleeping. And no, no one was with me. I have no alibi. I've seen the shows. I know I'm open season with no alibi, but that's the truth."

"You told me about Jennifer's mom," Susan said. "But I heard you were the one who was possessive. I heard you were the one doing the stalking."

"You must've been talking to Anja." Glenn snickered and raised his hands. "Okay, I'm going to tell you some more of the truth because I got nothing to hide. Yeah, I was a little jealous. I thought maybe Jen was closing her legs for me and opening them for someone else, so I followed her around sometimes. Just to make sure she wasn't cheating."

"And was she?"

"Not that I ever saw. She'd chill with her friends. Hang with that priest a lot. She did a lot of volunteering for her aunt's church. She was, like, mental the way she could turn on her good and bad sides like a switch. Hang with the priest in the day sorting food for the homeless, then snorting lines with me at night. It was crazy." He paused and took a deep breath, still trying to regulate himself. "Anyway, one day Anja spots me following Jen, and Anja starts following *me*. She told Jen about it, and this whole thing blew up. I guess Jen couldn't take her mom stalking her and me stalking her. I get it. She broke up with me for good, but by then, I was cool. I needed to move on anyway." He paused and looked down toward the ground. "You wanna hear the real kicker?"

"Sure."

"I think the person who was really jealous out of all of us was Anja. Me and Anja dated the summer before I met Jen at the bonfire. Nothing serious. A booty call for both of us. But as soon as Jen and I started going out, Anja was all over me. It was crazy. I never said anything because I didn't want any shit to go down between them since they were, like, best friends. But I always thought that was weird how Anja wanted me more as soon as she knew Jen and I were a thing. You need to check her out. She might've turned you onto me to get the spotlight off of her. Jealousy can make chicks do some crazy shit."

Susan grabbed her phone off the ground and motioned for Liam to help Glenn up.

"I think we're done."

"Cool."

"You know you're under arrest, right?"

Glenn brushed the dirt off his pants and wiped his hands on his shirt. "I figured. Won't be my first time."

Susan took her cuffs from her belt. "Probably won't be your last."

# 16

The Lewisboro Police Department had jurisdiction in Cross River, so Susan had a unit meet her at the gas station, and she and Liam handed Glenn Baker over to the officer. She wrote up a quick summary report on scene, explaining her reason for needing to interview Glenn in connection with her homicide case, the subsequent chase through the woods, and the discovery of narcotics on his person. The pills were a mishmash of opioids, but he had enough in his possession to warrant some attention. The officers took him away for booking, and she and Liam headed south. They still had a full day ahead of them.

They arrived at the Hawthorne headquarters to meet with John Chu in the hope that he'd discovered something in the evidence from the crime scene. When they got off the elevator on the basement level, the noise from the department upstairs was gone, leaving a vacuum of silence that could be unsettling if you weren't expecting it.

The forensics lab was one giant room, painted white with white shades over half windows and white tiled floors. There were six office labs lined side by side on their left and a data center room for computer and technological forensics on their right. Behind the data room was a conference room and beyond that, John's office.

Susan could see him sitting with his back to them, huddled over a microscope. As she and Liam crossed the floor, she waved to the other techs walking in and out of the other offices. John spun his chair around when she knocked on his door.

"We were in the area. Thought I'd pop in to see if you found anything so far."

"We found a few things," John replied, climbing out of his chair. "Whether or not it's connected to the case, I won't know for a bit. Those woods were full of junk. We took everything we could find. Come on—I'll show you."

She and Liam backed out of the office and followed John into the conference room. The long table had been draped in plastic, and the chairs had been pushed against the wall. Clear bags filled with soiled litter were stacked on the table. There must've been a dozen of them.

"We already went through the Moores' garbage," John explained. "That's in the other room. Nothing unusual. I'll email you the pictures we took of everything. This stuff from the woods will take longer. Some of it is a decade old, and some of it was from the last party someone had out there."

"Must've been some party."

"We're in the process of sorting through it, determining the age of the trash, and further determining if it's something that would link us to the victim or the perp from that night." John took a few items out to show them. "As you can see, we have everything from beer cans to used condoms to glass bottles to socks. It was a mess back there."

"Anything stand out?" Liam asked.

"Maybe. There was a piece of cloth caught on one of the branches near the murder site on the northwest side of the woods. Preliminary analysis shows it's a fabric made of polyester and silk. Hardly unique, but we're running a further breakdown to see what we can find from there. We also found a set of shoe prints in the mud that weren't consistent with the others on-site."

"What do you mean?" Susan asked.

"The tread marks led from the opposite end of the woods, coming in south toward the Moore home. There's no doubt they're from sneakers and don't match the treads from any responding personnel from the scene or from the members of the Moore family. We'll get you a brand and style, but it's the size of the print that's puzzling. It appears they're either from a child or a very small woman."

"How small?"

"If the prints were made by a child, I'd put them at about five feet, between the ages of thirteen and sixteen, depending on if they're male or female. If we think a small woman made the tracks, age wouldn't matter as much. I'd put an adult female at five feet."

"What about an adult male?"

"Possible, but unlikely. This is a size five we're talking about. That would be a pretty small male. Not impossible, of course. But I'd say child or petite woman would be more likely."

Liam looked at all the bags of trash. "This is quite the needle in a haystack," he said. "You find a murder weapon?"

"Negative."

"How about Jennifer's cell phone?"

John shook his head. "No phone either."

"I called in and ordered phone records from her account this morning," Susan said. "We should be getting them in a day or so."

"How did the sweep on the interior of the house go?" Liam asked John.

"The blood type from our victim matches the blood you found at the bottom of the stairs," John replied. "We're waiting on DNA to confirm. After the house was cleared, we did a full vacuum and luminol spray. Aside from your usual things like carpet fibers, food particles, human hair, and skin flakes, we found traces of fiberglass, gypsum, perlite, clay, and cellulose in the finished basement. The minerals found were most likely from the ceiling tiles. We're analyzing that further."

"You find any more blood?"

"No, but when we swabbed the surfaces, we found that the floors, both upstairs and downstairs, as well as floors and furniture in the parents' bedroom and bath, had been cleaned with a compound made up of sodium percarbonate and sodium carbonate. These substances form oxygen and hydrogen peroxide when mixed with water."

Liam stepped forward. "And if materials stained with blood are cleaned with products containing active oxygen, the luminol, phenolphthalein, and human hemoglobin tests we use give a negative result. You wouldn't find anything."

John nodded. "Exactly. You guys smelled the bleach, which we confirmed was also used. But if something happened inside the house, it could be cleaned up with a product as common as OxiClean or Clorox Oxi Magic, and we wouldn't pick it up with the luminol."

Susan circled the table slowly, looking at all the bags of trash, recalling what she'd seen inside the house. The missing rug from the main bedroom that was in one of Anja's pictures from a few weeks ago. Everything being so clean. Mindy Moore almost catatonic with shock. Noel Moore speaking for the family. The boy, Charlie.

"Something happened in that house," she said. "There's no debating that now. Liam found blood inside after Mr. Moore said no one went near the body. You found a cleaning product that was used throughout the house and would hide remnants of blood. We're missing a rug that would've been harder to clean than the hard surfaces. It all fits. Something went down inside that house." She looked up at John. "Could you tell if the body was moved?"

"Doesn't look that way, but double-check with Emily Nestor after the autopsy. See how the blood settled."

"I agree," Liam said. "It looks like something happened in the house."

"We have to keep digging," Susan said. "There's no way we can go to the DA with what we have. Not with the kind of lawyer the Moores hired. Everything has to be provable. We can't speculate."

"But maybe we should start concentrating more on the family," Liam replied.

"Exactly. Anja and the ex-boyfriend both said Mindy Moore was like a prison warden when it came to watching over Jennifer. And Anja said that Mindy and Jennifer were known to have some serious fights. What if one of their fights escalated to the point of triggering something, and it all went to hell from here?"

"Sounds as plausible as anything else we have."

"The family knows more than they're sharing. That much is clear." Susan turned away from the table. "I'm going to get a warrant for some financial records on the family. I want to see what Mr. Wall Street is all about. And I want to talk to the family priest, Father McCall. Let's find out what brought a teenage girl to his doorstep in the first place. Maybe she talked to him about something we should know about."

"I'll find out where the rectory is," Liam said.

"Something's not right. I can feel it. That family is off."

# 17

The house was dark when Charlie and his father returned home, but as soon as they turned into their driveway, lights from the half dozen news vans came to life, and reporters and cameramen spilled from the sliding doors. They rushed across the street and up to the barricade the police had erected, snapping shots and shooting footage, the reporters shouting questions and providing a kind of play-by-play. A single Lewisboro police officer manned the barricade and kept everyone back as the car sped into the garage and the door shut.

Charlie walked in through the mudroom like he'd done more times than he could count, but at that moment it felt like he was walking into a stranger's house. Everything seemed out of place. From the silence that was so uncharacteristic, to the fact that every single light had been out, to the heavy feeling of dread that filled all the rooms at once, he felt like this was the first time he was seeing the house he'd grown up in. It was foreign to him. Someplace that wasn't really his. He wanted to leave and walk back in again, hoping that the lights would be on and dinner would be on the table and his mother and Jen would be waiting for them to eat. The sadness and guilt and overwhelming grief was starting to crush his frail frame. It was all too much.

His father put down the gym bag he'd packed their stuff in and walked ahead of him, turning on the lights as they made their way from the foyer to the family room and farther into the kitchen. They didn't speak, and in fact hadn't said much of anything since leaving the hotel. One second Charlie was watching the television, and the next his father was telling him that the police called and said they could return to the house. That had pretty much been the extent of their conversation.

"You want something to eat?" his father asked, pulling the refrigerator door open and peering inside. "Looks like we got some leftover taco stuff or a couple of burgers that I made a few nights back."

"I'll have a burger."

"Coming right up."

Charlie walked into the family room and plopped down on the love seat that faced a row of windows. All he could see was his reflection staring back, but he knew that beyond the darkness that filled each pane was their patio, their yard, and the woods. He focused, trying to see the first line of trees that his sister would've walked through, but he couldn't see anything. Just a scared boy sitting on a love seat looking back at him.

The door to the microwave shut, and the burger began warming. Charlie took his phone from his pocket and turned it on, his thumb immediately hitting the Instagram app more out of habit than anything else. He began scrolling, looking through his feed, trying to get his mind off everything that had happened. But just like when he went in to look the night before, and that morning, and again when they'd finished lunch, his feed was full of messages and questions about his sister. He was tagged in tributes to Jennifer and linked to conspiracy theories and news stories that had already begun to emerge. His DMs were filled with questions about what happened and condolences for his loss and mini stories about what a great person his sister had been. Jen's face, smiling and laughing and making funny expressions, was on post after post. Pictures, videos, snaps. It was too much. He shut the phone off and tossed it onto the coffee table, choking back tears that wanted to come.

The microwave finished its countdown, and a digital bell began to chime. Charlie wiped his eyes and climbed from the love seat. He walked to the kitchen table just as his father slipped the burger onto a bun and served it to him on a paper plate. He gave him ketchup and a glass of lemonade but forgot a napkin.

"I wish I had time to make something better."

"This is fine."

His father leaned against the counter near the sink and folded his arms in front of him. "Listen, we're going to have to get up pretty early tomorrow. I have to take care of some arrangements for Jen, and I want to go see how your mom's doing. I think they might let her come home. I'm going to drop you at Bobby's house. You'll spend the day with him. I already called his folks, and his mom said it was fine. Okay?"

Charlie took a bite of the burger. "I'd like to see Mom too. Can you pick me up, and we'll go together?"

"You'll see her when she gets here. I don't want you to see her in the hospital. That's not right."

"I'm not a baby, Dad. I can handle it."

"I know you can."

Charlie fell back in his chair. "I can handle whatever I need to, okay? I'm going into high school next year. You can tell me whatever you have to about what happened the other night. I'm serious. All these secrets aren't cool. I'm part of this family too."

His father pushed off the counter and walked to the kitchen table. He sat opposite Charlie and scratched at the stubble on his cheeks. "I know you can handle whatever I need you to handle," he said softly. "There's no doubt about that. But right now I have to figure things out myself, and then we'll talk. I promise. I know I can't hide anything from you, and I'm not keeping secrets on purpose. But with the police sniffing around and the way these reporters like to tell their own stories about things, the less you know, the better. Everyone is going to start looking at me and your mom as suspects. Especially the police. That's how these things go. So the best thing you can do for all of us is to stay quiet about that night and be patient."

"You act like I can't deal with what's happening. I've been dealing with keeping secrets around here all my life. Do you even know about the fights Jen and Mom would have?"

"Of course."

"And the punishments Mom would give her if she messed up? Dad, she'd do some crazy things to Jen when you weren't here. Mean things. And then, when you got home, everyone would act like it was normal and nothing happened. Do you know about all that?"

His father stared at him for a moment, then slowly nodded. "I do. But that was before Jen changed her ways. They don't fight like that anymore. That's all in the past."

"Yeah, but now you were away again, and Jen's dead. Mom's in the hospital." He took a deep breath. "I know what I saw the other night. I know what I saw."

His father reached across the table, grabbed Charlie's hand. "You don't have to worry about any of that. Let me handle things for the time being, and everything will be taken care of. You stay quiet and stick to what we talked about when it comes to the police."

"Okay, but what about Mom?"

"She'll be fine."

"What if she—"

His father held up his hand. "No more. Tomorrow you go to Bobby's house, and you don't say anything about anything."

"Duh."

"I'm sure they're going to pry a little. Ask you about what happened and how you're holding up and how Mom's doing. Just answer as plain as you can. You're fine. Mom's fine. You don't know what happened. Just like that."

Charlie rolled his eyes. "I know, Dad. I'm with you. Don't worry. Family before everything else."

His father blinked away tears. "That's right," he said. "Family before everything else."

"And families have to love each other."

"Correct."

"No matter what?"

"No matter what."

# 18

Susan and Liam made their descent down onto the Scarsdale train station's platform as the 9:10 p.m. train pulled in. Despite the hour, dozens of commuters exited the six cars and began making their way to the parking lot across the street. The moon hung low on the horizon, the sky itself full of stars.

Arthur Breen emerged from the next-to-last car and walked toward the stairs that led to Christie Place. He was average height, average build, balding, tan. He was attractive, dressed in a slim-fitting, well-tailored blue-pinstripe two-piece; starched white shirt; thick red tie. The walking personification of a Wall Street banker. Susan pointed him out, and they worked their way around the others to get to their guy.

"Burning that midnight oil?" Susan began when they reached him.

Arthur turned around and stopped in the middle of the staircase. He looked at them and put on a kind smile. Susan could tell he was working out who they were, so she opened her sport coat and showed him her shield. His smile faded, and his eyes grew dark.

"Do you mind if we talk for a second? I called your office a few times today, and your receptionist kept telling me you were busy."

Arthur pointed up toward the street. "I really do have to get home."

"No problem. We'll walk with you."

Susan climbed the stairs with Arthur. Liam was behind them.

"I'm not answering any questions without my lawyer," Arthur said.

"You don't need a lawyer," Susan replied. "These aren't those kinds of questions. I just want to know some basic info for our files. Please."

Arthur held her gaze for a few seconds, then looked straight ahead.

"You're Jennifer's godfather, right?"

"Yes."

"And you've known Noel since you guys started at Lehman together?"

"Yes."

They reached the top of the stairs.

"Tell me about you and Noel. What's your relationship?"

Arthur shrugged as his eyes welled. "We're like brothers. He's family. They all are. We met at Lehman, and when that all fell apart, we ventured out on our own and started our own wealth management firm. I have a pretty robust networking group from my contacts at Yale, and those contacts have contacts. Next thing I know, we're sitting in front of some of the wealthiest people in the world, pitching our little firm. But Noel is the one who's so good at it. He knows how to push the right buttons and talk the language just enough so that he can get the big money interested without confusing them. I tee them up, and Noel closes. That's been the foundation of our partnership since the beginning. He can't hook the big fish without me, and I can't land the big fish without him."

"And together you've made a nice living for yourselves."

"You could say that. Yes."

They began to walk toward the corner that connected to the covered parking lot.

"Did you know Jennifer had a boyfriend?" Susan asked. "Kid's name is Glenn Baker. Ring a bell?"

"No," Arthur replied. "And I didn't know she had a boyfriend."

"Apparently, this kid got kind of stalky. Started following her around and taking pictures of the people she was with. Kept trying to get her back. Nonstop phone calls and texts. That kind of thing."

They arrived at the corner, and Arthur turned toward them. "Do you think he had something to do with what happened to Jen?"

"Maybe. I can't rule anything out at this point." Susan looked at the light and saw it was red. Still time before they had to start moving again. "I've heard from some people that Mindy was a pretty strict mother. Especially with Jennifer. You know anything about that?"

"Not really. Mindy had her rules as any parent would. Not a big deal."

"Yeah, but I heard there were screaming matches and fights that could get physical sometimes. You ever witness anything like that? Noel ever mention it at the office?"

Arthur snorted a laugh. "I thought you said you had questions that wouldn't involve me needing my lawyer. Now you want me to help you jump from a mother disciplining her kid to murdering her kid? Get lost."

Susan put up her hands. "I didn't say that. I'm just curious about how crazy their fights got. That's all."

"Mindy loved Jennifer. We all did. End of story."

The light turned green, and Susan placed a hand on Arthur's shoulder to keep him from crossing the street.

"We'll be done by the time the next green comes around. I promise."

"You're wasting your time."

"Talk to me about the relationship between Jennifer and Charlie. Was it healthy? Strained? Violent?"

Arthur turned to face them. His face was glowing red from the traffic light. "It was a regular brother-and-sister relationship. What are you even getting at? Now you think Charlie might've killed Jen? Wow, you guys really have no idea who you're looking for, do you? A boyfriend. A parent. A sibling. Talk about a wide net. Hey, I was a family friend. Put me on the list too. Oh, and don't forget their gardener and housekeeper and handyman too. Jesus. We have a killer on the loose, and you're wasting your time focusing on the one set of people who loved that kid more than anything in the world. This is crap. All of it."

"Okay," Susan said. "Last question. I met the family priest at the house the other day, and I'm told Jennifer was active at her aunt's church and that he and Jennifer had become friends. Father McCall. You know anything about him? Ever meet him?"

"Now the priest is a suspect too?"

"Did you ever meet him?"

Arthur nodded. "Yes. A couple of years ago Jennifer found religion even though it wasn't something Noel or Mindy ever really pushed inside the house. Mindy's sister, Sidney, is quite religious, though, so I'm guessing she had something to do with Jen's sudden interest in God. Anyway, Jen was active in the church and always volunteering. She and Father McCall struck up a friendship." He stopped talking for a moment and looked toward the ground. "I met him a few times at family gatherings. Nice enough guy, but you never know, right? Wouldn't be the first time a priest broke a critical commandment."

The light turned green again, and Arthur stepped off the curb.

"I lied," Susan said. "I have one more question, and then you can go."

He stopped but didn't turn around.

"Where were you the night Jennifer died?"

"At home. Sleeping. With my wife next to me and my three kids in their rooms down the hall. We have cameras inside and outside the house. You're welcome to view them so you can see I went to bed and didn't get up until the next morning. No one left the house that night. You can go check them out right now. I'll let my wife know you're coming."

"That won't be necessary."

"Then leave me alone." Arthur walked across the street just as the traffic light was turning red again.

# 19

The party store was crowded, but the number of shoppers still paled in comparison to the overall size of the place. Liam walked with Susan down an aisle full of birthday party accessories that held so many items he wasn't sure there'd ever be a party big enough to use everything offered on-site.

"This place is huge," he said, looking around in awe. "I didn't realize parties had so many different themes. Other than Halloween, I've never gone to a party where I had to dress up in costume."

"Me either," Susan replied. "The last party Eric and I went to was like a basic masquerade theme, and that was for his firm's charity event. Other than that, we just hung out with friends over dinner and drinks. Maybe a board game or charades."

"I think we might be considered lame."

"I wear that badge with pride."

They laughed, and their shoulders bumped lightly as they walked. For a moment, Liam thought about placing his hand next to hers, just to see what it would feel like, but he pulled away with his next step.

"I still have so much planning to do," she said. "One minute I'm thinking about motives and evidence, and the next minute I'm worrying about piñatas and streamers and whether we should go with Mylar balloons or the cheaper rubber ones."

"Sounds like the typical life of a state police investigator and single mom. Also sounds like you're doing a great job with both. You got this."

"Thanks." Susan looked away, her cheeks blushing just a bit. "My mom's a huge factor. She's such a help. If I didn't have her watching over the kids while I'm working these crazy hours with cases, I don't know what I'd do. She's the best."

"Yes, she is."

It felt nice to be out with another adult, even if it was at a party store for Susan's kids. It was easy with her. Never any preconceptions or awkwardness. They were a good team. He felt at peace when she was around, and the twins were just the icing on top. He'd always wanted kids, but it hadn't been in the cards for him and Vanessa. Then Kerry Miller happened. Then everything went down with his brother. It was a struggle for him to feel safe in any kind of a relationship. With Susan, it just felt right.

"What do you think about this eighteen-year-old girl hanging out with a middle-aged priest?" Susan asked.

"I don't know," Liam replied. "Might sound stranger than it actually was. Maybe she wanted some religion in her life. Maybe she wanted to try and offset some of her darker side. We'll have to find out."

"Yeah."

"I'm more concerned about the family."

"What do you mean?"

Liam stuffed his hands in his pocket. "We keep looking at people outside the family. The ex-boyfriend. Noel's partner. But none of that jibes with the blood in the house and the parents' bedroom being cleaned up like it was except for Jennifer's killer being someone inside the family. Noel was in Florida, so he's out. That leaves Mrs. Moore or their son. In any other scenario, it wouldn't make sense to clean up the mess."

"Maybe they were forced to clean it up by someone else?"

"Then why not tell us?"

"Fear?"

Before Liam could reply, a store employee turned the corner and stopped when he saw them. He was a skinny guy, all arms and legs.

"Officer, state police!" the man said as he clapped his hands. "I'm glad you came back." He took a step forward and extended his hand to Liam. "Dennis Sinclair. Store manager."

"Liam Dwyer. Nice to meet you."

"You must be the father of the birthday twins."

"No." Liam smiled. Now it was his turn to blush. "Just a friend."

Dennis turned his attention back to Susan. "So how'd your case work out? All solved?"

"We're working on it."

Dennis clapped his hands again. "What can I help you with? Have you given any more thought to the ideas I gave you?"

"Actually, we have," Susan replied. "We're going with the petting zoo. The twins thought it was a great idea."

"Excellent!" Dennis exclaimed. "Come up front, and I'll give you the name of my guy at the petting zoo company. And I'll set you up with the party package that goes with the theme so you don't have to waste time picking things out à la carte."

Susan smiled. "Sounds great. We'll meet you up front."

Liam watched Dennis disappear down the aisle, whistling as he went.

"That's a guy who loves his job," he said. "I wish I could be as fulfilled at work. I'm jealous."

"You'll feel fulfilled when we catch whoever killed Jennifer," Susan said as she placed a hand on Liam's back and gently pushed him forward. "That, I can promise. Getting the bad guy is always the best part."

# 20

Before the door was even open all the way, Charlie was swallowed into Monica Teagan's embrace. His face was mashed against her large bosom, and her arms surrounded his ears. He could hear her muffled voice speaking to his father.

"Oh, Noel, I'm so, so sorry."

"Thank you, Monica."

"Is there anything I can do? Anything you need?"

"No, thank you. Taking Charlie for a few hours is help enough. I just need to see to a few things with Jen's arrangements. I'll try not to be too long."

"Nonsense. You take as much time as you need. We'll be here. Whatever you need."

"I think they're going to let Mindy come home today."

"That's good news."

His father tapped him on the back.

"I'll see you in a few, bud."

"Okay," Charlie replied into Mrs. Teagan's chest. "I'll see you later."

Mrs. Teagan shut the door and lifted her heavy arms off Charlie's shoulders. She held him at arm's length from her body. His father often described her as big boned, which seemed accurate. Bobby described his mom as tall and fat. Whatever. It didn't matter. What mattered was, since the day the Teagans arrived in the neighborhood four years earlier, she'd been one of the kindest people he knew. She was the type of person who would always buy them extra snacks whenever Charlie slept over and would drop whatever she was doing to drive them someplace. She let Bobby have small parties in their basement and might even look the other way if kids brought a little beer and some vape sticks. Bobby was her only child; therefore, he was her everything.

They stood in the foyer, quiet, her hands still grasping his arms, holding him away from her but not letting go. She twice opened her mouth to say something and twice closed it. She cleared her throat and put on a half smile.

"I am so sorry about you sister," she managed. The corners of her lips were quivering. "I can't imagine what you're feeling right now. I won't even try."

Charlie tried on a smile of his own. "Thank you."

What else could he say? What was the follow-up after thank you?

"You want me to make you some breakfast?"

"No, that's okay. Me and my dad ate on the way over."

Tears began to well in Mrs. Teagan's eyes. "I simply cannot wrap my head around this. I saw Jenny the other day when she came to pick you up. We were talking about her leaving for Duke. She was so excited." She wiped away tears that began slipping down her cheeks. "I'm going to tell you the same thing I told your dad. If you need anything. Anything. You just ask. Understand?"

"Yes."

"Good. Now, go see Bobby. He's in his room, and he's just as broken up about this as I am. He loved your sister very much. She was always good to him."

Charlie wondered if Mrs. Teagan knew the extent to which her little boy loved Jen. The fact was, Bobby was obsessed with her, and had been for as long as Charlie could remember. The older they got—and the older his sister got—the more Bobby's infatuation with her grew. It had become commonplace for Bobby to come to Charlie's house under the guise of hanging out, but with the real purpose of trying to catch a glimpse of Jen or, even better, to strike up a little small talk.

Whenever Jen would engage him, Bobby's face would turn bright red and the stammer he claimed to have conquered in kindergarten would suddenly rear its head. Charlie teased him about it, as did his other friends, but Bobby never cared. He swore he'd marry Jennifer Moore one day, come hell or high water. Now there was simply no chance of that ever happening. Ever.

Charlie went upstairs to Bobby's room. Half of the texts and Instagram comments he'd received were from Bobby, asking what had happened and imploring him to admit that it was all some kind of sick joke. Most of the texts and DMs had gone unanswered. Charlie hadn't had the strength to read any more about his sister's death.

Bobby was sitting on his bedroom floor, legs crossed in front of him, back leaning against his bed. He had on his red-and-white middle school lacrosse jersey and a matching pair of mesh lacrosse shorts. His moppy blond hair was in his face, covering his eyes and nose. He had his AirPods in and was looking down at his phone.

Charlie watched his friend for a moment, standing just inside the bedroom. Bobby looked peaceful, something Charlie had been trying to pull off himself but wasn't sure if it was working. He was a ball of emotion and couldn't tell if people knew. Fear, anger, sadness, bewilderment. Guilt. They were overwhelming him, but he knew he had secrets to keep. For himself and for his family. He also realized that as the hours passed, the reality of his sister being dead was becoming more permanent and the shock he'd felt at the beginning was wearing off, replaced with a sadness he feared would eventually destroy him.

Bobby looked up from his phone and pulled one of his AirPods out. His eyes were red and double the size they should have been. Charlie had never seen eyes so swollen. Dirt streaks revealed the path his friend's tears had taken down his face. Bobby sniffled once and exhaled a choppy breath.

"Hey."

"Hey," Charlie replied.

"So it's true? I mean, one hundred percent true? She's gone?"

"Yeah. She's gone."

"Fuuuuck." Bobby shut his eyes tight and let his head fall back against the bed. He started crying softly, sniffling and sobbing.

Charlie stood and watched. He had no idea what to say or how to comfort him, and thought perhaps the situation should be reversed. It should have been Charlie who was crying and Bobby consoling him and telling him everything would be okay. Why was his friend more upset than he himself was that Jen was dead? It didn't make sense. Why wasn't he sad enough?

"I loved her, you know."

"I know."

"No, I mean it was real love. True love. I thought about her every day. She was the one."

"She knew you loved her. She didn't mind."

"I was going to marry her. We were going to have a family. I would've waited forever to make her mine. Now . . ."

Bobby started crying again, a little harder this time. He cupped his hands over his face, and Charlie could see his shoulders shaking.

"You wanna go check out where they found her?" Charlie asked. He didn't know what else to say, but he knew he had to get over to the site to see if the police had found what he had buried. "I haven't been there yet, and I'd like to see it. There's a lot of rumors up online, and I was thinking I could go there and look myself and answer some of those rumors with the truth. It might help."

Bobby wiped his eyes with his jersey. "We can't go. The police have it all taped off. I saw pics online."

"We can go into the woods through the walking path instead of my yard. No one will know we're there, and we'll just duck under the tape."

"But won't we be messing with evidence or something?"

"Yeah, maybe. But do you care? I'd like to see where my sister died. Maybe it'll help me process it or something. Plus, I might be able to see enough to shoot down some of the bullshit that's getting posted. You coming?"

"Are you going even if I don't go?"

"Yup."

"Okay, then," Bobby said. "I'll go." He climbed to his feet and grabbed a hat that was hanging on a coatrack in the corner. "Let me do the talking with my mom. She's not going to want us outside with the news vans in the area and all that."

"Yeah, no problem."

"I can't let you go to that place alone. Maybe it will help. Maybe we can squash some of the bullshit. I owe her that much."

"You don't owe her anything."

Bobby didn't answer. He shoved his phone in his pocket and walked out of his room. Charlie followed, hoping he'd sounded natural when he said he just wanted to see the place Jen died at.

He already knew where she'd died. He knew *exactly* where.

# 21

Liam was already at the Lewisboro headquarters when Susan walked in.

"Hey," she said as she dropped her bag on her desk. "You're in early."

"Couldn't sleep, so I thought I'd get a head start on the day. I got the priest's address in Yorktown."

"Excellent."

"You got me thinking when you said someone could have killed Jennifer and forced Mindy Moore to clean it up. It's plausible, so I dove in a bit deeper on Noel's firm, Phoenix Capital."

"What'd you find?"

Liam reached across his desk and handed Susan a file filled with screenshots and articles that he'd printed from the internet.

"Nothing more on the firm itself, but I started researching this Uriah Sitchel, the client that Noel was in Florida visiting. From what I can tell, Noel and Arthur are not only wealth advisors for Uriah; they're also business partners. They use Uriah as a marketing tool to show the other rich and famous people out there that if Phoenix Capital is good enough for him, it should be good enough for them."

Susan closed the file and handed it back. "Uriah Sitchel's a big name here in New York. He's like a one-man real estate empire. Almost single-handedly rebuilt lower Manhattan after 9/11. The guy's worth more than Bloomberg. A billionaire and then some."

Liam pushed another sheet of paper across the desk. "Phoenix Capital has partnered with Uriah on a few of his projects. Sometimes they act as brokers to help raise capital for a build. Sometimes they're his investment banker and invest proceeds from a sale or liquidation. Right now they're helping him put up Hudson Tiers on the west side."

The paper was an article with a photo of the three men standing shoulder to shoulder. Noel Moore, Arthur Breen, and Uriah Sitchel.

"I came across this buried in a financial newspaper for the Wall Street guys," he continued. "It wasn't big news as far as mainstream media is concerned, but in the financial world, it was huge."

"How huge?"

"Huge enough that there might be a motive for one of the richest men in the world to kill his wealth advisor's daughter."

Susan sat up in her chair. "Talk to me."

Liam passed another sheet of paper across the desk and pointed to a picture of a group of men, maybe late thirties, sitting on a bench on the Google campus. "The first guy on the left is Ziggy Dennings," he explained. "Ziggy was a member of the team that invented the algorithm that can track what people search for online and target ads based on those searches. After about ten years, they sold to Google and made hundreds of millions in profit. But Ziggy was a minority owner, so when the company sold, he walked away with twenty million while the others walked away with ten times as much."

"Poor guy."

"Ziggy and Uriah were friends dating back to their college years at Yale, and Arthur also had his Yale connection with Uriah, so Uriah introduced Ziggy to Phoenix Capital, and Phoenix managed Ziggy's sudden windfall. After a while, Noel and Arthur brought Ziggy an opportunity to invest in a pharmaceutical start-up called Duel Pharma. They were making a drug to target and kill ovarian cancer. It was supposed to be a slam dunk, so they put half of Ziggy's money into it and planned to turn ten million into eighty-five million."

"But it didn't happen."

Liam shook his head. "The drug was in the last phase of approval and got squashed. No one knows why, but there's speculation that a competitor with deep pockets paid off someone at the FDA to kill it so the competitor could be first to market with a similar drug. Duel's stock fell to a penny. Ziggy lost half his fortune. Just like that."

Susan closed the file and sat back in her seat. "He must've been upset."

Liam nodded. "I would think so. He jumped off the Whitestone Bridge last year."

Susan looked at Liam, and he waited.

"In the world of rich white men," she said, "that must've been embarrassing for Uriah to have made an introduction that ended up ruining a man's life."

"Had to have been. Ten million dollars is a lot of money, but a man like Uriah Sitchel holds more value in his reputation. That misstep must've been a black mark on his ability to make proper connections. A chink in his networking armor."

Susan placed her elbows on the table and folded her hands together. "You know, people like Uriah Sitchel are not the kind of people who accept losing. They're not used to it. They haven't been told no in decades, and they have no perception of what it's like to be a regular person. People like Uriah Sitchel can get upset if someone promised them something and couldn't deliver. They could get equally upset if they're embarrassed in front of their friends. If someone like Noel and Arthur created the impression that Uriah can't accept losing and isn't as strong as people perceive him to be, that could cause a problem when doing business in the future. People like Uriah Sitchel would never be okay with that. Ever. People like Uriah Sitchel wouldn't think twice about taking something someone loved to prove a point. He might even be powerful enough to make someone else clean up the mess."

Liam smiled. "He knew Noel wasn't going to be home because Noel was going to be with him."

"I think we need to get to Florida to talk to Mr. Sitchel."

"I'll book us a flight."

# 22

They told Bobby's mom that they were going to take their bikes to their friend Mike's house around the corner. Mrs. Teagan was reluctant at first, but Bobby assured her he'd call when they got there and call her when they were coming back. After a few rounds of worry and assurances, she let them go. They rode to Mike's, but never bothered to knock on his door. Bobby called his mom from the edge of Mike's driveway and let her know they'd made it. He then hid his phone in a pile of firewood next to Mike's driveway, knowing his mother would keep tabs on them through the tracking app she'd made him download. When they were done in the woods, he'd come back for the phone and call her to say that they were returning to the house, and she'd never know they'd been anywhere else. The plan was perfect in its simplicity.

It was only about two miles between their houses, and Charlie and Bobby rode cautiously, looking out for police cars or news vans. They turned off Old Corner Road and followed Pine Brook Road until they hit the entrance to the walking path. They ditched their bikes behind an old dumpster and went the last half mile on foot.

The morning was cool, the rising sun still caught behind the trees. It would be another two hours before it sat high in the sky, baking everyone beneath it. The two boys walked without speaking, dead leaves and fallen twigs crunching and snapping underfoot.

"Did you hear anything that night?" Bobby asked, breaking the silence.

Charlie thought about what a loaded question that was. He shook his head. "Nah. I was asleep until morning. I came down for breakfast, and my dad told me something happened to Jen."

"Did you see your mom?"

"Yeah, she was down with my dad. But she was all messed up. Like she was a statue. Just sitting there and staring. It was freaky."

"And then the cops came?"

"Yeah."

"And they started working back where Jen was?"

Charlie shrugged. "I guess. They kept us in the living room the whole time. And when they talked to us, they mostly talked to my dad. I didn't really hear or see much. Next thing I know, we're sleeping at a hotel and my mom's in the hospital. It's so crazy."

"What was Jen doing back there?"

Charlie didn't answer. Instead, he stopped and peered through the thicket of trees. "There it is. You see the yellow tape? That must be the outer part of the crime scene."

"Wow, that's a huge border," Bobby said. "That's nowhere near where Jen was."

"How do you know where she was?"

"All the posts online said they found her where the high school kids have their hangout. In the clearing. This isn't anywhere near that."

"I guess they were collecting evidence from as far out as they could. Come on."

Charlie pushed through a section of weeping willows. Their low-hanging branches brushed against his arms, tickling his skin. The woods were dense here. They weren't following any paths or trails. This was rough and uncut, and in their sneakers and shorts, it made for a slow-going hike.

"Hey, hold on a minute."

Charlie turned around to find Bobby standing on the other side of the willows. He was hugging his arms, looking at the police tape they could see a little clearer now. His face was pale, and there were new tears in his eyes.

"What's wrong?"

"I changed my mind. I don't want to see it. I don't want to go."

"We need to find out what's really there so we can stop all the lies that're online."

"No. I can't go. I can't."

Charlie walked back a few steps toward his friend. "Why are you freaking out?"

"I can't go. Please. Let's leave."

"We just need to look around once. I want to see where she was found. I have to see for myself."

Bobby turned away and started retreating to the path. "I'm not going."

"I need your help."

"I'm not going."

Charlie ducked past the willows and ran to catch up with Bobby. He took him by the shoulder and spun him around.

"Get off!" Bobby yelled.

"What's the matter with you?" Charlie snapped. "You said you were coming. You said you loved Jen."

"I do!"

"Then come see where they found her so we can tell those assholes online to take their rumors and shove them."

"No! I'm not going! Get it through your head! I don't want to see!"

Charlie watched Bobby run back to the path that would return him to their bikes. He could hear his friend crying as he went, his figure growing more distant as the density of the woods swallowed him. Charlie looked over his shoulder one last time, concentrating on the yellow police tape. His mind flashed again with the images from that night.

The blood.

The bedroom.

The towels.

His father's fear masked as anger.

"Wait up!"

Charlie sprinted toward Bobby, who was already a good two hundred yards ahead of him, the one question he'd ignored circling in his mind.

He knew why Jen had been out in the woods that night.

*Who else was out here with her?*

# 23

Father McCall opened the door to the rectory before Susan and Liam had a chance to climb the stone steps and knock. He was dressed in a simple black cassock and collar. His eyes were sad. He clutched a handkerchief in his hand.

"Good afternoon," he said.

"Good afternoon, Father," Susan replied. "We appreciate you meeting us."

"I thought we could talk around back, in the garden. It's such a beautiful day. I'd hate to waste a second of it inside."

"Lead the way."

They followed a brick path around to the back of the small stone rectory. The church itself, Saint Mark's, was across a large field and attached parking lot. Susan could see the tips of the two spires reaching up over the tree line.

"Any news on Jennifer?" Father McCall asked. He walked with his hands behind his back, head down.

"Nothing we can share with you," Susan replied.

"I understand."

"How long have you known the Moore family?"

"I met Sidney, Mindy's sister, when I was first assigned to this church about five years ago. She's always been a very active parishioner and one of our best volunteers. It seems to sadden her that her sister's family doesn't practice their faith, so Sidney used to bring me around to their family functions in an attempt to try and steer them back toward the church. And one day, completely out of the blue, Jennifer approached me with a glass of iced tea, and we talked on the back steps of the house for hours. She had so many questions and was so interested in what God preaches and how she might be able to serve him. I never saw anything like it. Most visits she'd wanted nothing to do with me and avoided me at all costs. Then one day, God speaks to her, and she ends up being one of his children and one of my friends. Now this."

The brick path ended at a horse fence that marked the boundary of a large flower garden. They walked inside and sat on two benches that faced one another. Father McCall wiped his eyes while Susan watched bees and butterflies hop from roses to tulips to sunflowers to daisies. The different colors and the unique smells that drifted through the air were awe inspiring. The twins would love a place like this. It was amazing.

"When did this happen?" Susan asked. "The family function and Jennifer wanting to find God."

Father McCall thought for a moment. "Summer. Two years ago."

"And you guys kept in touch?" Liam asked.

"Oh yes," the priest replied. "We were very close. I can't believe something like this could've happened to such a sweet girl. These are some of the mysteries of God I'll never understand."

"What did you and Jennifer discuss in the beginning?" Susan asked.

The priest looked up at the radiant blue sky. "Nothing much at first," he replied. "Small talk. I figured she was trying to see how comfortable she would be talking with someone like me. As I said before, religion wasn't something that was practiced by the family aside from Sidney, so I reasoned that a talk at a family picnic was one thing, but taking it to the next level and actually practicing the faith was another. I eased her into it. She came to church with Sidney and stayed after the service some days to learn about the sacraments and what would be expected of her in the faith. The official talks eventually became personal ones." He shifted in his seat. "She told me about her family and the disagreements she had with her mother. We talked through that, and she eventually opened up about her drinking and drug use. From what she told me, she was trying to get all that under control before leaving for college. She was struggling with some demons. No doubt about that."

"Tell me about the family."

Father McCall sighed. "I feel like I'm talking out of school."

"We're just trying to gather all the facts we can so we can figure out what might've happened to Jennifer."

The priest nodded and paused for a few beats. "Jen talked about how her mother could be . . . overbearing and how her father was often absent from the house. She never mentioned anything specific, but I could tell there was a level of abuse there. Maybe not enough to need the police, but something was off. Her parents were driven by success and material items, but she was wired differently. Despite growing up wealthy, Jen didn't seem to care about money as much as the people around her, and that made her feel alienated sometimes. I think that's why she ended up with that boyfriend. Glenn was the antithesis of rich, successful people. I think she was drawn to him purely for the fact that he was unlike the circle of friends her family expected her to be with."

"Did Jennifer seem scared of Glenn?" Susan asked. "Did she express concern for her safety?"

"No. He was more of an annoyance than anything else."

Susan watched a butterfly hover over a daylily, then land gently on the flower. "Did Jennifer seem depressed or anxious in general?"

"No. In fact, she seemed much better as it came time to leave for Duke. She was so looking forward to starting fresh. It was like a new light had been lit within her." The priest leaned forward and balanced his elbows on his knees. He looked back and forth between Susan and Liam. "It doesn't matter how many times I pray on this; I just can't believe Jen was killed with such violence. Please promise me you'll catch whoever is responsible. Please."

Susan could see the anguish in the priest's eyes and reached over to place her hand on his arm. "We're going to find who did this," she said. "I promise you. We'll find them, and we'll bring them to justice."

Father McCall tried to smile and patted her hand. "You can't lie to a priest, you know. It's against the rules."

"I wouldn't, and I'm not," Susan replied. "We'll find Jennifer's killer if it's the last thing we do."

# 24

Jennifer Moore's body was the only cadaver in the examination room. She'd been placed on the first of three stainless steel tables, closest to Dr. Nestor's office space. There was a white sheet covering everything except her face, which was pale but peaceful. No markings or scratching or trauma of any kind. All the damage had been from the neck down.

Dr. Emily Nestor snapped a file from her desk and opened it. "Okay," she began. "Jennifer Moore, eighteen, female. Time of death looks to be between midnight and three in the morning, based on the blood settling in the body and organ shutdown."

"The mom found her around eight, so I guess that makes sense," Susan said.

"Cause of death was definitely the excessive loss of blood from stabbing. One punctured a lung, and one nicked the heart, but the loss of blood led to her death."

Liam stepped up to the table. "Any defensive wounds?"

"None," Nestor said. "So your theory that she was killed quickly stands up." She reached under Jennifer's head and lifted it. "You can see where I shaved, there's a pretty severe gash on the back of her head. Someone hit her pretty hard. If she was knocked out before she was stabbed, that would explain the lack of defensive wounds."

"We found plenty of rocks in the clearing where the body was found," Liam said. "A lot of them had spatter. John collected them."

"If he finds one with skull fragments or hair, that's probably what the perp used to knock her down."

Susan pulled away the sheet that was covering Jennifer's body. She bent over and examined the knife wounds in her stomach and chest. Nothing too grotesque. No mutilation of any kind. A simple in and out as far as she could tell.

"There's some bruising around the wrists and ankles that are separate from our crime," Nestor continued. "These bruises are old and almost healed. There's also some bruising on the buttocks. Nothing severe. Like she was hit with something. Spanked, maybe?"

"Mom was a disciplinarian," Liam said.

Nestor paged through the file. "I also found evidence of a past abortion. Hard to tell how long ago that took place, but I'd say in the last five years. She's only eighteen, so she probably didn't reach puberty until around thirteen. There's your five-year window."

"Can you tell the last time she had sex?"

"No, but I'm fairly sure she hadn't had sex the night before or morning of her death. There was no discharge or semen or traces of any spermicides found."

Susan turned away from the body and began pacing the room. "Glenn Baker said she was a virgin. That was why he thought she wouldn't have sex with him. He kept calling her a tease, like she would pretend she wanted it, but when push came to shove, she'd put a stop to things. But maybe that's the natural reaction of someone who's had a teenage pregnancy and had to go through the trauma of terminating it. She wanted to push through and become sexually active again, but every time she tried, she'd relive the trauma. She'd get to a certain point and wouldn't be able to go any further."

Liam was chewing his bottom lip. "If we can find the clinic that performed Jennifer's procedure, they might have the father listed on their paperwork. Could lead us somewhere."

Susan nodded. "I agree. We need to find the father."

"And that five-year window might be able to be shortened to two years," Liam said. He walked around the examination table. "If there was one thing that could cause a young woman to seek religion out of the blue, a terminated pregnancy might be it."

Susan looked down at Jennifer's body. "You think she confessed to Father McCall?"

"Only one way to find out."

# 25

The number of news vans out in front of the house looked like it had gotten bigger since he'd been at Bobby's. Charlie's father whipped down the street and pulled into the driveway as quickly as the police officers could pull back the wooden horses.

The house was dark and quiet again, so different than what he was used to. Charlie walked behind his father, who was helping his mother through the mudroom, down the hall, and into the family room. He placed her in the same chair she'd been in the morning the police had come, only this time, instead of looking blankly out the window into the backyard and woods, she let her head fall back, and she closed her eyes.

Charlie watched for a moment, then went around the house turning on the lights. He flipped on the television and plopped down on the couch. The Yankees were playing the Rays.

"Mom, is this too loud?" Charlie asked, looking over at his mother, who remained motionless. "Mom?"

"It's fine," his father replied from the kitchen. "You want something to eat?"

"No. I already ate at Bobby's."

His father walked into the family room carrying a glass of water and a bottle of pills. He put the water down and shook two of the pills out into his hand. "Who's winning?"

"Yanks. Five to one."

"Nice."

Charlie watched as his father bent down next to his mother and slipped the pills between her lips. He grabbed the water and helped her sip from the glass. When he was done, he wiped her chin, placed the glass back on the coffee table, kissed her on the top of her head, and made his way toward the stairs.

"I'm going to go take a shower, and I need to make a few calls. You okay down here with your mom?"

"Sure."

"Don't answer the phone or the door."

"I won't."

Charlie watched his father climb the stairs and took notice of how *old* each footstep sounded. His dad usually bounced up the stairs, but now it was just the drum of each foot pounding the tread with a long pause in between. It was unnerving.

Despite the sunny afternoon, heavy drapes covered the wall of windows that stretched across the back of the house. His father had left them drawn after more news vans started showing up. He was afraid they'd eventually sneak through the barrier tape and start taking pictures, so they were shut both day and night. So much had changed in such a short period of time.

Charlie climbed off the couch and approached his mother. She was sleeping, head tilted to the side, a dull snore emanating from her chest. She looked troubled even in sleep, like she wanted to cry or scream or yell but the drugs in her system prevented her from doing so.

"Mom," Charlie whispered, shaking her gently by the shoulder. "Mom, can you hear me?"

She continued to sleep, unmoving.

"Mom."

Charlie glanced back toward the stairs to ensure they were still alone.

"Mom. Please. Wake up. I need to talk to you."

He shook her again, a little harder this time, but his mother was like a rag doll, lifeless. He leaned in next to her ear, so close he could still smell the disinfectant soap from the hospital.

"Mom. I'm sorry." Tears began to blur his vision; his voice cracked from crying. "I'm sorry for what I did. I'm sorry for taking Jen away from you. I didn't mean it. I need you to know that. I didn't mean it."

There was no verbal reaction or movement from his mother, but he knew she'd heard him. He knew because he could see the single tear break away and run down her right cheek. That was all the answer he needed. He laid his head on her lap and cried as quietly as he could so his father wouldn't hear.

# 26

Father McCall was no longer dressed in his cassock and collar. He answered the rectory door in a white T-shirt and a pair of blue khaki shorts, no socks or shoes.

"I'm so sorry for coming unannounced," Susan said as he stepped back and allowed her and Liam to gather in the foyer.

"No worries," Father McCall replied. "If I knew you were coming, I would've put on my costume, though."

He chuckled, but neither Susan nor Liam reciprocated.

"I just have a quick question," Susan continued. "Did you know Jennifer had an abortion?"

The priest gazed at the floor. "Yes."

"Was that the reason she sought you out two years ago?" Liam asked.

"It was." Father McCall retreated a few steps and sat on a bench that was stacked with copies of the previous Sunday's newsletter. "I didn't know anything at first. It was about six months in when she started broaching the subject. She danced around the details with her questions, but I knew what she was getting at. Eventually she confessed to what she'd done, and I forgave her. That was the point when she became more active in the church. It was like a weight had been lifted, and she was reborn."

"Did she ever tell you who the father was?"

"No, and I never asked. If she wanted to tell me, she would have. She never did."

"Is there anything else you haven't told us that might be pertinent to our investigation?" Susan asked.

The priest held up his hands in surrender. "I wasn't keeping this from you. I never really thought it would be pertinent to your case. Still don't. It was two years ago."

Susan turned and opened the door. "Two years or two days, I need to know everything that might point us in the right direction. You think about all of your talks with Jennifer, and I'll call you later to discuss *anything* that you think could mean something. Got it?"

"Yes. I—"

Liam walked out of the rectory, and Susan slammed the door behind her before the priest could say another word. She couldn't help but feel that time was somehow running out.

# 27

Susan and Liam walked into her house, and Susan could hear the twins in the yard talking about the puppy Casey wanted for her birthday. She hung her bag on the coatrack and went into the kitchen.

"And the dog would live with us here in our house instead of in the cage at the shelter, where it's cold and all the other dogs are always barking. Our dog could sleep at night without the other dogs waking it up, and we could call it Pixie if it's a girl or King if it's a boy."

"But what if it pees or poops on the floor? Mom might get mad, and I'm not cleaning it. That's gross."

"We'll get one that knows to go outside like a good dog."

"I'm still scared about the chickens."

"I already told you. The dog and the chickens will be best friends. I'll make sure."

"What color would you get?"

"I want a white dog with brown spots. I think those are the prettiest. And I want it to have blue eyes, and it can't be too big, or it'll knock Grandma over, and it can't be too small, or we might step on it by accident. I don't want to hurt it."

"You're getting a dog?" Liam asked.

"No," Susan replied. "We're definitely not."

She opened the patio door and stepped outside. The twins were feeding the chickens that congregated around them, pecking at the ground, while Beatrice was cleaning the coop and harvesting eggs.

"Guys! I'm home!"

"Hi, Mommy!"

"Hi!"

"Liam's here!"

Liam stepped outside. As soon as they saw him, the twins tossed the rest of their feed and ran to the deck. Liam positioned himself at the top of the stairs, arms outstretched.

"Hi, guys."

"Liam!"

"Hi, Liam!"

Casey and Tim fell into Liam's arms, and they hugged.

"Are you coming to our birthday party?" Casey asked. "It's going to be a petting zoo. Animals are going to be here!"

"Yes, I'm coming for sure," Liam said. "In fact, I already helped your mom pick out some stuff for the party. We're going to have fun. I can't wait."

"Did you see the pony?" Tim asked. "We're going to have a pony to ride on."

"I didn't see the pony, but I heard he's going to be awesome. Maybe I'll even go for a ride."

Casey giggled. "You can't ride the pony. You're too big!"

The twins laughed as they followed Susan and Liam down the stairs into the yard. Beatrice pulled her head out of the coop and waved with a handful of eggs.

"Hi, guys."

"Hi, Mom. You need any help?"

"Nope, all done."

Susan picked up a few morsels of feed and tossed them to the chickens that approached. Liam stood next to her and did the same.

"Nothing fancy tonight," Beatrice said as she walked toward them. "Spaghetti and meatballs. More than enough if you'd like to eat with us, Liam."

"Thanks, Beatrice," Liam replied. "That'd be great." He stepped forward and put out his hands. "Let me help you with those eggs."

Beatrice transferred some of the eggs to Liam, and the three of them walked back to the house. As soon as they stepped inside, Susan heard the news report playing from the small television on the counter next to the bread box. Donna Starr reporting from outside the Moore home.

*"It's been two days since the body of eighteen-year-old Jennifer Moore was found behind her home by her mother, Mindy Moore, in the early morning hours. Residents in this high-end and tight-knit community are shocked that such violence could take place in a town that so many felt would never be touched by such evil."*

The broadcast shifted to a handful of prerecorded interviews of residents expressing their shock, disbelief, and heartbreak over what happened to poor Jennifer, then cut back to the live feed from Donna.

*"The police have closed off the area around the Moore home, and I've been told by sources that the police are considering both the woods where Jennifer's body was found as well as the inside of the Moore residence to be active crime scenes. That alone is an indication that the police have not yet ruled out family members as suspects."*

"We haven't ruled anyone in or out," Susan yelled at the television. "God, I hate when they speculate to change the narrative."

"They have to get those ratings up," Liam said. "That's the game."

"And who's leaking to this girl? I never said anything about the inside of the house being treated as a crime scene."

*"We'll keep digging into this story for our News Twelve viewers. This is Donna Starr, on the scene. Back to you."*

Susan turned off the television and leaned on the counter, her arms folded across her chest. "Okay," she said. "Let's eat some dinner and spread this case out. We need to see what we have and where we think it might be heading."

---

With the kids asleep, Beatrice in her room watching television, and empty plates from spaghetti and meatballs sitting in the sink, Susan and Liam studied the notes and files spread across the love seat. They had Susan's notes from her interviews with the best friend, Anja York; the ex-boyfriend, Glenn Baker; the business partner, Arthur Breen; and the priest, Father McCall. The other reports, including forensic findings and the preliminary findings from the autopsy, were on the coffee table.

Susan flipped through the photos taken from the crime scene in the woods as well as pictures from inside the house. She stopped on the photo of Noel Moore's suitcase that remained just inside the front door where he'd dropped it the night he returned from his trip to Miami to see Uriah Sitchel.

Liam ended the call he was on and slipped his phone back in his pocket. "That was John Chu. The subpoena came through and he got Jennifer's cell phone records. He said he's going to use a computer system to break down the numbers into clusters so we can see who she's been calling and texting the most, and then we'll see if we can find out who those numbers belong to. He said she didn't use the phone much for voice calls, but there are a ton of texts."

"Typical teenager."

"I wish we could see more than just the numbers."

"If we find her phone, we can." Susan placed the photos back down and grabbed the preliminary autopsy report. "Did you ask if he found a rock with hairs or skull fragments?"

"Yeah. He said he didn't see anything yet, but he'll keep us posted."

Susan tapped the report with a pen she was holding. "We need to get Jennifer's medical records. Hopefully documentation about her abortion is in there with the name of the clinic she had it done at. I'd like to see if the records contain the name of the father."

Liam snatched a sheet of paper from the file. "Okay, so Jennifer is hooking up with someone two years ago and gets pregnant. She has the pregnancy terminated and turns to her aunt's church to find God and connects with the priest Aunt Sidney's been bringing around. We need to find out who Jennifer might've been dating back then. That's probably the father."

"Yeah, probably. But if it's some scared teenage kid who wasn't ready to be a parent any more than Jennifer was, where does that get us? I feel like our focus should be on the family. Something happened in that house, and someone cleaned it up. Why?"

Liam read through the paper he was holding. "This small footprint that was found in the mud at the scene wasn't Mindy Moore's. She's a size nine. And we already found Jennifer's flip-flops at the scene. Noel Moore's foot is obviously too big. The boy is the only one that's close to a match."

"You think Charlie Moore killed his sister?"

"I don't know. You'd remove a large area rug from your bedroom and clean your en suite bath to help cover up your son's involvement with your daughter's murder, wouldn't you? You'd want to protect your kid. Protecting that boy could be all the motivation Mindy Moore needed to clean up a crime scene. She cleans it up, fakes an episode of catatonia; Noel hires a super lawyer to keep them shielded from the people investigating their daughter's murder. It makes sense on some level."

"But the footprints we found were coming toward the house from the opposite side of the woods. If it was Charlie, wouldn't he just follow Jennifer out the back door to kill her?"

Liam slipped the paper back into the file. "Maybe he went a different way to throw her off track. Catch her by surprise."

"Maybe." Susan stood up and stretched. "Let's see what Uriah says tomorrow and if it fits into your hired-gun-and-make-them-clean-up-the-mess theory. After that, we'll take a closer look at the kid."

# 28

They took the first flight out of Westchester County Airport and were on the ground in Miami by seven in the morning. Detective Raul Fernandez from the Miami PD met them at their gate and escorted them to his car. The coordination between the two departments had been flawless. Lieutenant Carter called the captain in Miami and worked out all the details. It was to be a quick turnaround and an informal interview. Uriah Sitchel wasn't officially a suspect, but Susan wanted to meet him face-to-face and look into his eyes to see if she could detect a man who might have vengeance on his mind when it came to Noel Moore.

Detective Fernandez drove in silence for the first few miles. Susan sat in the passenger seat, and Liam was in the back. The morning rush was heavy and reminded Susan of bumper-to-bumper traffic in Manhattan.

"So what do you like this guy for?" Fernandez finally said, breaking the quiet. "Come all this way."

"We don't like him for anything," Susan replied. "We're just creating proper timelines in a homicide we're working, and the father of the victim was with Uriah the night of the murder. We're simply checking things out."

"Couldn't do that from a video conference?"

"We could. Chose not to."

It took them a half hour to make their way to the Miami Beach waterfront. Fernandez pulled into a cobblestone driveway as iron gates opened to allow them access. A winding road lined with palm trees and tropical flowers led them to the doorstep of Uriah Sitchel's sprawling estate. White stucco walls, dark windows, terra-cotta roofs, etched glass. It was incredible.

An assistant was waiting at the front door and escorted them around the back of the house to a stone patio where Uriah was sitting at a glass table overlooking Biscayne Bay. Off in the distance, cruise ships and tankers dotted the horizon with the sun suspended just above the waterline.

Uriah was a middle-aged man of average height. His tan skin offset his white hair and goatee. He was fit, but not overly so. The top buttons of his Hawaiian shirt were undone and showed the beginning of what would be a fairly chiseled chest. He stood from his chair and smiled when he saw them, before shaking each's hand and motioning them to sit. As soon as they did, a group of three women brought out plates of food and coffee.

"I know you had an early morning, so I thought we'd have a proper breakfast," he said. "I hope sausage, eggs, and pancakes are okay. We have coffee, orange juice, and grapefruit juice as well. I'd offer you a mimosa, but I know you're on duty."

"Thank you," Susan replied as a plate was slid in front of her. "That's very kind."

"No bother at all. I was crushed to hear what happened to Jen. Anything I can do to help in your investigation or make your short stay more comfortable, I will do. And as I said on the phone, you didn't have to come all the way down here for me. But go ahead and ask me anything. I'm here to help."

Susan took a sip of her coffee. A warm breeze blew her hair away from her face, and it felt good. "How long have you known Noel?"

"I met Noel through Artie. Artie was on a team at Lehman who worked with me and my firm. After 2008, I was on my way to bring my business to Merrill, but Artie reached out and asked for a meeting.

He said he was starting his own firm. I had no intention of bringing my business to a boutique, but we had our Yale connection and alumni take care of one another, so I agreed to meet. He brought Noel with him, and the entire time Noel was pitching, all I could think of were the possibilities that were ahead for this guy. He was a financial genius, and the ideas he had were so original I couldn't say no. I started with a few million and eventually brought my entire portfolio to him. He's been like family ever since."

"And from what I could tell, you help Noel and Arthur recruit other clients in your circle of friends and associates. Is that right?"

Uriah nodded and slipped a forkful of eggs into his mouth. "I make introductions. There's no formal agreement or anything. Noel's genius and Artie's care for his clients grew the firm into what it is today. All the credit should go to them."

"And all the blame," Liam said.

Uriah looked at him. "What do you mean?"

Liam cut into a piece of sausage. "Ziggy Dennings? Duel Pharma?"

Uriah held Liam's gaze for a moment. Susan was about to say something to break the tension that suddenly crept across the table when a smile appeared on Uriah's face.

"I like people who are prepared before a meeting," he said. "Shows good character. Too many folks are in a rush these days and just gloss over information that could prove vital in a negotiation. The fine print or the buried story is usually where the meat and potatoes of a deal are. I don't get why people have become so impatient with the little things."

"Ziggy lost big on the Duel Pharma deal," Liam continued. "Ended up jumping off a bridge because he couldn't handle the losses. You made the introduction. And your reputation took a bit of a hit because of it."

"Nah." Uriah brushed the accusation away as if he was swatting a fly. "My reputation is rock solid. And Ziggy took the coward's way out. Some investments are good and some are bad. We know the risks going in. Ziggy got screwed, no question about that. But if he'd held on, he could've gotten back in the game. He chose to jump. That was his decision. It had nothing to do with me, and it wasn't Noel's fault either. Sometimes you just lose. Simple as that."

Susan played with her eggs, pushing them around like the twins did when they weren't hungry. "Would you say you're satisfied with Noel's performance as your wealth manager?"

"One hundred percent satisfied."

"And can you confirm his whereabouts on the night in question?"

"I had my car pick Noel up at the airport on August twelfth. He stayed with me at this house for three days, and we drove him back to the airport the night of August fifteenth. Next thing I know, Artie calls me with the news about Jen's murder." Uriah placed his glass down on the table and leaned in. "I know what you're thinking, but Noel had nothing to do with what happened. He's a good man and loves his family more than you can know. I'm afraid you came here for nothing."

"Maybe we didn't come here to get your take on Noel," Liam said. "Or at least, that might not be the only reason we came."

Uriah fell back in his seat, laughing and holding his stomach. "Oh, man! We got Mr. Conspiracy Theory over here. What, you think that I ordered a hit on his daughter because Noel made a wrong move with Ziggy Dennings? That's an interesting take. I like it."

"Am I wrong?"

Uriah wiped his mouth with the napkin from his lap. "Look," he said softly. "If I'd wanted to send a message to Noel by killing his daughter, I sure as hell wouldn't have had her killed behind their house. I wouldn't advertise the murder and make it easy for the authorities to investigate. With the kind of money I have, I can buy the assurance that there would be no way anyone could trace anything back to me. I could buy a car accident or an accidental drowning. Maybe an allergic reaction. I don't need the spotlight, and Jen's murder was too obvious for someone like me to be involved with, so you can cross me off your list and fly back to New York."

# 29

They landed in New York at 11:57 a.m. and drove straight to the Lewisboro police station. The Uriah Sitchel interview had been a bust, but Susan felt better having seen his face and been in his presence during the interview. She was confident he had nothing to do with what happened to Jennifer Moore but would keep him open as a suspect for now.

Maria Hicks sat in an empty office they were using instead of an official interview room. The last thing Susan wanted to do was intimidate the woman who had voluntarily agreed to come to the station and talk about her employment with the Moore family. Susan sat next to Maria, and Liam sat on the side of the desk instead of behind it. It was the best they could do, given the amount of available space.

Maria was an older woman, sixties, thin, pale, with white hair that was cut short. No makeup. Pleasant smile. Her hands were folded on her lap, and Susan could see the arthritis taking hold. All those years of manual labor couldn't have been easy on her joints, but her smile was easy and her eyes bright. She seemed relaxed, which was a nice way to start things off. She reminded Susan of her own mother. Something about that smile.

"We appreciate you coming in to see us today," Susan began.

"It's not a problem," Maria replied. "Whatever I can do to help you find who killed Jenny. It still doesn't feel real."

Susan took her phone out of her pocket and handed it to Liam. "I'd like to record this interview, if that's okay. Easier when we make our notes later."

"Sure. Yes."

Liam began filming and nodded for Susan to begin.

"For the sake of this recording, my name is Investigator Susan Adler of the New York State Police, Troop K. I'm assisting the Lewisboro Police Department in the homicide of Jennifer Moore. Sitting with me for this interview is the Moores' housekeeper, Maria Hicks. Ms. Hicks, have you agreed to be recorded during this interview?"

Maria nodded. "I agree."

"Good. We can begin." Susan took out her file and opened it. "Can you tell me how long you've been working for the Moore family?"

"Twelve years. Jenny was six when I started, and Charlie was one. I got the job through my friend, who was Charlie's nanny. She stayed on until Charlie started kindergarten and then moved to another family in the city. But I stayed. They liked me. I liked them."

"What are your scheduled hours?"

"I work Monday through Friday. Begin my day at nine and end it right after the dishes from dinner have been put away. That's usually around seven."

"And you're the only person on staff?"

"Yes. They offered to get me help as I got older, but I told them I'm fine. It's not the square footage of the house; it's the efficiency of your day. I have a set list of tasks to complete each day, and as long as they get done, I'm fine being alone."

"How is it working for them?"

Maria shrugged. "It's fine. When the kids were little, things were always messy and out of place, and I worked hard to try and keep up. As the kids got older, things got easier. I love those kids. They've always been good to me. Respectful. I hear stories from the other nannies and housekeepers around here, and the kids are ten times worse than the parents. Spoiled. Entitled. No respect for the staff. But Mr. and Mrs. Moore raised Jenny and Charlie the right way. They're good kids."

Susan made a few notes. "What can you tell me about Mr. and Mrs. Moore's marriage? What have you seen over the years?"

"As far as I could tell, it was a good marriage. Mr. Moore worked like a dog, and Mrs. Moore did most of the parenting. That was the way they did things. Of course, I've heard them argue from time to time, but all married couples do that. Never saw them have a big fight or anything. Just little arguments."

"Tell me about what happened the morning of Jennifer's murder."

Maria fell back in her seat and let out a breath. "I got up, showered, got dressed. Was about to eat my breakfast when the phone rang. It was Mr. Moore telling me not to come in that day. I think I can count on one hand how many times he told me to stay home over the years. Sometimes if the weather was really bad or the house had the flu. But as soon as he said it, I knew something was wrong."

"Did you ask him why he wanted you to stay home?"

"I didn't have to. He told me something happened to Jenny and that the police were coming. Then he started to cry, and he hung up. I called back, but it went to his voice mail. A few hours later, a woman I know who works down the street called me and filled me in. I saw the rest on the news."

More notes. Susan paused to reset the conversation. "Tell me about Mrs. Moore's relationship with Jennifer."

Maria's brow furrowed. "When Jenny was little, they were inseparable. They went everywhere together. Did mother-daughter trips on the weekends. You could actually *feel* Mrs. Moore's love for that child. They were best friends and mother and daughter all wrapped up into one."

"And then?"

"Then Jenny grew into her teen years."

"What does that mean?"

"Do you have children?" Maria asked.

"Twins. A boy and a girl. Six years old. Almost seven."

"Then, you'll see. Once they hit thirteen or fourteen, they want to start exploring the world for themselves. They want to stretch out and push back, and suddenly they don't want to listen to Mom and Dad. They want to figure things out for themselves."

"Is that what happened with Mrs. Moore and Jennifer?"

"Mrs. Moore has always been a perfectionist. She knew what she wanted, how she wanted it, and when she wanted it done. We never had a problem because I do what I'm told and I don't ask any questions. And when Jenny was younger, she didn't know any better, so she did what she was told too. But as she got older, she started rebelling. Bad grades. Bad friends. Sneaking out at night. Missing curfew."

"So they fought."

"Yes." Maria sat up in her seat. "I'd say between fourteen and sixteen, Jenny and her mother had some nasty fights. Mrs. Moore doesn't know this, but sometimes after an argument, I would sneak into Jenny's room and try and explain to her why her mother was so angry. But she didn't want to hear it from me either. Then, all of a sudden, during her sophomore year of high school, things changed, and Jenny's grades improved and the friends got better and she was home on time. Her mother stayed on her, but Jenny accepted it and knew what was expected of her. I can't say that the distance between them was ever resolved, but there was some kind of resignation with Jenny for sure. I think she finally realized it was easier to go along to get along."

"Do you know who Jennifer was dating back around the time she matured? Sophomore year?"

Maria smiled as she thought back. "There were always boys and girls around. Hard to tell if they were just friends or dating. I really couldn't tell you."

"What about names? Could you provide names of who she was friends with back then?"

"I'm sorry. I can't."

Susan made a few notes. It appeared the fighting with her mother ended around the time of her abortion, which was also the time she sought out Father McCall and became more active in her church. The pregnancy termination had really affected her.

"How about Charlie?" Susan asked, looking up from her notepad. "How was his relationship with Jennifer?"

"Brother and sister. They loved each other, and they argued. To be expected."

"Did they ever have any knockdowns like Jennifer had with her mother?"

"No," Maria replied. "Not that I saw. Just sibling stuff. Nothing serious."

"Did you ever see a mean streak in Charlie?"

Maria paused, looking back and forth between Susan and Liam. "No. Why are you asking me that?"

"No reason," Susan replied. "Just covering all our bases."

"Charlie wouldn't hurt Jen."

"I'm not implying that."

"He wouldn't pull her hair, let alone *kill* her."

"Understood." Susan closed the folder and placed her hands on the table. "Let's switch gears a little. I need to ask you about your schedule."

Maria's shoulders relaxed. "Okay."

"When was the last time you cleaned Mr. and Mrs. Moore's bedroom and bath?"

"I do the bedrooms and bathrooms on Mondays and Fridays. So I guess last Monday was the last time."

"That was two days before Jennifer was killed."

"Correct."

"What kind of cleaning material do you use for the bathrooms?"

"Clorox mostly. Lysol. Maybe some Windex for the windows and mirrors."

"Do you know if any of the products contain sodium percarbonate, like you would find in Oxi products?"

"No idea. You'd have to check the labels. I keep everything in a cabinet in the laundry room."

"There were no cleaning products in the house," Susan said. "We thought you might've brought them in with you."

Maria shook her head. "No. I keep them there. I don't know where they'd be if they're not in the laundry room. I've kept them there for as long as I can remember."

Susan pulled an envelope out from under the file and opened it. She reached inside and came away with a small stack of photos the crime scene team had taken.

"Last question," she said as she handed the pictures to the housekeeper. "These are photographs of the inside of the Moore house, taken by our team. I want you to look through them and tell me if anything looks out of place or different. Can you do that?"

Maria nodded and began flipping through the pictures, one after the other. Susan watched her. Liam continued filming. The room was quiet.

"No, this isn't right," Maria said, pointing to a photograph that was halfway through the pile. She handed it back to Susan.

Susan looked at it and knew she was on to something. It was a shot of the parents' bedroom. "What's not right about it?"

"The area rug under the bed is missing."

"When was the last time you saw the rug there?"

"The day before Mr. Moore called me and told me not to come in. The day before Jenny was killed."

# 30

With his mother sleeping soundly in the bedroom, Charlie sat in the hallway on the second floor, listening through the laundry chute that was next to the bathroom and led to the mudroom one floor below. Jen had showed him the trick a few years earlier when he'd gotten in trouble for throwing rocks through the windows of an abandoned gas station out on Old Post Road. The police had come and escorted Charlie and Bobby back to their houses. No charges were filed, boys being boys and all, but his mother had been embarrassed and furious. Jen had taken him by the hand that afternoon and led him to the chute, carefully opening their end and sticking his ear up to it. As soon as she did, he heard his parents in the family room discussing his punishment. He'd known the verdict before they'd ever called him down to discuss it. It was a neat trick and came in handy in situations such as these.

Uncle Artie was in the family room. He could hear his father pacing between the family room and the kitchen, making his end of the conversation a little harder to follow.

"I don't care that she was on the train platform when I got off," Artie said. His voice was shaking. "I get that she has to check everyone out who's involved with the family. But Noel, she went to see Uriah. That's too much. She got on a plane and flew down to talk to him."

"She was checking my alibi," his father replied.

"No, she could've checked your alibi with a phone call or a video chat. She went down there to see if he was involved."

"Why would she suspect him?"

"Because of what happened with Duel Pharma and Ziggy Dennings."

"Jesus." His father's voice was almost a whisper. "She did her homework."

Footsteps traveled into the kitchen.

"Noel," Artie said. "I need you to listen to me like I'm your brother, here. It's time to start thinking a little more proactively to get the spotlight off of you and your family. You need to get out in front of this."

"Get out in front of what?"

"Everything. Look, I know you probably haven't been paying attention to the news or looking at social media, but it's not just the cops that're starting to question whether or not your family was involved in Jen's death. People are starting to talk. I heard them on the train, and a couple of guys at the office had this roundabout way of asking me about it. People are starting to speculate about you and Mindy. There was an article in the *Daily News* that tried to connect you and Mindy to what happened to Jen. It was mostly bullshit, but if enough people read it and repost it and gossip about it, it won't matter that the reporter was reaching. The rumor will become the truth. How long do you think it'll take before a journalist finds out that the state police flew down to Miami to interview the man you were with the night of Jen's murder? The second that information goes out, you'll become the main suspect in the eyes of the general public. A few articles about your possible connection to what happened to Jen and a few more about some bad calls like Duel Pharma, and we're out of business. The clients we have don't want the spotlight on them, good or bad. And they certainly don't want their wealth advisors suspected of murder. We need to change the narrative."

Footsteps back into the family room.

"So what am I supposed to do?"

"Call a press conference. Do an interview. Let the regular people hear *from* you instead of reading *about* you."

"I can't. My lawyer would flip. She keeps telling me to stay quiet. What if I say something that I shouldn't? What if I'm taken out of context and make things worse?"

"You can't make things worse," Artie said. "Jen's dead. Mindy's practically catatonic. Clients are starting to call, Noel. Screw your lawyer. If people make up their minds that you guys are guilty, staying quiet won't matter. It'll be too late to change their opinions, and then where are you?"

Charlie could hear his father begin to cry.

"I'm scared."

"You should be. This is scary." Artie crossed into the kitchen. "Get in front of this. You can preempt the narrative. You can make your own story and get the public on your side. It's the only way. Do it for your family."

Charlie gently closed the cover of the chute and climbed to his feet. He walked down the hall and looked inside his parents' bedroom. His mother was an unmoving lump in the center of the mattress, and although he knew he was looking at a room that was clean and tidy, with everything where it should be, all he could see was the blood on the carpet, the spatter on the dresser, and the piles of red-stained towels stacked next to the bathroom. He turned around and bent to see the mark on the opposite wall in the hallway where he'd hit his head. The drywall was cracked a little. He wondered if the police had caught that.

"Charlie! Come down here a sec. Uncle Artie and I need to talk to you about something."

"Coming!"

He stared at the hardwood floor he was standing on and thought he could see droplets of blood, but when he blinked, they were gone. A voice in the back of his mind spoke.

*You did this. It's your fault she got killed. Tell them the truth. Tell them what happened.*

But he knew he couldn't. Not now. Not ever. If he told them the truth, they would never forgive him. They would never understand that Jen was being a bitch to him and it was the only way to get back at her. If he told them what he'd done, they'd put him away in jail forever. He'd never see anyone again.

Charlie paused when he got to the top of the stairs. The voice was relentless in his mind.

*This is all your fault. You killed your own sister.*

# 31

Liam sat in a conference room in the basement of the Lewisboro police department, next to the locker rooms and gym. It wasn't a large space, nor was it the most modern tactical room he'd ever sat in, but it was useful being off the main floor, and the computer screens set up at each station made sharing notes and files far easier than having to make copies and passing sheets of paper along.

Sergeant Dunes sat across from Susan, and the Lewisboro police chief, Chief Haslet, sat across from Liam. Chief Haslet was almost as large as Senior Investigator Crosby. He was built like a rugby player, all girth and thick legs. But his white hair gave away the fact that he was on the back end of his career, and the wrinkles under his eyes told Liam that he'd seen his fair share over the years. John Chu was on the speakerphone in the center of the table. Liam had never been on the investigative side of a recap meeting such as this. He was always playing the role John was about to play. He still felt out of place, like a third wheel on a team that was otherwise a well-oiled machine. But he was learning, and that was the main thing. If there was a contribution to make, he'd make it. Until then, he was determined to stay in the background and absorb as much as he could.

"I want to draw everyone's attention to the first attachment I sent you," Chu began. His voice crackled over the speaker. "This was found in the woods behind the Moore house on the outskirts of the crime scene perimeter. Could be nothing, or it could point us in a direction we need to go in. Hard to tell with all the rest of the junk back there."

Liam pulled up the image and immediately recognized the character. It was a chrome Darth Vader pendant.

"You locate the necklace this goes on?" Susan asked.

"No," Chu replied. "Just the pendant."

"Looks like it's a little beat up, but clean," Sergeant Dunes said. "Not sure I'd consider it part of the junk that's back there."

Liam looked at Susan across the table. "Obviously something a kid would wear. This, plus the child-size shoe print we found . . ."

Susan nodded. "Charlie Moore was back there. Had to be."

"Second attachment has to do with phone records," Chu continued. "I was able to group the numbers that had been called more than once. As I mentioned to Investigator Adler and Mr. Dwyer yesterday, it appears Jennifer didn't use the phone for voice calls too often. Most of the numbers we see on the records are texts. Most of the voice calls were able to be traced back to the Moore residence, Mr. and Mrs. Moore's cell phones, her brother's cell phone, Anja York, and Glenn Baker. There's a cluster of calls from Duke University's administration office. The rest were one-offs to department stores, her beauty salon. Things like that. She also made seven calls to Saint Mark's Church in Yorktown."

"She's active in that church," Susan replied.

"What about the texts?" Chief Haslet asked.

"The same numbers that showed up on the voice calls from her family and friends were tenfold on the texting," Chu said. "We're still working on her social media accounts."

Everyone around the room nodded.

Chief Haslet motioned to Susan. "Update on your end?"

"Waiting for Jennifer's medical records to come in. Should be here shortly. Liam and I looked at the ex-boyfriend and the client Noel was visiting in Florida the night Jennifer was killed. We'll continue to keep an eye, but we think they're clear. We're turning our focus on the family. With the addition of this Darth Vader pendant and the small shoe print we already found, we may take a closer look at the kid."

"You need to be careful there," Haslet replied. "He's a minor."

"We got confirmation from the Moores' housekeeper that the area rug in the main bedroom was there the day before Jennifer's body was found, which means it was removed the day or night of her murder. We add that to the blood Liam found on the stair banister and the fact that we could smell bleach in both the parents' bed- and bathroom, and we know something happened inside that house. That points to the family. And the only family home that night were Mindy Moore and her son, Charlie."

"I agree that things appear to be pointing to the Moore family," Haslet said. "But let me make one thing crystal clear: everything we have is circumstantial. Nothing is concrete at this point, and until it is, I will not disrupt this community with false accusations or shoddy police work. If we're going to bring charges, they need to be on the back of airtight evidence."

"Yes, sir."

Liam raised his hand to get everyone's attention. "Just a quick update on some other pending things we had in the file. I checked with the waste removal company that the town contracts. They said garbage pickup at the Moore address takes place on Mondays. That means the garbage was already picked up two days before Jennifer was found, and wouldn't be picked up again until the investigation was already underway. If the area rug from the bedroom was discarded after the murder, it's doubtful the rug was discarded through the trash pickup."

"What about a dump?" Sergeant Dunes asked. "He could've gone to County Waste."

"We could check hours of operation," Liam replied. "But the timelines might be off. If Jennifer was killed by one of her family members in the middle of the night, they'd have to wait until morning to dispose of the rug and drive back and forth to the dump. Could work, but it could be tight considering how early they called 911."

"Anything else?" Chief Haslet asked.

"I just had a thought," Liam said. He leaned forward in his seat and spoke into the phone. "John, can you tell us who the last person was to call and text Jennifer Moore?"

"Sure," John replied. A cluster of computer keys clicked on the other end of the phone. "Okay, the last call in was from an 888 number. Probably a telemarketer or something. Came in at six thirteen p.m." More clicking. "Last outbound call was the day before to Mindy Moore's cell."

"How about the texts?"

"Last text Jennifer sent was to her brother at one twenty-one the morning of her murder."

"What about the last incoming text?"

"It was a reply back from her brother. One twenty-two. That was the last text Jennifer Moore ever received."

# 32

As soon as the man in the shadows turned on the two spotlights, Charlie could feel the heat. He squinted and tried to see beyond the brightness but caught only the faint outline of the two cameras that were pointing toward the couch he and his father were sitting on. There was a small crew of about six people he'd seen when he was ushered inside the fancy room. Now all he could hear were their movements in the darkness behind the lights. The entire scene was unnerving.

Uncle Artie had come back to the house just after lunch with news that he'd secured an interview with Donna Starr from the local News Twelve channel. Artie told Charlie to take a shower and put on a pair of khakis and a golf shirt; then he told his father to do the same but suggested a suit rather than anything casual. The two men briefly talked about whether they should include his mother, but she was sleeping again, and they decided her current state—whatever that meant—was too unpredictable and could end up making things worse. They left her at home.

Artie had driven them to the Doubletree in Tarrytown and walked them up to a suite on the third floor, whispering instructions to his father the entire time. Charlie had largely been ignored, and he was aware that he was being used as some kind of a prop to elicit sympathy from the viewers. He was there to remind the audience that his mother or father couldn't possibly have done anything to his sister. Not with another child they had to love and look after.

"Hey, bud," Artie said as he gently tugged on the back of Charlie's neck. "You hanging in there?"

"I guess."

"I'm proud of you. I'm proud of how strong you're being for your mom and dad and how you're doing right by your sister. I don't hear any complaining or anything negative coming from you, and that tells me that you have the right kind of character. You're growing into a fine man, and I'm proud of you."

Charlie nodded. He wasn't sure what to say. The compliments made him sick to his stomach. "Thanks."

Artie smiled and ran a thumb across Charlie's cheek as if wiping a tear that wasn't there. "Anything you need, just ask me. I want to help."

Donna Starr appeared from behind the lights and sat in a chair that was off to the side of the couch.

"Will Mrs. Moore be joining us?" she asked. She smiled at them both when she sat.

"No," his father replied. "She wasn't feeling up to it."

Donna's smile hardened. "I understand. Perhaps a follow-up interview at your house with the entire family could work. We'll see what we can do."

Artie stepped into the shadows, and Charlie watched as a man snaked a microphone wire under the collar of Donna's suit jacket. The same man had done the same thing with their microphones earlier.

"I don't want either of you to worry about anything," Donna said. "We're here to clear the air and get some misconceptions out of the way. There's no gotcha moments coming. This is purely an interview that will allow you to say what you need to say."

His father nodded and took a sip of water from the glass on the coffee table in front of them.

"How about you, Charlie?" Donna asked. "Are you going to be okay?"

"Sure."

"Can I ask you a question if I have to?"

"Yes."

"Excellent."

The man finished with her microphone, then walked away. A voice asked if they were ready, and everyone confirmed. The voice then began counting backward from five and stopped speaking at two. On each of the cameras, a single red light came on, and Donna smiled.

Showtime.

"Good evening. My name is Donna Starr, and this is a News Twelve Special Report. I'm here with Noel Moore, the father of Jennifer Moore, who was found murdered in the woods behind her house in the tranquil and upscale community of Lewisboro, New York, three days ago. The homicide has rocked the town, with residents frightened and anxious that a killer may be among them. Over the course of the last few days, rumors have begun to circulate about one of the Moores being involved in Jennifer's death. Mr. Moore contacted me earlier and asked if he could come on the air to address these rumors. Mr. Moore and his son, Charlie, are with us now."

She smiled as she paused, adding to the tension. Charlie could feel sweat forming on the back of his neck. The lights were so hot.

"Noel, tell us about that morning."

Charlie watched his father recount the story about that morning that he knew was full of lies. He listened to the details about them coming down for breakfast and his mother wandering into the back to see if Jen was running and how she returned to the house in shock. He bit his lip when his father talked about going out into the woods and finding Jen and calling the police. But what really caught him off guard was the way his father kept choking on his words. How he kept having to stop to keep himself from crying. Charlie hadn't seen this side of him. The emotion and the sorrow. This was new.

"I can't imagine making a discovery like that," Donna said softly. "I'm so sorry."

"Thank you," his father replied, dabbing his eyes with the palm of his hand.

"How is your wife?"

"She's in shock. She's at home now after spending a few days in the hospital."

"What have the police said?"

"Not much. We're obviously cooperating fully, and they've been in and out of our house, but so far they haven't shared anything with us."

"Do you find that strange?"

His father turned up his hands. "I don't know. I've never been in a situation like this before."

Donna paused and repositioned herself on the chair. "Noel, I need to get to the point of this interview, so I'm going to come out and ask. Did you or your wife have anything to do with what happened to Jennifer?"

Charlie held his breath, not knowing exactly what his father was going to say.

"Absolutely not. That's why I wanted to come here today and get out in front of this before the rumor mill started. Lewisboro is a small town, and Mindy and I have been part of that community for twenty years. I know people are whispering and have suspicions. I know what people are saying online. And I've seen what the larger cable news channels are intimating. But that's all for drama and ratings, and I refuse to allow my daughter's murder to be a tool in a ratings game. I lost my little girl. She was *slaughtered* a few hundred yards from our house. We need to use all of our resources and concentrate on finding who did this. The faster the police investigate Mindy and me, the faster they can clear us and look to find whoever really killed Jen. But I can't allow the public to pass judgment on us, and I won't. Mindy and I loved our daughter like we love our son. We were a loving family, and now everything's changed. We need to find the person responsible for this."

Donna took a very staged breath and looked toward Charlie.

"What can you say about your sister?" she asked.

The heat from the lights was bad enough, but now Charlie could feel all the eyes on him, waiting for his answer. Words vanished from his mind. He had no idea what to say. What could he say about Jen?

"It's okay," his father whispered, patting him on the leg. "I'm right here."

"Jen was the best big sister anyone could have. She was kind and cared about me and helped me. I miss her."

He looked at his father and could see he was crying. That made Charlie want to cry, too, but he clenched his teeth and fought it. Not like this. Not on camera with the world watching. He wouldn't give them the moment they wanted so bad.

Donna turned her attention back to his father. "Noel, what's next for you and your family?"

"We have to get my wife healthy again, and we have to bury our daughter." He started sobbing, hard and silent, his face in his hands, his shoulders shaking.

Charlie watched the cameras watching his father, and he suddenly wanted to jump up and smash them all to pieces. He didn't want other people seeing his father like this, at his weakest and most vulnerable. His dad was strong, powerful, like a superhero. There wasn't anything he couldn't do, and all they wanted was to see him cry like a baby so they could promote their show.

"It's okay," Donna whispered. "Take your time."

"If anyone knows anything about what happened, I'm begging you to come forward," his father whimpered. "Tell us what you know. It can be anonymous. I don't care. We just need to find the person responsible. Please."

Charlie closed his eyes and leaned back on the couch.

*The person responsible.*

*More like the* people, *Dad. The people responsible.*

# 33

Susan and Liam were in their makeshift office at the Lewisboro headquarters uploading their reports and interrogation notes into the system. Susan's stomach rumbled from the dinner she never had a chance to eat. It was almost seven. She was about to go and grab something from the break room when her cell phone rang.

"This is Susan Adler."

"It's John Chu. I got Jennifer Moore's medical records."

She snatched a pen from her desk. "What'd you find?"

"Regular teenage kid as far as her records go. Gynecologist did confirm a terminated pregnancy in the exam notes. Happened at age sixteen."

"Any mention of the father?"

"No, but there's a secondary note referring to where the procedure was performed. Women's Family and Health Center of New York. They're on Staten Island."

"Wow. Quite a trip from here to Staten Island."

"Probably didn't want to be anywhere near her hometown. Go to a place where no one could possibly know you. Makes sense."

"Thanks, John. Email me the records when you're done looking through them."

"Will do."

She hung up the phone and was about to update Liam when Sergeant Dunes almost fell into their office.

"Turn on channel twelve. Now."

Liam got up from his seat and grabbed the remote for the flat screen that stood in the corner atop a file cabinet. As soon as Susan saw Noel and Charlie Moore sitting on a couch with Donna Starr off to the side, perched on the edge of an overstuffed wingback chair, she knew.

*"The faster the police investigate Mindy and me, the faster they can clear us and look to find whoever really killed Jen."*

"This is not good," Susan said.

"Yeah, no kidding," Dunes replied. "The chief is going ballistic. Did you have any idea this was in the works?"

"Of course not. We haven't officially interviewed any of the Moores yet. I'm surprised his lawyer would even allow this. Charlotte Walsh seems more tactical than an interview with a community news channel."

*"If anyone knows anything about what happened, I'm begging you to come forward. Tell us what you know. It can be anonymous. I don't care. We just need to find the person responsible. Please."*

"The chief needs you and Liam to hang out," Dunes said. "He's putting together a press conference to try and counter the interview. A lot more people are going to have an interest in our progress now, and he wants to address it head on."

"What time?"

"One hour."

"We'll be there."

Dunes left the office, and Liam walked back to his desk and folded his laptop closed. He stuffed it in his bag and stood. "We better get up to the chief. United front and all."

Susan unplugged her computer and slipped it into her bag. "I agree. Let's go."

# 34

The size of the news teams that had descended on the police station seemed to be doubling by the hour. Susan couldn't believe the number of reporters standing outside the main entrance, waiting for the press conference to begin. There had to have been at least twenty-five correspondents with microphones and recorders at the ready, with another fifteen cameras lined up in the back near Bouton Road, ready to capture every moment. Susan and Liam stood off to the left of the podium from which the chief planned to speak. Sergeant Dunes was on the opposite side along with a small cluster of her fellow uniformed officers. Onlookers from town pulled over to watch.

Chief Haslet walked out of the department's front doors and made his way to the podium. He unfolded a piece of paper he was holding and cleared his throat.

"I want to thank everyone for coming on such short notice," he began. "I'm going to make a brief statement, and then I'll open it up for questions."

He looked at Susan and Liam, and they both nodded. He then turned and looked at Sergeant Dunes. She did the same. Everyone was ready.

"As you all know, three days ago the body of eighteen-year-old Jennifer Moore was discovered in the woods behind her house. The Lewisboro Police Department, along with an EMT unit, responded immediately. Upon assessing the situation and knowing we'd need the full resources of an in-depth homicide investigation, we called upon the New York State Police to assist. They assigned Investigator Susan Adler and forensics specialist and consultant Liam Dwyer to the case."

He motioned to Susan and Liam as he spoke. The cameras briefly turned to them, then went back to the chief.

"Investigator Adler and Mr. Dwyer have been working hand in hand with my officers for the past three days to gather evidence, create a proper timeline, and put the investigation together in the most professional and meaningful way possible, and by meaningful I mean we're putting together a case that will not only uncover who is responsible for Jennifer's murder, but one that will provide the evidence needed to bring charges and a conviction in the court of law. Things like this take time. We have not ruled anyone out, nor are we solely focused on any one suspect. The case remains open and active as we work toward finding the party responsible for this heinous act and bringing them to justice."

He pushed away from the podium, then leaned in again.

"I saw Mr. Moore's interview this afternoon. He spoke about the media and the public making innuendoes when it comes to the Moore family's possible involvement. And like Mr. Moore, I don't appreciate those innuendoes either. I might also add that I don't appreciate innuendoes made toward this department that we might be focusing on someone in particular and ignoring other evidence that could help us find the person responsible for Jennifer's death. That couldn't be further from the truth. We've invited Mr. Moore to come in to the station for an interview on several occasions, and my people have tried to talk to Mr. Moore at his home. Mr. Moore's legal counsel has prevented us from doing so."

Chief Haslet looked past the reporters in front of him and focused on the cameras in the back.

"I would again like to invite Noel Moore, Mindy Moore, and their attorney down here so we can get some answers to our questions, gather details we need a bit of clarity on, and, as Mr. Moore put it, clear people who need clearing so we can get to the task of finding the person who killed Jennifer. I can only hope I'm taken up on my invitation this time." A pause. "I'll open it for questions."

As hands went up across the crowd and Chief Haslet pointed to the first reporter, Susan scanned the audience. She saw Donna Starr standing off to the side, and their eyes locked. Susan motioned for her to meet around the back of the building.

"Hang tight a sec," she whispered to Liam.

Liam nodded, and Susan broke away from the stage as more questions came, one after the other. She walked behind the building to find Donna in the officers' parking lot.

"You're pretty brave coming here," Susan began. "Disrupt a police investigation and then hang out for the cleanup."

Donna pushed her hair out of her eyes, her tight grin never fading. "I told you we could be allies and help each other out, but all I got was 'no comment' and 'leave me alone,' so I had to go out on my own. This is what happens."

"We're trying to find a murderer. This isn't some reality show people can tune in to each week."

"I'm not saying it is. I'm just reporting the news. Besides, he called me. I didn't go after him for any of this."

"You're glamorizing a homicide in the hope you'll get the attention of the networks in the city. Whether Noel called you or you called Noel, the fact that you've been hovering over every aspect of this investigation tells me you're in it for the ratings."

Donna gave a broader smile as she turned and walked away. "Sorry," she said. "No comment. I have to go ask more questions now. Stay tuned."

# 35

Charlie was beginning to doze off on the couch in the family room when all the ruckus began. He'd been watching a rerun of a blooper show he loved when a combination of the doorbell ringing and someone pounding on the front door exploded through the house. His father ran down from the second floor and stuck his head in, pointing at him.

"Stay here."

The pounding and the ringing didn't end until his father unlocked the dead bolt and pulled the door open.

"You have to be *kidding* me."

Charlie recognized the shrill voice immediately. His father's lawyer.

Heels clicked on the marble tile in the foyer, then into the living room. His father was wearing socks, so Charlie didn't hear him follow her after the door was closed and locked. There was a brief moment when he thought he should go up to his room and let the adults talk, but that moment passed as soon as the yelling began. He was stuck where he was, pretending to be asleep but listening to everything.

"What the hell was that I just saw on the news?"

"Do you mean the interview?"

"No," Charlotte barked. "I meant the three days of rain in the forecast. Of course the interview. The *unscheduled* interview. The *unsanctioned* interview. The interview I had no idea you were planning and had no heads-up was going down today. The interview I, as your attorney, would have advised you against doing because all you've done now is create doubt in the minds of everyone who watched it."

"What are you talking about?" his father shot back. "The entire interview was about how Mindy and I were innocent and how I was standing up for my family so I could try and squash the rumors that were starting. I need people to stop looking at us like we had something to do with Jen's murder. I think it went well."

"I think you should stick to the stock market or whatever the hell it is you do. Deciding what's a good and bad move during a murder investigation is my job."

"I had to do something."

"No!" Charlotte was enraged. "You were specifically instructed to do nothing. That interview made you vulnerable. Before the interview, you were a family grieving behind closed doors with a family attorney who was working with the police during the investigation. After the interview, you're a smug rich guy with a drugged-out wife who's hiding behind his high-priced lawyer and blocking any attempt the police have made to get you to come in for a formal interview. Big difference."

"I don't know what you're talking about."

His father's voice was softer now. Defeated. Beaten. Charlie wanted to run into the living room and pull him out of there, but he was too frightened to move.

"Lewisboro's chief of police gave a press conference to counter your interview, and the number one thing he did was stress over and over that they've invited you to come in and give your statement and you've refused. It doesn't matter that you refused because I told you to. It doesn't matter that refusing to come in is common with investigations like this. All the public needed to hear was that your daughter was killed, the police wanted you to come in so they could walk through what happened, and you keep saying no. He did a real good job making you look like a proper person of interest."

"My god."

A bag thumped on a table, and Charlie jumped.

"So here's what we're going to do, because they've forced our hand. You and I are going to go in to police headquarters, and you're going to give your interview. I'll be with you and I'll guide you, but we need to do this in order to get the public back on our side. They painted you into a corner. The only way out is by giving your statement."

"That's fine," his father said. "I have nothing to hide. I should've given it the day they were here. You told me not to. You made me look guilty, and I'm not."

"I don't care either way. My job is to keep you and your wife out of jail. Stop making my job harder than it already is."

The lawyer and his father continued to argue, then began to come up with a plan about his visit to the police station the next day. Charlie listened closely so he could hear what time they'd be leaving. He wanted to get back into the woods since Bobby screwed it up the last time he tried to go. He just needed a few minutes at the crime scene. In and out.

No one would even know he was there.

# 36

The following day, Sunday, came with a welcome surprise. Chief Haslet called Susan to let her know Noel Moore had agreed to an interview Monday and that he and his attorney would be arriving at the station promptly at ten. She spent the rest of the day splitting her time between the twins and preparing for the interview, knowing this would be her one and only shot to get to the bottom of questions that still lingered. It was important that she didn't waste anyone's time, and she was quite aware that Charlotte Walsh would be waiting to pull the plug the first chance she got. Before long, day turned to night and Monday morning arrived. It was time.

Susan made it in to Lewisboro by eight and spent two hours going over notes and reports, forming her questions carefully. By ten, Noel and Charlotte were in the interview room, waiting. Susan was ready.

Noel straightened up in his seat when she came in. Charlotte remained pin straight in her chair. They nodded their hellos, and Susan sat across from them, placing a folder down in front of her along with a notepad and pen. Chief Haslet was watching from the observation room along with Sergeant Dunes and Liam.

"I appreciate you meeting with me."

"My pleasure," Noel replied. "I'm glad we could finally make this happen."

"Before we get started, I have to let you know that we're being recorded through audio and video from those two cameras in the room." She pointed, and Noel acknowledged both devices.

"Okay."

"That okay with you, Miss Walsh?"

Charlotte rolled her eyes. "It's fine."

"Good. Let the record show that Noel Moore and his counsel, Charlotte Walsh, both recognized the presence of audio and visual equipment in the room that will be used to record this interview." Susan looked up at the camera facing her. "This is file number three-three-six-Lewisboro PD. The interviewee has agreed that this conversation will be on the record. My name is Investigator Susan Adler of the New York State Police, Troop K. Right now we're at the Lewisboro Police Department in South Salem, New York. I've been assigned to investigate the homicide of Jennifer Moore, and I'm here with the father of the victim, Noel Moore."

Susan took a breath and grabbed her pen, but Noel held his hand up.

"Look, I just want to start things off by apologizing if I caught anyone off guard with that interview I did. Charlotte here tells me it wasn't the wisest thing to do, but I was starting to see rumblings online and in the news that kept suggesting me or my wife might have had something to do with what happened to Jen. I felt like I needed to end those rumors as quickly as possible. In retrospect, I probably should've just ignored everything and let you do your thing."

"Thank you for that," Susan replied. She let her shoulder sag to give off the perception that she was relaxed, hoping Noel would relax as well. "I will admit we were taken aback by the interview. It's unusual for a family member of a homicide victim to do something like that while the police are still in the initial phases of the investigation. But I get it. In this day and age with social media and the rumors that would quickly get out of control, you felt like you had to protect your family and present the facts. I probably would've done the same."

"Thank you."

Susan flipped her notepad open.

"Let's get started. I'd like you to walk me through the morning of your daughter's death," she said. "From the second you got up until the second the first set of police responded."

"I thought this had already been covered," Charlotte interrupted.

"I'd like to cover it again. Make sure I got my facts straight."

Noel looked at his attorney, and she nodded. He placed his hands on his lap, and his head dropped a little.

"The alarm went off, and Mindy and I got up. We went into the bathroom and brushed our teeth and whatnot. I went down to make the coffee, and when we didn't see Jen, Mindy went to wake her up. Charlie had camp a little later so we let him sleep, but Jen needed to get up since she was going out with Mindy that day. Mindy came down a few minutes later and told me Jen wasn't in her room, so we figured she went out for a run."

"How often did Jen go out for runs?"

"Couple times a week."

"Always in the woods?"

"Mostly, but sometimes on the track at the high school."

"Okay. Go on."

"We don't normally go into the woods looking for her, but on that morning, Mindy noticed Jen didn't take her Fitbit with her, and we all knew how long it took her to get ready after a run. She and Mindy were going shopping for the rest of the things she needed for college after breakfast, and I know they wanted to get there early and beat some traffic. We figured she might've lost track of time, so Mindy went into the woods to see if she could catch her coming around the trail that's back there."

Susan took notes. "How often did she run without the watch?"

Noel shrugged. "I have no idea. Mindy just mentioned she saw it in her room and that she didn't have it on, which is why she went into the woods to look for her."

"How do you know she hadn't gone to the track?"

"She would've had to drive out to the high school to get to the track. All the cars were still there. Plus, she mostly ran on the track in the evening."

"Okay. Keep going."

"While Mindy was back behind the house, I called Jen on her cell, but it rolled to voice mail. Next thing I know, Mindy comes inside the house in pure shock. I mean, she was out of it. Mumbling about Jen being in the woods and that there's so much blood. I obviously knew something was wrong. I thought Jen was hurt, so I ran out there. That's when I found her."

"How did you know where to look?"

"Mindy said she was back where the kids hang out. I knew where she was talking about."

"Did your wife have any blood on her when she came into the house?"

"Not that I noticed. She was wearing the same thing she had on when the officers arrived, and the CSI guys collected all of the clothes we were wearing. If your guys found blood, I didn't see it."

"What did you do when you got to Jennifer?" Susan asked. "Think for a second and walk me through it. Take your time."

Tears began to well in Noel's eyes. He sniffled, and his bottom lip trembled. "I stopped about five feet away when I saw her. There was so much blood. I could see the cut on her chest and the way she was lying on the ground. I knew she was dead."

"Did you touch her?"

"No."

"Did you approach her?"

"No. I stayed there for like a minute, maybe? Then I ran back to the house and called 911. By then Mindy was practically catatonic, and I sat her in the family room. We waited for the police, and Charlie woke up. I told him something happened to Jen, and we all stayed in the family room until the police arrived. That's pretty much it."

Susan skimmed the initial report Noel had given the responding officers as well as what he'd told her when she arrived on scene. Everything he'd just said coincided with what he'd told her that day.

"You left your wife to go check on Jennifer in the woods."

"That's right."

"Was she in the same spot when you came back in the house?"

"What?"

"Was your wife standing or sitting in the same place as when you left her?"

Noel finally looked up. "Yes. She was holding herself up on the edge of the kitchen counter. I remember that. When I came back inside, she was still there."

"And you sat her in the family room."

"Yes."

"Did you go upstairs yourself? After you called 911? Maybe to check on your son or to get something for your wife?"

"No," Noel replied, shaking his head. "I stayed with Mindy the entire time until the police came."

"When Charlie came down, did he stay in the family room the entire time?"

"He just told you that," Charlotte interrupted.

Susan ignored the lawyer. "Mr. Moore? Charlie?"

"Yes," Noel said. "My son stayed with us in the family room the entire time."

More notes.

"Mr. Moore, can you tell me the last time the en suite bathroom was cleaned?"

"What does that have to do with anything?" Charlotte asked. She looked at Noel.

"I'm just trying to establish who was where, and when," Susan said. "Can you tell me how often your cleaning lady comes?"

Susan could see Noel's leg begin to bounce up and down. He stared at her for a moment. Charlotte was doing the same. No one said a word. She knew their minds were churning, trying to figure out what road she was leading them down.

"I believe I told you that our housekeeper comes every day."

"Ah, you're right." Susan tapped her file. "I'm sorry. You did tell me that. And you stated that you called her that morning and told her to stay home because of what happened."

"Correct."

"So we know the bathroom wasn't cleaned that day. What about the day before? Do you know if your housekeeper cleaned the bathroom the day before the murder?"

He shrugged. "Maybe. Mindy handles all that. I'm usually working, and by the time I get home things are just . . . done. The bathroom may have been cleaned the day before. I really couldn't say."

"Why is this relevant?" Charlotte asked.

Susan ignored the question and took an eight-by-ten glossy picture from inside her folder. She slid it across the table.

"This is a picture of your bedroom. One of the forensic techs took it. I'd like to know where your rug is."

Noel stared at the photo, and from her angle, Susan could see his face turning a light shade of red. She leaned forward and traced her finger along the lines of the faded hardwood floor, then slid a second photo across the table. This one was the prom photo of Jennifer and Anja York in the bedroom with the rug on the floor.

"So there was an area rug here as recently as June," she said. "And it looks like it had been there long enough for the sun to fade the floor around it. It's gone now, and when I talked to your housekeeper, she said the rug was there the last time she was at the house, which was the day before your daughter was killed. What happened to the rug? Where is it?"

"You talked to Maria?"

"Yes. And just so we're all clear, she said she hadn't cleaned your bathroom in three days. She said she does the bed and bath on the same day. But man, when I went in there that morning, I couldn't get over how spotless it was. I could still smell the bleach. Our team picked up on that too."

Noel's leg was bouncing furiously now. He stared down at the photo and back up at her. "You're implying that we had something to do with what happened to Jen," Noel seethed as he glared at her. "You're just like the rest of them."

"I'm not implying anything. I just want to know where the rug is."

"How are you supposed to find out who's responsible for my daughter's death when you're wasting time on me and my family?"

"I'm trying to look into your family, clear you, and move on. Isn't that what you said you wanted me to do in your interview with Donna Starr? So where's the rug? What happened to it between the day your housekeeper was there and the morning your daughter was murdered?"

Noel's eyes glassed over with a fresh set of tears. "We had nothing to do with what happened to Jen. Why can't people understand that? We didn't do anything."

Charlotte quickly stood from her seat and pulled her client up. "We're done here," she said. "Let's go."

Susan watched them leave, bemused. "Thank you for coming in."

Noel and Charlotte left without saying anything further. A few seconds later, Chief Haslet and Sergeant Dunes walked in.

"Nice job," the chief said.

"Thanks," Susan replied. "We still don't have enough to bring charges, but at least he knows we're not taking any more of his crap."

"You held back on the fact that we found blood in the house," Dunes said. "And that Darth Vader pendant."

"For now, yes. I also held back on a lie he just tripped up on. He said he called Jennifer's cell to see where she was while Mindy went into the woods to look for her. Phone records show Jennifer's last incoming call was from an 888 number around six p.m. the night before she was found. We'd need her actual phone to see if the call came in unanswered, so I held back. And the blood is too easily dismissible by someone as skilled as Charlotte Walsh. The pendant and the phone record don't prove anything either. But if we keep them and build on them, it could end up turning into something."

"I get it."

Susan picked up her notepad. "The clothes the Moores were wearing the morning they found Jennifer didn't have any blood on them. I'm guessing they changed before they called us, which means whatever they were wearing at the time is probably with the rug."

Liam hurried into the room carrying Susan's bag. "Hey, I don't know what's up, but your phone's been ringing the entire time you were in here."

She took her bag and rifled through it, coming away with her phone. When she saw the screen, her heart leaped into her throat. Eric had called seven times and left two voice mails. Her mother had called three times.

Something had happened. She retrieved the last voice mail.

*"Hey, Susan. Where the hell are you? Call me. We're at the ER at Mid-Hudson Regional. Casey fell on the monkey bars and broke her arm. They're taking her into surgery in like twenty minutes. You really need to get here."*

She checked her watch. That call had come in sixteen minutes earlier. She'd never make it.

"I have to go," she said as she quickly gathered her things into her arms and started for the door. "Family emergency. My kid broke her arm. She's at Mid-Hudson Regional." She looked at Liam. "Stay here and get the transcripts printed from the interview. I'll meet you at the hospital."

"Yeah, sure. Go."

She was gone, running to her car and climbing into her sedan, her ex-husband's voice echoing in her mind, the urgency in his tone.

*You really need to get here.*

# 37

Susan leaped out of the elevator before the doors had a chance to open all the way. She jogged down the pediatrics wing of the hospital as she read the signs directing her to the surgery center. After several twists and turns down the corridors, she found Eric standing just outside the waiting room, dressed in his suit from work. Beatrice was sitting inside with Tim. They were both coloring.

"I'm here," she panted as she almost fell into her ex-husband's chest.

Eric pushed himself off the wall. "Where were you?"

"I was in an interview. We can't bring our phones in. I didn't know you were calling."

"I called the barracks too."

"I wasn't there. I was in Lewisboro. The barracks left me a voice mail too. I just didn't have my phone. I'm sorry. What's going on?"

Eric sighed and pushed his jacket behind him so he could put his hands on his hips. "She went into surgery like ten minutes ago."

"What happened?"

"Apparently Casey was on the playground at camp and she started climbing the monkey bars and goofing off with her friends, and she fell from the top, hit the bottom bars, flipped over, and landed on the ground."

"Were the counselors there?"

"Of course. It just happened so fast. No one could react in time. One minute she's laughing and playing; the next she's on the ground. They called 911, and she was brought here."

Guilt washed over Susan like a tidal wave. "I'm sorry I didn't pick up the phone. I didn't know."

Eric took a step forward, closing the gap between them. "It's okay. You're here now."

"But I didn't get to see her before they took her in for surgery."

"You'll see her when she comes out."

They both turned when they heard footsteps. Liam came around the corner and stopped.

"Is she okay?" Liam asked.

"Yeah. She fell off the monkey bars at camp and broke her wrist," Eric explained. "They need to put a few screws in, so she's in surgery."

"She must've been so sacred," Susan said.

"How long is the surgery scheduled for?" Liam asked.

"Hour and a half."

The three of them made their way into the waiting room. Eric went in first while Susan and Liam lagged behind.

"I got the transcripts loaded into the system," Liam said.

"Not now," Susan whispered. "We'll talk later."

They walked inside, and as soon as Tim saw Liam, he jumped up from his seat and ran to give him a hug. Susan put on a smile as her son started explaining everything that had happened, including the fact that he didn't get a chance to make watermelon heads with his arts and crafts team because Casey fell. As usual, Liam took it all in stride, keeping pace with the conversation while at the same time participating in it. He was so good with her kids. So natural.

Susan glanced at Eric, who was watching Tim and Liam. He looked up and found Susan's eyes, but before he could linger on them, she closed hers. How could she keep doing this? How long could she juggle being a mom and being a cop before something collapsed? She'd have to let Liam take the lead on the case for a bit so she could make sure Casey was okay and nothing was triggering Tim. But then what? How many cases would she have to hand off for the good of her children? How long could she keep doing this?

A fresh set of tears wanted to break through, and she let it. There was no holding back now.

# 38

As the afternoon began to give way to dusk, Charlie came down the stairs to find his father sleeping on the couch in the family room. His mother was in her bedroom, asleep as well, the crying having stopped after she'd been given the medicine her doctor had prescribed. He studied his father, and there was no question he was out, snoring quietly with each gentle exhale. Without wanting to waste any more time, Charlie snuck out the sliding door and walked through the backyard toward the edge of the woods.

He'd been planning to do this while his father was at the police station, but Aunt Sidney had come over to babysit and never let him out of her sight. This was the only opportunity he saw aside from sneaking out in the middle of the night, and there was no way he was doing that after what happened. It was now or never.

It would still be a few hours before the sun was gone, but with the thick canopy of trees above, the woods were dark with shadow. Charlie tried his best to follow along the broken branches and stomp the undergrowth so his path to the crime scene would be mixed in with the path the police had taken during their investigation. It was important to hide the fact that he was out there. No one could know.

Birds sang somewhere in the background, but overall, the woods were quiet. Scary. The feeling of isolation, despite his house only being about a hundred yards away, was overwhelming. He couldn't see anything other than the brush that surrounded him, and the path to the hangout spot was tight, making things seem even more closed in.

Charlie pushed past the branches and stepped through the bramble. After a few more feet, the path opened up, and he stopped when he reached a piece of police tape that stretched around a small clearing that he knew had once been filled with crates and beer bottles and remnants of burned wood from a fire. Now there was nothing. No cigarette butts or used condoms or empty Styrofoam containers from the diner. No trash or red Solo cups or busted taps from ancient kegs. The police had taken everything. Every piece of anything had been bagged and tagged, as the cops on TV shows always said. But they hadn't touched the small pile of river rocks he'd stacked a few days earlier. They were still there, just beyond the spot where Jen's body had been found.

He stepped under the police tape and shuffled onto the actual crime scene. He stopped when he saw the dried blood that had pooled on the ground. He could see some spatter on the leaves around the clearing. He'd never seen an actual crime scene before, and it was nothing like the movies and shows. He could smell the blood even though he knew that was impossible. He could feel the sense of dread that permeated this part of the forest. The birds had stopped singing, and everything was completely silent. That was it. That was the spot where his sister had taken her last breath. That was the spot where she knew she was going to die.

Charlie kept to the edge of the police tape as he made his way to the pile of rocks. He knelt down and moved them away, tossing each one to the side. The ground underneath the rocks was still loose, and he dug his fingers into the earth, feeling around for it, his fingers searching the soil.

He felt the edge of the chain and gripped it, gently pulling up until it snaked its way out like a worm coming up from the soil. He placed it in his palm and studied it. A thin gold bracelet with hearts on the ends. Jen's bracelet. The one he'd buried.

"Hi, Charlie."

Charlie jumped and fell backward, closing his hand around the bracelet as he tumbled onto his butt. Footsteps scurried across the leaves, and suddenly the reporter lady was standing over him.

"Oh, I'm so sorry," she said. "I didn't mean to frighten you."

Charlie opened his mouth to say something, but he couldn't. The thumping of his heartbeat filled his ears. "I . . . I . . ."

"It's okay," the woman said. She took a step back. "I'm Donna. Donna Starr? Remember? We did the interview with your father."

Charlie nodded and scrambled to his feet.

"I saw you walking across your yard when I was shooting some B roll for tonight's broadcast," Donna explained. "I just wanted to make sure you were okay."

Charlie put his hands in his back pockets to hide the bracelet. "You mean you wanted to stalk me in case you could get some cool video of me standing at my sister's murder scene."

"No, it's not like that. I don't even have a camera with me. I can respect your privacy."

"Yeah, right. That's why we have to keep the shades closed all the time. Even in the day."

There was a moment of silence as they both looked at the ground where Jen's body had been discovered.

"You know, we can be friends," Donna said quietly. "We can help each other."

"How?"

"Sometimes the police find things during their investigation, but because they need to find more, they don't tell anyone right away. I have lots of friends in the police, and sometimes they tell me things the rest of the people don't know. If that ever happens and I find out something that you don't know yet, I could tell you."

"And what do I have to do for you?"

"Same thing. If you see or hear something that other people don't know yet, you tell me. We'll keep each other informed so we can find out who killed your sister. We can be friends and work together. No one has to know. It can be our secret. How does that sound?"

"I guess it sounds okay."

Donna smiled. "Good." She pushed at some fallen leaves with the toe of her tennis shoe. "So what are you doing out here?"

"Nothing. I needed to see where they found Jen, and no one would show me, so I came myself."

"Why were you kneeling in the dirt?"

"Saying a prayer."

The reporter nodded. "Does your dad know you're here?"

"No. He's sleeping. And he can't know. I'd get in trouble."

"Don't worry. I won't say a word."

"Can I be alone now, please? I'll be done in a minute."

"Sure," Donna replied. "And you'll call me if you hear anything. I'll do the same for you."

Charlie didn't reply, but she took out her business card and placed it on the ground. Then she left the way she'd come. He waited until she disappeared. As soon as he felt he was alone again, he pulled his hands out of his pockets and studied the bracelet, wondering if she'd watched him dig it up and if he'd suddenly become something she knew that the police didn't.

He stayed for a little while longer, then walked back toward the house. His father was still asleep when he came back inside, and Charlie snuck past him on his way upstairs. He pushed his parents' bedroom door open to check on his mother, but the bed was empty.

"Mom?"

He walked through the room and knocked on the closed bathroom door. He could hear the water running.

"Mom? You need anything?"

No answer.

"Mom."

Nothing.

Charlie turned the knob and opened the door just enough to poke his head in. When his eyes focused and his mind told him what he was seeing, it was as if he'd gone back in time a few nights earlier. The blood. The vacant look in his mother's eyes. The fear that crept from his stomach to his throat.

And then he heard himself screaming. Screaming for his father. Screaming for help. Screaming to make it all go away.

Screaming to God to stop hurting his family.

# 39

Liam climbed up the front steps and stopped when he got to the door, quickly stepping aside to allow two officers to exit the Moore house. Once again, the property was full of pulsating red lights and emergency personnel. Another crowd of neighbors and reporters had gathered across the street, eager to see what twist the story had taken. As soon as the officers were clear, Liam walked inside and met Sergeant Dunes in the foyer.

"Where's Investigator Dwyer?" Dunes asked.

"Had a family emergency," Liam replied. "You got me for now, and I'll relay everything back to Susan in the morning. For now, you're in charge."

"Copy that."

They walked down the hall toward the kitchen.

"The 911 call came in about forty minutes ago. EMTs arrived on scene to find Mrs. Moore in the tub of the en suite bathroom upstairs, both wrists cut with a razor. The kid found her."

"Where was Mr. Moore?"

"Fell asleep on the couch in the family room. Woke up when he heard his son screaming. He's the one who placed the call."

They turned the corner to find Noel Moore and his son, Charlie, sitting at a small table nestled in the corner of the kitchen, overlooking the patio in the back. Noel looked disheveled and generally unkempt. His hair was askew, and his eyes were almost vacant and rimmed red. His skin was pale under the pendant light hanging over the table, and his T-shirt seemed to hang off him. It looked as though he'd lost weight in the few days since the investigation had begun.

Charlie Moore was a mess. He was huffing breaths and sobbing, constantly running his arm across his nose to wipe it. His eyes were twice the size they'd normally be, and dirt stained his face where tears continued to fall. His head was hung when they walked in, and although his father looked up to acknowledge Liam and Sergeant Dunes, the boy ignored them, trapped in a nightmare he was undoubtedly reliving over and over.

Liam felt a bit untethered. He'd been at the hospital when Susan got the call from Lewisboro dispatch about the 911 call coming from the Moore house, but Casey had just gotten out of surgery, and she was unable to respond. She'd asked Liam to go in her place, and he'd agreed without hesitation. But now that he was on scene, he realized he'd never been anything close to a lead investigator on a case, and he knew he had no real jurisdiction. He didn't know what to ask or what subject to broach. He was a man who investigated through science. This was all too new to him, and he had no idea how to take that important first step.

"Mr. Moore, can you tell us what happened?" Dunes asked.

Liam felt his shoulders relax just a bit as the sergeant took command.

Noel looked at both of them and did a half shrug. "I have no idea. I was watching TV, and I guess I fell asleep on the couch. Next thing I know, Charlie's screaming, and I run upstairs to find Mindy in the tub. I saw the blood and her wrists, and I knew what she did. I called 911, and you all showed up."

"Did your wife give you any indication that she was planning to hurt herself? Did she hint at it, or did something happen today that might've triggered her to act this way?"

"Not that I know of. She's been kind of in and out of it since she found Jen. Wasn't talking. Hardly eating. But nothing specific that would ever make me think she'd try and kill herself." His eyes filled with tears. "How could she do this?"

Dunes waited for a beat. "Have any reporters been harassing you or calling the house or trespassing? Maybe your wife had an interaction with someone from across the street, and that triggered something?"

"No," Noel replied. "We keep the phone off the hook, and she hasn't left the house since she got home from the hospital. I think it's just the loss she's feeling. I think it crushed her to the point of her not wanting to have to feel it anymore. But she can't be in her right mind. She would never do this to Charlie if she was thinking straight. This is all too much."

Noel put his head in his hands and cried quietly. Liam watched the boy, who was still sobbing uncontrollably and looking down at the table. He wanted to reach out and hold him and tell him that he knew exactly what he was feeling. He knew what it was like to have a mother so sick with grief that she would do things she wouldn't ever normally do. He'd lost his father and watched his mother slowly go insane over it. He knew what it was like to have a normal childhood one minute and something unrecognizable the next. When the family unit was torn, that tear could be deep and unmendable. The tears Charlie Moore cried were familiar. They were tears of confusion and anger and fear and loss. Liam knew those tears well. He'd cried them himself too many times to count.

"Is my mom going to die?"

The boy's question cut through the silence like a knife. He'd raised his head and was looking at the sergeant.

"The EMTs think she's going to be okay," Dunes replied. "You got there in time, and your dad called 911 right away. You both saved her."

The boy slid off the chair and dug into the back pocket of his shorts. He came away with something and placed it on the table.

"I didn't save my mom," he said. "I'm the reason she's like this in the first place. It's because of me that she was so sad she tried to kill herself. It was me. My fault."

Liam took a step closer. He couldn't help himself. "What are you saying, Charlie?"

The boy focused on Liam. "I'm saying my mom tried to kill herself because of what I did to Jen."

"And what was that?"

More tears ran down the boy's face. "I killed her. This is all my fault."

---

Noel Moore leaped from the table and grabbed his son. "Don't say that!"

"I did!" Charlie cried in response. "I killed her, Dad. I'm sorry. I didn't mean to. I didn't know what was going to happen."

The boy fell into his father's arms, and he cried another set of uncontrollable tears. Sergeant Dunes stood motionless in the kitchen, watching everything play out. Liam fumbled in his pocket and came away with his phone. He started recording the conversation.

"I need to record this for the investigation," he said and noticed his voice was shaking just a bit. He took another step closer and knelt down. "Charlie, tell us exactly what happened the night your sister was killed."

"No!" Noel snapped. "I want my lawyer. Get Charlotte over here."

Charlie immediately pushed away from his father. "No, Dad. Let me tell them. I don't need that mean lady to yell at everyone again. I need to tell them what happened."

Before Noel could reply, Charlie started talking.

"Jen was always obsessing over that stupid bracelet." He gestured toward the piece of jewelry he'd pulled from his pocket and set on the table. "She loved that thing more than she loved us. Always freaking out about where it was and running to put it back on as soon as she got out of the shower. It was weird. So the day before she died, I asked her to give me and Bobby a ride to Target so I could get a new game for my Xbox. *Toad Wars.* She said no. I begged her to take us, and she was just being a bitch and kept saying no. She had nothing to do that day—she was just sitting in the family room surfing channels and texting. By the end of the day, *Toad Wars* was sold out, and all my friends were posting about it and how cool it was and how they were able to get a copy."

"So you were angry that she didn't take you to get the game and you missed out," Dunes said.

The boy nodded. "So the next morning when she was in the shower, I took her bracelet and ran to the back woods and buried it so she'd never find it. I marked where I put it with a pile of rocks like we learned about in history how the Indians used to mark graves. She was totally freaking out about losing it. Going on and on, accusing everyone of taking it. Me and Mom and Bobby when he came over. I kept a straight face and kept telling her I had no idea what she was talking about. By the end of that day, she was losing it. Crying and freaking out. I couldn't take it anymore. I finally texted her in the middle of the night when I could still hear her crying and told her where it was. I figured she'd wait until morning to get it, but I heard her run out of the house as soon as I sent the text. I fell asleep, and then the next morning she was dead."

Sergeant Dunes nodded as the tension in the room dissipated. "But you didn't actually kill her."

"She was out in those woods because of me. Because of my stupid prank. If I didn't take that bracelet, she would've been asleep in her room and would be alive right now. It's all my fault. I killed her."

Charlie started crying again and fell back into his father's embrace. Liam stopped recording and walked to where the sergeant was standing.

"What he says confirms what John told us about her phone records," he said. "Jennifer's last text exchange was between herself and her brother. It fits."

"Let's take the bracelet as evidence for now," Dunes replied. "I'll have one of the officers bag it."

"Sounds good."

Sergeant Dunes approached Charlie and his father, who was still trying to console him.

"Charlie," she began. "We found a Darth Vader pendant in the woods when we were back there in the clearing. Is that yours? Did you lose it by accident while you were hiding your sister's bracelet?"

The boy looked at her, and his eyes widened. "A Darth Vader pendant?"

"Yeah, like the kind you'd hang from a chain. Is it yours?"

The boy gave a quick nod. "Yeah. It's mine."

Sergeant Dunes walked back toward Liam, who had retreated to the door.

"So now we know why there were small footprints in the mud, what the text exchange was that Jennifer had with her brother that night, and we know why Jennifer was in the woods in her PJs in the first place," she said quietly. "Fills in a lot of holes."

Liam nodded. "All of them except the most important ones. Why was the parents' bedroom and bath cleaned up like it was? Where is that rug? And if Jennifer Moore was out in those woods on a whim, who was hanging around the property to kill her?"

# 40

Another day. Charlie sat in his bed thinking about everything that had happened the night before. His confession was a giant weight lifted from his shoulders, and the fact that the police didn't want to put him in jail for the rest of his life was a welcome surprise, but the images of his mother in the tub still danced in his mind, endlessly reminding him that if he hadn't been such a little shit to his sister in the first place, Jen wouldn't have been out in the woods and she'd still be alive and his family wouldn't have been changed forever. But another thought danced alongside those horrible images of his mother's attempted suicide. Now that the threat of impending incarceration had been lifted, it left room for more questions that needed to be asked. Who killed his sister that night? And why?

Charlie thought about the detective lady who'd asked him about the Darth Vader pendant they'd found in the woods. He'd lied and said it was his because he didn't want to put the police on Bobby without talking to him first, but that pendant was absolutely Bobby's. There was no question. It was Bobby's favorite thing in the world. His good luck charm. He'd gotten it during a trip to Disneyland. He'd always thought Vader was the best character in the Star Wars series, so it made sense. And according to Bobby, the moment he put it around his neck, good things started happening in his life. He won a contest on that vacation that allowed him to visit a VIP area in the park and get his picture taken with all the characters that the normal public didn't have access to. They got a free meal at one of the hardest restaurants to get into because he had found a lost phone, turned it in, and was rewarded by its owner. It sounded dumb, but that wasn't the only time it worked. When Bobby got home from Disney, the pendant became legendary. His mother's cancer went into remission. His father got a promotion at work, so his folks stopped arguing about money all the time. His classes in school got easier, which got him good grades, which then got him the newest PlayStation after he made the dean's list. He attributed all of it to the pendant, and it became folklore among his friends. Bobby never took it off, and no one else at the school had one like it. You could only get it at the actual Star Wars: Galaxy's Edge park. They didn't sell them in stores or online. So Charlie knew the pendant was Bobby's, and knowing that made him furious. Why was it in the woods next to where his sister was murdered? What did Bobby do?

Charlie turned on his phone and waited for it to boot up. As it did, hundreds of chimes and rings sounded off, and he felt his stomach clench. More haters. More people either accusing him and his family of killing Jen or trying to take part in their loss. News had undoubtedly spread about his mother's attempted suicide, which meant there would be even more accusations and people he didn't know talking shit. People were assholes one way or the other.

His Instagram was filled with people tagging Jen in posts and all the different hashtags that had been set up in her memory. Friends were trying to reach out to see if he was okay, but in reality he knew they just wanted to be part of the excitement of a murder investigation. He looked at his Twitter feed, and it was more of the same with a bunch of comments about his mom. His email was full of the same crap too. Vultures. Every last one of them.

He flipped over to his texts and messaged Bobby with shaking hands.

You around?

He saw the three dots appear, which meant Bobby was answering him.

Heading to football practice

What time u coming back?

Around lunchtime

K Talk later

How's your mom?

OK

Thinking of her. Thoughts and prayers, dude

He waited before answering, swallowing the anger and the fear and the confusion that were drowning him.

Peace

Charlie put his phone down, and as soon as he did, he heard a noise downstairs. He figured it was his aunt. His father had gone to the hospital after the police left and Aunt Sidney had come to stay with him. She'd probably gotten up to make breakfast.

The wind blew against the house, and Charlie glanced out his bedroom window as he walked from his room into the hall. It was sunny, but in the distance he could see dark clouds filling the sky. It looked like a storm was coming. Their first rain since Jenny's death. He peeked inside the guest bedroom and found his aunt sleeping soundly. The covers were pulled up to her shoulders, and he heard her breathing heavily, in and out. An empty bottle of wine sat on the nightstand next to the lamp.

Noise from downstairs again.

"Aunt Sidney," he called. "Wake up."

She didn't move.

"Aunt Sidney."

Nothing.

Charlie ran back inside his room and grabbed his phone. He kept it in his hand, ready to call 911 if he needed to. He went downstairs, and when he reached the landing, he heard rustling from the basement. He looked for evidence of a break-in. A busted window. A broken door. A bent screen. But there was nothing. Everything appeared as it should have. Maybe it was his dad, and he hadn't heard him come home. That was the only thing that made sense. Who else would be in the house?

More rustling from the basement. Charlie walked into the kitchen and carefully opened the basement door, which led to a playroom, a movie theater, and a storage area. He stood at the top of the carpeted stairs, his thumb hovering over the emergency button on his cell phone.

"Who's there?" he cried in his deepest, most authoritative voice. "Is that you, Dad? Come out now or I'm calling the police."

More rustling. Quieter this time. Footsteps shuffling around the concrete floor. Whoever it was, they were in the storage area.

"Who is that?"

A door closed.

"I'm calling the police!"

Footsteps went quiet as they walked across the carpet. Closer toward him.

"You don't want to call the police on me," a voice replied. "I'm one of the only friends you got."

Charlie relaxed as soon as he heard the voice. He watched as Uncle Artie turned the corner and began climbing the stairs. "You scared the crap out of me."

"Sorry, bud." Artie stopped at the top step and planted a quick kiss on the top of Charlie's head.

"What're you doing here?"

"I told your dad I was stopping by to take you fishing." He held out his hands, which were gripping two rods and a tackle box. "You need to get out of the house and get your mind off all the stuff that's been going on. A morning out on the lake will do that."

"I don't even like fishing."

"It's not about the fishing. It's about a change of environment. And you need one."

Charlie backed away from the basement door and allowed Artie to pass by. Artie put the gear down and walked into the kitchen. He opened a cabinet door and pulled out two bowls. "You want some cereal?"

"Sure."

"Coffee?"

"Yuck. No, thanks."

Artie chuckled as he poured two bowls of Frosted Flakes and prepared a pot of coffee.

"I'm sorry about what happened to your mom."

"Thanks."

"I talked to your dad. He said she's going to be okay. He said your quick thinking saved her. He called 911, and you put pressure on the wounds. That's hero stuff, my friend."

"Didn't feel like a hero."

"I know. And I know this is a lot for you. All of it. For what it's worth, you're handling it like a champ. You didn't need this thing with your mom, but some people cope differently, and she's suffering big-time right now. She's not thinking straight."

"I know."

"She's scared and sad and not herself. What she did has nothing to do with you or your father. She's just distraught over Jen and didn't know how to handle the pain."

Charlie didn't say anything. There really wasn't anything to say. His mom tried to kill herself after his sister had been murdered. His world was spinning completely out of control.

Artie paused, and the house grew quiet again. He took a spoonful of cereal. "So what were your plans today before I came into the picture?"

Charlie swallowed his own cereal. "I need to stop by Bobby's house."

"Yeah? You guys hanging out?"

"Something like that."

"I can drop you off after fishing if you want."

"Okay. That would be great."

Aunt Sidney stumbled into the kitchen. She looked exhausted. Her eyes were bloodshot, her pupils nothing more than tiny black dots. Her hair was a mess. When she saw Artie, she stopped and quickly tried to fix herself.

"I didn't know you were here," she said. "I look like who-did-it-and-ran."

"Nonsense," Artie replied. He poured a second cup of coffee and slid it across the island. "You look like an aunt who came to the rescue last night. I'm glad Mindy's okay."

Sidney sipped the coffee. "Yeah, me too."

Charlie finished his cereal and hopped off his stool. "I'm going to get dressed. Artie's taking me fishing, and then he said he could drive me to Bobby's house."

"You hate fishing."

"That's what I said."

Artie laughed. "It's not about the fishing!"

Charlie and Sidney laughed too. It was a sound that house hadn't heard in a while. It was a sound, Charlie suddenly realized, that he'd desperately missed.

# 41

Susan sat in her car, staring at the Cortlandt barracks as the engine idled. Her head was still heavy from lack of sleep, and her lower back ached from sitting in the unforgiving hospital chair all night, but she knew she had to get back to work. She'd missed the night before with Mindy Moore's attempted suicide and Charlie's confession about burying his sister's bracelet, and although there was no question she wasn't herself, either mentally or physically, she had a job to do. There was no escaping that fact, even when she felt like the balance between mother and investigator was off kilter yet again.

Casey had made it out of surgery without issue. The surgeon had placed two tiny screws to hold the broken pieces of her wrist in place, and she'd been put in a cast while the ulnar bone healed. The entire family spent the rest of the afternoon with Casey, who had slept most of the time, drifting into consciousness just long enough to eat or use the bathroom, but the anesthesia had done a number and her tiny body wasn't used to it, so she slept and snored, and they all watched and waited. There was nothing more any of them could do.

When it got close to dinner, she'd received the call about Mindy Moore and sent Liam to assist on her behalf. She'd then asked her mother to take Tim home while she and Eric stayed behind. After another few hours, Eric announced that he needed to leave and go to the office to pick up some paperwork he was supposed to have gotten earlier that day, and Susan caught up with Liam while she remained beside her daughter's bed, ensuring she'd be there whenever Casey woke up. That was, after all, what a child expected of their parent: to simply be there.

Susan climbed out of her car and made her way inside the barracks. As she walked onto the investigator's unit, she saw Liam sitting at his desk.

"Hey," she said.

Liam spun around. "Good morning. You okay?"

Susan fell into her chair and looked up at the ceiling, fighting off the urge to simply close her eyes and go to sleep. It felt good to be back at the barracks, back at her desk and in her chair. It felt like she'd come home. But this wasn't home. This was work. She couldn't keep blurring those lines.

"I guess I'm as good as I can be. Thanks for covering for me last night."

"Happy to help."

Crosby emerged from his office and walked toward them. He sat on the edge of Susan's desk. "How's Casey?"

"Fine. She'll be fine."

"You know you can work from home. There's no reason for you to have to come in here or stay in Lewisboro if you need to be with her."

Susan blotted her eyes with the back of her hand and sat up straight. She didn't want to cry in front of the guys. "It's okay. Eric and my mom are there now, and she's being discharged later. I'll leave to bring her home then, and if I need to stay at the house, I'll let you know. For now, I'm better here."

"Give her a kiss for me."

"Will do."

Crosby clapped his hands and cleared his throat. Sentimental time was over. "Okay, fill me in on what we've got so far. How's Mrs. Moore?"

"She'll be okay," Liam replied. "They're going to keep her for a few days in the psych unit and see where things go from there."

"We need to talk to her the second we're allowed to."

"Yes, sir. I left explicit instructions for them to call us when that time comes."

"And the kid told us why the vic was in the woods when she was, but we still don't know who met her there or why she was killed."

"Yes," Liam said. "But I think this leans us even more toward the family being involved. No one knew Jennifer was going to be in those woods to get that bracelet until Charlie told her where it was buried and she ran out to get it. The odds of someone being in the woods at that exact moment with the motive to kill Jennifer are astronomical."

"Maybe Jennifer wasn't the target," Crosby replied. "Maybe some nutjob was in the woods, and the girl created an opportunity. Wrong place, wrong time."

"But we still keep coming back to the blood in the house, the missing area rug, and the bleached bathroom," Susan said. "None of that fits with a random act of violence from a stranger in the woods."

Crosby nodded, thinking. "And the father was away."

"Correct."

"So that leaves the mother. The mother who's practically catatonic. The mother who hasn't given a statement to the police because of her mental state. The mother who's so grief stricken that she tried to kill herself last night."

Susan sat up in her seat. "The mother who has a history of altercations with the victim."

"There you go. We have our primary suspect."

Susan's phone started to ring, and she pulled it out of her pocket.

"Casey?" Crosby asked.

"No, John Chu." She connected the call and put it on speaker. "Hey, John, it's Susan. I have you on speaker with Liam and LT here."

"Hello, everyone," John said. "I have some interesting information to share."

"Go ahead."

"So when we were at the Moore residence the day the investigation began, you had me take DNA swabs and prints so we could discount the family when we were doing our analysis."

"Yeah, that's right."

"Well, we got the DNA results back. Everything was normal except one test. We ran it again to confirm and got the same result."

"What'd you find?"

"Jennifer Moore doesn't have a DNA match with anyone else in the Moore family."

Susan looked at Liam and Crosby, then leaned in closer toward the phone. "What are you saying, John?"

"I'm saying Jennifer Moore is not a member of the Moore family in any way. There is no relation. She's not their kid."

# 42

The clouds Charlie had seen earlier when he'd looked out his bedroom window were hovering overhead, but the threat of an impending rain was no longer there. The thick cover of gray had begun to break apart, and although the sky was still dark for the most part, rays of sunshine were beginning to peek through. By midday it promised to be sunny again.

He and Artie sat in a rowboat in the middle of Lake Waccabuc among a handful of other boats that had not been scared off by a morning shower. They both had rods in the water as the current pushed them along, a gentle breeze nudging them from west to east. Neither of them had caught anything, but Charlie'd had fish take his bait off the hook twice. That was all the action thus far.

There was very little conversation. Artie had tried to talk about dumb stuff like camp and the upcoming soccer season Charlie had no interest in taking part in, and after a number of one-word answers and Charlie's unwillingness to push the conversation any further, the last half hour had been mostly silent.

"You still got your bait on that hook?" Artie asked, breaking the quiet.

Charlie nodded. "The rod hasn't moved, so I guess. Should I reel it in and check?"

"Give it a few more minutes, then we'll take a peek. I'm thinking of rowing into the corner by where that tree fell. We might be able to catch something in there."

Charlie looked back out toward the water. The last time Artie had taken him fishing, Bobby had come with them. That had been a fun day. "Can I ask you something?"

"Of course. Anything."

"Do you think it's possible to love someone and hate someone at the same time?"

Artie slowly began reeling his line in, trying to entice a fish to bite. He kept his focus on the water in front of him. "I'm not sure what you mean, bud."

"I mean, is it possible to love someone, but at the same time hate them so much that you could hurt them?"

"Sure," Artie said. "Sometimes you hear stories about people who love each other hurting the person they love. It happens." He paused. "Are you talking about your mom?"

Charlie had begun reeling his line in as well. Nice and slow, like Artie had taught him earlier. He stopped, startled. "My mom? No. What are you talking about?"

"Nothing. Nothing. I didn't mean—"

Artie started rambling, but Charlie wasn't listening. He thought about the night before when the ambulance had brought his mother to the hospital. He'd told the sergeant and the man the truth about his part in his sister's murder, but he'd continued to lie for his father when he said he'd gone to sleep after sending Jen the text and had come down the next morning to find out what had happened. That lie had come so effortlessly. Just rolled off his tongue like it was nothing. He didn't even have to think about it. His brain just helped him along. Maybe the lie was easy to tell because the truth was something he knew he couldn't face.

*Is it possible to love someone, but at the same time hate them so much that you could hurt them?*

Charlie closed his eyes and was immediately back in his parents' bedroom. He could see the blood and the vacant look in his mother's eyes and the expression of horrified panic on his father's face.

*Is it possible to love someone, but at the same time hate them so much that you could hurt them?*

He remembered the fights his mother had with Jen and the arguments that always seemed to escalate. He could remember the shouting and the crying and the times she'd chased Jen around the house, pulling her hair and dragging her up the stairs. That was love and hate mixed together, right? That was a parent trying to discipline their child. Or was it something more than that? He didn't know, but nothing would make him believe that his mother had killed his sister. There had to be another explanation.

If his mother hadn't killed his sister, maybe his best friend had. And he needed to prove it. He needed to find the truth.

# 43

Charlie pretended he'd forgotten about Bobby's football practice when Mrs. Teagan answered the door. He'd waited until Uncle Artie had pulled away before ringing the bell; then he'd faked his surprise when she told him where Bobby was. It was all part of the plan, of course. He needed a way to be alone in Bobby's room to try and find why his Darth Vader pendant would've been out in the woods where Jen was killed. He couldn't snoop with Bobby there, and he wanted some ammo before just coming out and asking him, so he used the one time he knew Bobby would be gone and counted on Mrs. Teagan's kindness to let him in anyway, make him something to eat, and put him up in Bobby's room until practice was over. Things played out just as planned.

The room was a lot like his own. Light-blue paint on the walls, dark wood bed frame with matching dresser and nightstand, a large flat screen that was bolted right onto the wall, and the PlayStation underneath. Posters of Aaron Judge and Gary Sanchez covered one side of the room while Daniel Jones and Shaquan Barkley covered the other. Bobby loved the Yankees and the Giants almost as much as he loved Jen. The room was neat. Tidy. Everything in its place. Charlie stood in the doorway and scanned the space, trying to decide where to start. Their houses were almost identical, which meant their two rooms were laid out the same. He tried to think where he would hide something he didn't want anyone else to see and decided to go for the closet first.

The closet was a walk-in. Clothes were hung on hangers: shirts on the top row, pants on the bottom, dress clothes on the left, play clothes on the right. At the end of the closet was a wooden shoe rack. Dress shoes lined the first two rows, and sneakers were placed underneath. Everything was so sterile. Charlie had never realized Bobby was such a neat freak. He was always the one willing to jump in a mud puddle or dive into the lake with his clothes on for a laugh. He loved contact sports and tried to get as dirty as he could in every game he played. This room was the opposite of the friend he knew. He'd been in it a thousand times but never really noticed how meticulous everything was. He wondered if that was Bobby or his mother. Regardless, there was something unsettling about a kid's room being so well organized.

Charlie made his way through the closet, pushing back the pants and the shirts, searching for anything that might be hidden behind the clothes. He got down on his hands and knees and poked around on the floor, stretching his hands under the racks of pants until his fingers hit the wall. He carefully took each shoe and examined it along with the compartment itself. There was nothing. His last spot to check was a small three-drawer dresser that sat next to the shoe rack. He opened each drawer and found old Halloween costumes, certificates from school, athletic awards from peewee football and junior lacrosse, and a bunch of baseball hats. Nothing more. Nothing about Jen. Nothing that would tell him why the Darth Vader pendant was in the woods.

He made sure everything was placed back exactly how he'd found it, then stepped out of the closet and closed the door. His heart stopped when he saw Mrs. Teagan standing in the doorway, staring at him, and he fell backward onto Bobby's desk.

"I'm sorry," Mrs. Teagan said. "I didn't mean to scare you."

Charlie looked at his best friend's mother, and despite the lies that had come so easily earlier, he froze up.

"What're you doing in the closet?"

"I don't know," Charlie replied without thinking. "Just checking it out, I guess. It's so neat."

Mrs. Teagan chuckled. "Yes, Bobby likes things in their place. He's always been like that."

"I didn't mess anything up."

"It's okay. I was just coming to see if you wanted a snack."

"No, thank you. I'm fine."

"Okay. Holler if you change your mind."

"I will."

"And put the TV on or something. Play a video game. He'll be home soon."

Charlie nodded, and Mrs. Teagan left. He waited until her footsteps reached the bottom landing, then he got back down on his hands and knees and kept searching.

He looked under the bed, but there was nothing. He looked under the dresser, and that, too, was empty of anything suspicious. He went through Bobby's desk and found notebooks, a dictionary, and a bunch of user manuals and cheat sheets for his video games. That was it.

In the silence of the room, Charlie made his way over to the nightstand and pulled out the two drawers. Again, there was nothing that could explain why his friend's favorite thing would be at his sister's murder scene for the police to find.

He pushed the top drawer too hard, and it slammed shut. As it did, it rocked back and forth once and sent a picture sliding off the nightstand and down the back wall. He tried to catch it but wasn't quick enough, so he reached over and grabbed the edge of the frame with the tips of his index and middle finger.

"Come on," he mumbled.

As he got ahold of it, he saw the edge of a small spiral notebook tucked behind the nightstand, against the wall. Charlie replaced the picture on the nightstand and went back down for the notebook. The spiral spine was easy to grip, and he lifted it out of the tiny space. He sat on the bed and opened it, then flipped through the first few pages, the breath catching in his throat as his entire body began to tremble.

*What is this?*

The notebook contained dozens—maybe hundreds—of pictures that had been printed out and pasted in. They were all photos of Jen. Every single one of them. Jen at the house, in the yard, in the pool, at the supermarket, at her job, shopping with her friends, in the woods at the bonfires, smiling, laughing, talking, sleeping.

Charlie flipped through the pages faster and faster. His surprise was turning to bewilderment and then to anger. He knew his friend had a crush on his sister, but this was stalker level to the highest degree. A normal person, even a person with a serious crush, might take pictures and have them on their phone, but Bobby had taken the time to print them out and keep them in a scrapbook. It was crazy. And he'd even hidden in bushes to take some of the pictures. He'd followed her through town, hiding around corners and behind cars and trees. All those casual shots of Jen, who'd had no idea she was being watched.

Charlie turned to the last few pages, and he stopped. These were pictures taken at night looking up into Jen's bedroom window. He could see his sister in silhouette, standing in front of her mirror. In some she was clothed. In others, only a bra . . . in others, nothing at all. Charlie knew from the angle of the photo that there was only one place Bobby could've taken the pictures from.

Out in the woods. Behind the house. Right where his sister's body was found.

# 44

They walked through the main entrance of Putnam Hospital and were directed to the psych unit on the second floor. Mindy Moore was asleep again, sedated by the drugs that flowed from the IV bags hanging above her. She looked peaceful. Two bandages were wrapped around each wrist. The room itself was quiet but for a few noises from the monitors that tracked her pulse and blood pressure.

Noel was sitting in a chair next to his wife. It was almost the exact scene Susan herself had just experienced with Casey. She wondered if she'd had the same look of distress and concern on her face as Noel had on his. He looked disheveled and beaten, the absolute opposite of the man she'd seen on his firm's website or in the countless articles written about the upstart wealth management team gone big-time.

Susan walked farther into the room, and Liam followed, closing the door behind them. Noel spun around in his seat, and when he saw them, nodded a silent hello and turned back to his wife.

"We need to discuss a few things," Susan said calmly.

"I'm not supposed to be talking to you," Noel replied.

"It's important."

"Okay, but I'll need to call Charlotte."

"Yeah, fine. Call her. But we know about Jennifer's abortion. And we know she's not your kid. Not biologically, anyway."

The air in Noel's upper body deflated, and his entire frame sunk in a bit. He rose from his seat, then walked across the room and out into the hall. Susan and Liam followed him down the corridor until he stopped by the elevators.

"Was it the swabs you took that first day?" he asked.

"Yup."

"I thought that might cause more harm than good. But I figured if we refused, it would've looked suspicious. I decided to roll the dice and hope you guys didn't try and compare them. I was hoping they would just be for elimination purposes around the house."

"Well, they weren't," Susan said. "Talk."

Noel sighed and looked at them. "Jen's adopted."

"Why wouldn't you tell us that?"

"I didn't think it was pertinent. Whether she's adopted or not has no bearing on who killed her. We took her in as a newborn, so the thought of her not being our biological daughter never crosses our minds at this point. To be honest, I didn't think of it until you asked for the swabs."

"You should have told us."

"If I thought it would help you find her killer, I would have. But no one in the community knows, and we'd rather keep it that way." He brushed his hair out of his eyes. "Mindy couldn't have kids. For whatever reason, her body couldn't develop healthy eggs. We had a couple of early successes, but they were always followed by miscarriages, and after a while we felt it wasn't worth the hope and the disappointment. We adopted Jennifer when she was an infant, and it was a closed adoption."

"Did she know?"

"We gave Jen our last name and had a new birth certificate printed. It was dumb luck that she had the same hair and eye color as Mindy. Like it was meant to be. Then, out of nowhere, Charlie comes, and for whatever reason, Mindy was able to carry him to term. We had a family. We kept our secret. Charlie has no idea. Jen's always been our little girl and his big sister, and nothing will ever change that. She might not match our DNA, but she's ours in every sense of the word."

"Did . . . she . . . know?"

"No. We never told her."

"Do you know if she ever did a DNA test from one of those kits you can buy?"

"Not that I know of, but maybe."

"Did she ever start asking strange questions? Like maybe she found out and then was tip-toeing around the subject to see what you would tell her?"

Noel shook his head.

"Who was the adoption agency?" Liam asked.

"I can't recall," Noel replied. "It was a Catholic organization we got through the church in town, but I don't remember the name of it."

"Where's the paperwork?" Susan asked.

"At the bank in a safety deposit box with our other important documents. Will. Deed. Those kinds of things."

"We need to get that paperwork. Now."

"I have to check with Charlotte."

Susan took a step closer. "Don't make me waste time getting a subpoena. Tell Charlotte this has to happen."

"I'll try."

"Tell me about the abortion when she was sixteen."

Noel's face was white. "I didn't know about it until a year later. She never told me. Neither did Mindy. I found out when I was itemizing our medical bills for our taxes. I was shocked. I thought we were done with that kind of behavior from Jen by then. I couldn't believe it."

"Who's the father?"

"I don't know."

Susan huffed. "Come on, Noel. You know that's the first question you asked."

"I did ask," Noel replied. "But she wouldn't tell me. Mindy hounded her about it constantly, but she couldn't get her to tell us either." He stopped talking for a moment as a nurse walked by. "Do you think her adoption or her pregnancy is linked to her being killed?"

"I have no idea, but I'm sure as hell going to find out. Let's get to the bank so you can give me the paperwork on the adoption agency."

"Okay. Just let me touch base with Charlotte."

Liam pressed the elevator button and waited while Susan leaned against the wall, arms folded across her chest. "Anything else you've kept from us that you deemed unimportant?"

"No."

"We'll see."

# 45

When Bobby returned from football practice, Charlie was waiting in his room. Everything had been put back in its place, and the two friends spent the rest of the day together playing video games and shooting hoops in Bobby's driveway. Neither of them spoke about Jen and what happened, and Charlie decided not to mention the Darth Vader pendant. Not after the notebook he'd found with all the pictures of his sister in it. He wanted to do a little more digging and find out what was really going on, so they played the roles of best friends and went through the motions of hanging out on a typical summer afternoon. Charlie had been invited to eat over and spend the night, but he'd refused. By the time his father had come to pick him up, he was exhausted from his performance and just wanted to go home.

Charlie sat on his bed and held the phone up to his ear. Normally he'd use FaceTime, or at the very least the speakerphone, but he didn't want his father overhearing anything.

"Did you get everything?" he asked.

He could hear Donna Starr breathing on the other end,

"Yeah, I got it."

"All the pics? I sent every page."

"Yes. I got them."

"So what're you gonna do?"

"I don't know," Donna replied. "What do you want me to say? Bobby's a minor. I can't go snooping around his life, and I won't have permission to go around asking people about him. If I interview him, an adult would have to be present."

Charlie fell back on his pillow. "I'm not asking you to interview him. I want you to do some investigative reporting and tell me if my best friend killed my sister."

"That's quite a leap you're making. Do you really think Bobby could do something like that?"

"I don't know, but the police found his pendant in the woods near Jen, and I found that notebook proving that he was stalking her. That notebook was scary. You saw what I sent you. Stalker times ten! And some of the pictures he took were right around where Jen was killed. I also heard some policemen talking inside the house the morning we found Jen. They said a shoe print was in the mud. Small. Kid size. I mean, that can't be a coincidence, right?"

"But he's a small kid," Donna replied. "Wouldn't your sister just beat him up if he came at her?"

Charlie sat up and kicked his legs over the edge of the bed. "Bobby's not that small. He plays linebacker for the football team and he's a midfielder in lacrosse. And sure, Jen could kick his ass, but if she didn't see him coming and he hit her from behind or something, it's totally possible. I read online she was knocked out. He could have snuck up and hit her."

"But think of the way she was killed. You think your friend could *do* that?"

"Look, we can't ignore what I found. Something's up. I need you to find out what."

There was a rustling of papers on the other end of the phone. Charlie hopped off his bed and walked to his door. He opened it and stuck his head out to make sure he was still alone on the second floor. He was.

"Okay, look," Donna began. "I'll do some digging for you, but don't expect a feature piece. I'm working within very serious limitations, and I could get in a lot of trouble checking out a minor without parental or police consent."

"Don't go to the police. I don't know what we have yet."

"Yeah, no kidding. The second they see what you sent me, I'm out of the loop and they're running with what you found. I'll figure out how I'm going to handle things on my end. You just keep your mouth shut. Don't talk to anyone about this. Not your dad. Not Bobby. Not the cops. Let me figure it out first; then we'll see how far we need to take this."

"Okay."

Donna sighed. "If we really do have something here, I'll let you know before anyone else. I promise. Stay out of trouble. Let me do my thing."

# 46

Empty pizza boxes sat on the kitchen counter downstairs. The table was still occupied with the jigsaw puzzle, but progress had been made. The garbage can was overflowing with paper plates and napkins and plastic cups, and the sink was full of dishes. None of that mattered to Susan or her mother. They both sat at Casey's bedside, watching their little girl sleep.

Casey's arm was sticking out of the blanket, a tiny pink cast covering her hand, wrist, and forearm. Four black screws protruded from the plaster. The screws were fastened to a fixation plate that was supposed to help keep things stable.

"It's funny," Beatrice whispered as she looked at her granddaughter. "You wake up in the morning and everything seems normal and you think you're just going to have a regular day. Then something unexpected happens, and your world is turned upside down. She's played on those monkey bars all summer. Up and down. Up and down. I used to watch her when I'd come early to pick them up. I'd marvel at how agile she was. Then one slip, and we're at the hospital."

"*You're* at the hospital," Susan replied. "Grandma and Dad are at the hospital. Mom's not picking up her cell. Mom's at work. Again."

Beatrice turned and looked at Susan. "Don't start. I don't want to hear any of that. If you're going to sit here and berate yourself over an accident you weren't around for, then I'm leaving. I can't stand to hear people feel sorry for themselves. You were at work, and Casey had an accident. It happens. And I got news for you: it'll probably happen again. That's what this parenting thing is all about."

"I know." Susan wiped away a fresh set of tears. "But I've put all you guys through so much as it is, and it's all related to the job. I had a man, in this house, trying to kill you all. There's a fair amount of guilt that comes with that. And now I wasn't around when she fell, just like I wasn't around when the Bad Man came. That's not all right."

"I didn't say it was all right. I said it was life." Beatrice got up from her chair and shuffled toward the door. "These kids are your world, and believe me, they know it. They can feel it. It doesn't matter what happened today or what happened when the Bad Man came. They know you'll always be there for them, and that's the most important thing for a child to know about a parent. You're doing a fine job, kiddo. I'm proud of you. Keep your head held high. You've earned it."

"Thanks, Mom."

"I'll be downstairs in my room. I'm turning in."

"Wait."

Beatrice stopped and turned around.

"You like Liam, right?" Susan could feel her face blushing. She felt like a teenager again, hoping for her mother's approval. "I mean, he's grown on you, no?"

"I like Liam very much. And yes, he's definitely grown on me."

"How would you feel if we became more than friends?"

"Where's this coming from?" her mother asked, a slight smile creeping upon her lips. "I thought you were keeping it professional."

"I am. We are. Totally. But he's a good man. I'm wondering if I need a little more good in my life."

"We could all use a little more good in our lives." Her mother turned back around and stepped into the hall. "Good night, honey."

"Good night."

Susan leaned over her daughter and carefully stroked her hair. The doctors said they could take the screws out in six weeks and the entire cast off in eight. A little rehab would follow, and that would be the end of it. Best-case scenario. She'd been lucky. Casey looked so peaceful as she slept, but from the corner of her eye, Susan could see the cast and the screws and the plate and knew she should've been there. The job had gotten in the way again. She needed to balance her duties better as an investigator and as a parent.

Casey slowly opened her eyes. "Mommy?"

"I'm right here, honey. How are you feeling?"

"It hurts a little."

"Okay, I'll get you more medicine to help."

Casey's eyes were glassy and reflected the hallway light. "Mommy, how am I going to ride the pony at my party if I can't hold on with two hands?"

"I'll help you," Susan replied, her heart shattering into a million pieces. "And your dad can help too. And Liam."

"But what if I fall?"

"You won't. We'll hold on real tight and make sure you have a great time."

Casey closed her eyes again.

"I guess I'll have to pet the puppy with my good hand."

Susan smiled in the darkness. "We're not getting a dog, honey."

"Yes, we are. It's our birthday present. And the dog will be best friends with the chickens, and everyone will be happy."

Susan listened to Casey until she heard the steady breathing she was used to hearing, then got up and walked across the room, stopping at the door and looking at the baby monitor she'd taken out of storage. If Casey needed her, she'd be there this time.

"I'm sorry," she whispered. She blew Casey a kiss, then left and went downstairs, where Liam was waiting.

# 47

Liam was sitting on the couch in the living room, a file opened on his lap, a notebook and pen at his side. He studied the grid map he'd made, and it felt good to be back in the part of the investigation that called for analysis and examination. His mind calmed, and he was able to relax.

It had taken most of the afternoon to get the adoption paperwork from Noel Moore. As soon as he'd called Charlotte Walsh to let her know what was going on, she'd squashed the cooperation and demanded a subpoena. Susan had leaned on a few favors and gotten things rushed, and by late day, they had presented the subpoena and escorted both Noel and Charlotte to his bank, where they retrieved a copy of the adoption paperwork.

The agency was called Helping Hands Family Center, out of Newark, New Jersey. It was a Catholic organization owned by the Archdiocese of New Jersey. At the time, a nun named Sister Ann Michael ran the place along with a priest named Monsignor Wilson. The adoption agency no longer existed, but the organization itself was still around and functioned as a homeless shelter and food pantry. Liam had called and was told neither the nun nor the priest was associated with the organization anymore. Helping Hands was run by a nonprofit board of directors now. He scheduled a meeting for the following day.

Footsteps came down the stairs, and he looked up to find Susan on the landing. She crossed the foyer into the living room.

"Your mom just went to bed."

"Yeah, I know. She was in Casey's room with me."

"How's the princess?"

"Okay, I think. She's sleeping now."

"You want to talk about it?"

"About what?"

Susan's eyes were tearing up again, and she quickly wiped them with the tissue she was holding. Liam wanted to hold her and comfort her but knew doing so would be crossing a line.

"About how you not being at the hospital when Casey went into surgery is dragging up these emotions from the Randall Brock case."

"Yeah, I'd rather not."

"Okay. But just know that you can't be everywhere at once. Things are going to slip through the cracks sometimes. And this is coming from a guy who has a serial killer for a brother and never knew it until he was trying to frame me for murder."

Susan blew out a puff of air and sat down next to Liam. "We're damaged goods, aren't we?"

"Speak for yourself. I prefer being labeled one of a kind."

Susan chuckled and pulled the file from his lap to hers. "What're you looking at?"

"The forensic report from the Moore house. I'm trying to build a grid of what was found where so I can get a sense of the trace evidence we collected."

Liam watched as Susan flipped through the pictures from the crime scene and inside the house. She stopped at the photo of the luggage Noel had dropped when he came home that night, then moved on to the others.

"What're you looking for once you build the grid?"

"I'm not sure. Sometimes it's just easier to see things clustered as they were found. Every once in a while a light bulb goes off. I learned it back when I took an FBI course and used it in almost all of my cases in Philly. Just a best-practices kind of thing."

Susan closed the file and handed it back to him. She shut her eyes, letting her head fall onto the couch cushions. He watched her as she slipped off, her breath growing light as sleep came quickly. He reached out and pushed away a strand of hair that had fallen across her face. He studied her, knowing that he felt something he'd never thought he'd be able to feel again, but petrified to act on those emotions for fear of losing the friendship they had built over the last two years. He leaned his head back on the couch as well, and when he awoke, he discovered it was almost two thirty in the morning. Susan was gone, but she'd put a blanket over him and left a note asking him to stay until morning. Apparently bacon and eggs would be served. His favorite.

# 48

The seven o'clock mass was sparsely attended, and Father McCall had his parishioners out in under an hour. Susan and Liam met him in the vestibule.

"I see the angels have you up early," the priest said with a smile.

Susan shook her head. "More like the devils."

"Good point."

She unfolded a sheet of paper. "I had a few more questions for you, if you don't mind."

"Not at all. Ask away."

"When you and Jennifer met to talk, did she ever mention that fact that she'd discovered she was adopted?"

Father McCall took a step back as if Susan had nudged him. His hand rose to his heart. "No. I had no idea."

"You're sure? Maybe she didn't come out and say it but intimated things along the lines of not being a part of her family or feeling like an outsider. Anything like that?"

"Jennifer was always down on her parents, but not for the reason of being adopted. She hated the way her mother was so strict and often wished her father wasn't such a workaholic. The family's materialism got to her a bit too. Never an inkling of anything regarding being adopted."

Susan handed Father McCall the paper she was holding. "Any chance you know an old orphanage called Helping Hands Family Center out of Newark? The archdiocese ran it up until it converted to a homeless shelter and soup kitchen in 2005."

Father McCall took the paper and read through it. "I'm afraid that was before my time. I was on the West Coast in the nineties up until I got here five years ago."

"So I guess that means you wouldn't know Sister Ann Michael or Monsignor Wilson? They ran the place."

"Never heard of them. I can ask the others in the rectory. I'm not sure how long they've been in the area."

Susan took the paper back and stuck it in her pocket. "No need, but thanks. We're heading down there now."

"In that case, good luck. I hope you find what you're looking for."

"So do we."

Father McCall stood in the entranceway as Susan and Liam walked toward their car. He suddenly broke free and rushed down the stairs after them.

"Investigator Adler, I have one more thing."

Susan and Liam both turned around.

The priest fumbled with his words, placing his hands in his pockets and then taking them out again. He was nervous about something.

"I wasn't completely honest with you when we first spoke at the rectory," he said. "Jennifer did confide something to me and made me promise not to say anything to anyone. I take my oaths quite seriously, so I didn't tell you at the time. But it's been nagging at me because I think it could have something to do with your investigation, and now that you told me about her adoption, perhaps this can help connect some dots."

Susan walked toward the priest, closing the gap between them in three steps. "What is it?"

"About a year ago, Jennifer told me she'd been sexually abused. She never told me who was abusing her or why. Only that it had been an ongoing thing, and that's why she was taking the drugs and drinking as much as she was. She was trying to dull the pain she'd been feeling for so long. She was trying to escape the repeated assaults she'd been forced to endure. I implored her to tell me who was hurting her, but she never would. Eventually, I stopped asking for a culprit and instead concentrated on simply trying to help her through the anger and confusion and hurt she was carrying. With the help of God, and the talks we had, she was eventually able to cut down on the drinking and the drugs and got on a steadier path that led to her admission to Duke and a new chapter of her life that was waiting." He shook his head. "I don't know if the person who killed Jen was the same person who was abusing her, but I felt you had to know her entire truth."

Susan was gobsmacked. "We spoke to you two days ago," she said. "That's an eternity in an investigation like this."

"I know. I'm sorry."

"This could be the linchpin in the case. Maybe the person who assaulted her is the father of her baby. Maybe the pregnancy was a result of her rape. Maybe her mother knew what had happened, which is why they had such a tumultuous relationship. And yes, maybe the person who was abusing her is the person who killed her. Maybe that person wanted to get to her before she had a chance to start that new life at Duke you just talked about. What were you thinking keeping this from us?"

The priest bowed his head. "I'm sorry. That's all I can say."

Into Susan's stunned silence, Liam spoke. "Was the abuse still going on, or had it ended?"

"I got the impression it ended, but I'm not one hundred percent sure."

Susan walked around to the driver's side of her car as Liam opened the passenger door. She stopped and looked at the priest. "I'm going to look into this, and we're going to follow up. If you see me calling, you better grab that phone. We're not done."

"Again, I'm so sorry I didn't tell you straight away."

"Sorry doesn't cut it this time," Susan replied. "Not this time."

# 49

Helping Hands Family Center was on the southwestern tip of Newark, almost bordering the town of Hillside. Newark International Airport sat to the east of them, and the roar of low-flying jets either taking off or coming in to land was a constant.

Susan and Liam parked in one of the visitor spots in the center's lot and climbed out of the car. They'd left early, hoping to beat some of the traffic that would normally gridlock the bridges between New York and New Jersey, but a combination of their timing being a bit off and an overturned tractor trailer taking out two lanes of 95 made them much later than they wanted to be. They'd sat in traffic for well over an hour.

The sun was still in the process of climbing the sky, but the temperature was already well above eighty degrees. It was going to be another scorcher of a day.

"I don't know why we're having such a hard time getting people in this investigation to tell us what we need to know to find Jennifer's killer," Susan said as they walked toward the main entrance. "First Noel Moore *forgets* to tell us Jennifer was adopted, and then Father McCall feels *obliged* to keep Jennifer's sexual abuse a secret because she asked him to. What's going on?"

"Sometimes families with ties to money and prestige feel the need to keep secrets buried deep. Jennifer being adopted might not be a big deal to folks like you and me, but not having your kid be blood might be a huge deal in Noel's circles. I don't know."

"And how do you explain the priest keeping the abuse from us?"

"Maybe he saw it as a kind of confession. Felt obliged to keep that info between Jennifer and God?"

"Yeah, well, God's not trying to catch her killer. We are."

The Helping Hands Family Center building was a three-story brick structure, tan with black-trimmed windows. Some of the panes in the windows had been shattered or were missing completely, replaced by panels of plywood. Cracks in the pavement gave way to weeds, dotting the parking lot with bits of green and white and yellow from the clover and dandelions. A chain-link fence surrounded the property with a check-in point at the entrance. The sign carved in granite over the entrance read **ARCHDIOCESE OF NEW JERSEY.**

Phyllis Sable was the director of the organization. She was a middle-aged woman, attractive and petite. She stood at the top of the stairs that led to the entrance, a smile drawn on her face as she waited. She wore a white blouse and navy-blue pants. Her black hair was up in a bun. There was a warmth about her that Susan could feel immediately. Everyone greeted one another, then Susan and Liam followed Phyllis through the lobby and into a small cluster of offices where the administrative staff was set up.

"I'm sorry we're so late," Susan said. "The traffic was a nightmare."

"That's how traffic is around here," Phyllis replied. "Whenever you're planning to arrive, just add anywhere from fifteen to forty-five minutes because you never know what you'll hit." She pointed to a door in the corner of the room. "That's my office. We can talk in there."

Susan and Liam sat in two folding chairs in front of a large antique teacher's desk while Phyllis sat in a faux-leather office chair. The space was tight, cluttered, and full of paperwork and filing cabinets. A lone window let in the light, but other than that it was a bit dank and unwelcoming, the complete opposite of the woman who occupied it.

Phyllis folded her hands on the desk. "I know you've wasted some time sitting in that traffic, so why don't we get right to it?"

"Sounds good, thanks." Susan took out her pen and pad. "As I mentioned on the phone, we're currently involved in a homicide investigation in upstate New York, and we've come to learn that the victim was adopted from this facility eighteen years ago. We already have the adoption paperwork from the adopting father, so we don't need anything official that would require a warrant. We were hoping you could provide some information about Helping Hands back when it was a foster care facility."

Phyllis raised her hand, motioning around the office. "Right around 2000, the state decided it wanted to run the foster care system on its own in order to be more consistent with regulations and procedures. At the time, computers were really emerging, and the technology was being created to keep files in order, online, and searchable through different facilities. They wanted to be able to track each child through a single database, which these days sounds like common sense, but back then it was a big deal. Anyway, they rescinded the foster care license from Helping Hands, but to the state's credit, they did provide subsidies and grants to get us up and running as a soup kitchen and shelter so we were still able to provide to the community, which is our vocation. I was brought on as the director when we officially opened our doors to the homeless and hungry fifteen years ago, and I've been here ever since. We have two hundred and fifty beds, an on-staff doctor and nurse, and a full staff of counselors. We feed over one hundred families a day, and we offer breakfast, lunch, and dinner. Aside from the city grants, we're also aided by the archdiocese."

"So you weren't here during the transition from foster home to shelter?"

"No, I wasn't."

"Any idea what happened to all the records of the kids and the adoptions?"

"A lot was handed over to the state, since the children we had under our roof were being transported to state-run facilities. As for past records, I really couldn't tell you. I assume the archdiocese has them somewhere."

Susan wrote in her notepad. "And what about Sister Ann Michael or Monsignor Wilson?" she asked. "They ran the place when it was a foster home. Would they know?"

Phyllis cocked her head to the side. "If you don't mind me asking, what is it that you need to find out? You said you already had the adoption paperwork. That should tell you everything. What else are you looking for?"

"It was a closed adoption," Liam said. "No listing of birth parents or any information that could lead us to the victim's biological relatives. We were hoping someone who used to work here might remember something."

Phyllis thought for a moment, then reached into her desk and came away with a stack of Post-it Notes. "I do know that Monsignor Wilson died about six years ago. He was living at a rectory in Elizabeth at the time."

"Damn."

"But Sister Ann Michael is still alive. She's living in a convent called the Sisters of Christian Charity. It's about an hour west of here in Mendham. If you're already down here, it might be worth your while to pay her a visit. Not sure she'll have any memory of one kid who was adopted eighteen years ago, but who knows? Maybe today's your lucky day."

Susan took the Post-it she handed over and copied down the address in her notepad. "I appreciate your help," she said. "We'll pay her a visit and see what we can find."

---

Sisters of Christian Charity was more than the small run-down convent Susan was expecting to see. The place was magnificent, with manicured grounds, sprawling gardens, and a mixture of old and new architecture. The sedan's tires crunched on pebbles as they pulled up in front of the domed structure, which looked more like the Sacré-Cœur Basilica in France than something you'd find a few miles south of Manhattan.

"This place is incredible," Liam said as he hopped out of the car and spun around to take it all in. "I could use a place like this to retire in."

They followed a stone path that meandered through knee-high boxwoods and around several statues of saints that were mounted next to butterfly gardens and bird feeders. Susan could hear the buzzing of the bees and the gentle chirping of birds all around them. Somewhere in the distance, water was running from a brook or stream. The grounds were a blanket of pure serenity. She couldn't remember the last time she'd felt such peace.

A young woman stood at the end of the stone path. She was dressed in a blue-and-white habit and matching blue gown. A set of wooden rosary beads hung from a rope tied around her waist. She wore no makeup, nor did she need to. She was beautiful, her eyes so full of life, her smile both disarming and enchanting.

"Welcome to the Sisters of Christian Charity," she said as she spread her arms out before her. "I'm Sister Rose."

Susan shook the nun's hand. "I'm Investigator Adler. New York State Police. This is Liam Dwyer. He's assisting us."

"Mrs. Sable called to let us know you were coming. I understand you'd like to speak with Sister Ann Michael."

"Yes, we would. If she's available."

"I'm afraid that won't be possible. Sister Ann Michael is on our hospice unit. She doesn't have much time left."

"I'm sorry to hear that."

They followed Sister Rose up the stairs and in through the large double doors. Inside, the lobby looked like it was more upscale hotel than convent. A large crucifix hung on the far wall next to a winding set of stairs.

"This place is really nice," Liam said. "I can't get over it."

"Thank you," Sister Rose replied. "We're very active in our community and throughout the state. This isn't just a retirement home for us sisters. We are teachers in schools, we serve in our churches, we serve the sick as nurses and therapists and even dietitians. We're also pastoral ministers in our hospitals and nursing care facilities. We serve the dioceses here in New Jersey, but also New York, Pennsylvania, and Ohio. Sister Ann Michael came to us after the foster home she ran closed in 2005. She was an inspiration the way she took to her new vocation. Her diagnosis came six years ago. Breast cancer that spread. There's not much time now. We're all praying for her."

"I'm so sorry."

"Is there something that I can help with?"

Susan shook her head. "I doubt it. We're investigating a homicide, and the victim was a newborn orphan at the foster home back when Sister Ann Michael was running it. We're trying to search for the birth parents since it was a closed adoption and were hoping she might have records or remember something."

"I see," Sister Rose replied. "I wish I could help you, but our sisters in hospice don't spend too much time fully conscious. The drugs help with the pain, and when it's near the end, we try and keep them as comfortable as we can."

"I understand."

"I can tell you that no records of any kind have been transferred here from the orphanage. Everything that wasn't handed over to the state went to the archdiocese. We've also already cleaned out Sister Ann Michael's room. There were no notes of any kind there either."

—

When she was back outside with Liam, Susan let her head drop a bit. "I'd chalk this up to a genuine dead end."

Liam smiled. "Feels that way at least once in every investigation, doesn't it? Even from the forensics side. Come on. There are a few things we should look at."

# 50

The Lewisboro police station was quiet as afternoon turned toward dusk. The uniforms were out on patrol, and the dispatch desk was silent but for the occasional phone ringing and the mumble of the duty officer routing the call to the appropriate extension. The place was peaceful, but it wouldn't stay that way for long. Changeover was coming in another hour, and the patrols would start rolling in about fifteen minutes before that.

Susan and Liam walked into their office, each of them holding a cup of coffee. She plopped down in her seat and watched Liam do the same across from her. He opened the forensics file he'd been studying at the house the night before.

"You still working on your grid?"

"Yup. I wanted to go over John's reports. What're you going to do?"

"I'm going to try and figure out how all of it fits together. I'm not sure Jennifer's adoption is related to what happened to her. It was so long ago, and the records are buried at this point. I don't see a motive there. But I do see a motive with the sexual assault angle. If Jennifer told Father McCall about it, there's a chance she'd tell someone else. A friend or another adult. And being halfway down the east coast in North Carolina at Duke, far away from Lewisboro, might make her feel safe in telling her story. Keeping her quiet is a very plausible motive."

"And if we're connecting an event that happened inside the house the night Jennifer was killed to this new information about her assault, then maybe Jennifer did tell someone," Liam said. "Maybe she told her mom, and things went south from there."

Susan nodded. "Yeah. The mother who was a control freak and who was always trying to keep up appearances and make Jennifer into someone she wanted to see in the community instead of letting her daughter find who she was. There's no way she could let a sexual assault stain her family's name. Better to be consoled by those trying to help you through the tragedy of your daughter's murder than having those same people whisper behind your back with the news of your daughter's rape and molestation."

"It fits."

"It does."

Liam turned his attention back to his grid. "Talk through this with me for a sec. I need another set of eyes on this."

"Shoot."

"According to John's report, his team found a concentration of mineral wool, fiberglass, gypsum, and clay in the basement. It's the only area in the entire house it was found, and he found more than a trace. It's from the ceiling tiles the Moores have down there, but in the world of forensics, it's the equivalent of finding a pile of sand in the middle of the living room. And it wasn't in a neat pile. It was scattered around. Why was there so much ceiling-tile debris down there?"

Susan opened her laptop and scrolled through the crime scene photos. "We didn't find anything suspicious in the basement," she said. "No reason for there to be debris down there."

"Exactly. We didn't find any blood or clothing, and the room itself wasn't disturbed. Not like you'd think from people walking through it to get stuff from storage."

"So why the dust from the ceiling?"

Liam suddenly lifted his head. "Let me see those crime scene photos?"

Susan turned her laptop around.

He dropped the file and rolled his chair next to hers, then began clicking through the pictures, scrolling faster than the eye could see. He stopped when he got to the basement photos. His finger traced his grid after examining each picture.

"If I tighten the grid in the basement to sections of the room, I can narrow down where the dust from the ceiling was found, and we can see a concentration."

Susan leaned forward to look at what Liam was pointing to.

"That's the section in the unfinished part of the basement where most of the residue from the ceiling tiles came from," he said. "I didn't realize it at first, but this is a drop ceiling. I just thought the ceiling was done with tiles for wiring or small piping, but this ceiling drops significantly. You can see the area next to it with no tiles. It's like two feet taller."

"Okay."

"I think the reason why there was so much residue on the floor is because someone was messing around with the ceiling tiles themselves."

Susan's eyes widened. "Like maybe taking out the tiles to hide things and then putting them back."

"Exactly like that."

"Is the ceiling big enough to hide an area rug?"

"An area rug and then some."

Susan reached for her phone. "I'm calling the judge. We need a search warrant for that entire house. I think you and your grid just came through big-time."

# 51

Charlie sat on the floor in the corner of his room, half in his closet in case someone came in and he had to hide. He'd already checked on his father, who had been lying on the couch watching a documentary about China, his eyes staring at the television, although he was clearly unfocused, no doubt thinking about everything that was happening. Aunt Sidney and Father McCall were downstairs trying to talk to him, but all they got in return were grunts and nods. His father had been like that since coming home from seeing his mother at the hospital. That's when he knew it'd be safe to call the reporter.

He'd contemplated telling his father about what he'd found in the notebook he discovered in Bobby's room and the fact that he knew the Darth Vader pendant was Bobby's, but he figured that would just lead to more questions about why he didn't come forward sooner, and he was already walking on thin ice having not said anything about the bracelet until it was almost too late. Instead, he figured it would be easier to vet everything through the reporter first, and if there was something concrete to tell, he'd tell his father then.

Charlie stared at the woman's business card and dialed from his cell.

"Hello?"

"Is this Donna Starr?"

"Who is this?"

"It's Charlie Moore. Jen's brother."

A sigh on the other end. "Hello, Charlie."

"I wanted to check to see what you found out about Bobby."

"I didn't find anything out."

"Bull," Charlie snapped. "I've seen you on TV. You're really good at your job. I looked on YouTube and saw a bunch of stories you did. There's no way I gave you a lead like Bobby Teagan and you didn't look into it."

Silence.

"Tell me," Charlie pleaded. "I need to know. Did my best friend kill my sister?"

"Where are you?"

"At my house. In my room."

"Where's your dad?"

"Downstairs watching TV."

Papers rustled.

"Listen, Charlie. I need to tell you something. I'm only telling you now because we're friends and I promised that if I heard something before you did, I'd let you know."

"Okay. What'd you find?"

Donna's voice got lower. "Tomorrow all the major papers and the TV outlets are going to run the story about you burying your sister's bracelet in the woods, which will explain why she was out there in the first place."

Charlie could feel his stomach clench, and he thought he was going to throw up.

"I tried to see if we could sit on the story until later," Donna continued. "But it was out of my hands. Another station picked it up on the wire, and it snowballed from there."

"Are you going to run a story about it?"

"I have to. It's my job."

Charlie ended the call and slammed the phone down as the tears came. He collapsed on the floor, his mind racing. As soon as the stories were released tomorrow, everyone would know that he was the reason Jen was in the woods. They'd say he was the reason she got killed, and they'd be right. The tweets and posts about it would never stop. He'd be blamed for the rest of his life and he'd never be able to escape his one mistake. He'd be branded with it until the end of time, and the one person he thought could help—the reporter—would write her own story to help bury whatever might've been left of a normal life.

Pounding on the front door.

The doorbell rang.

Muffled shouts from outside.

Footsteps running across the house.

"Charlie!" his father called.

"I'm up here!"

"Stay in your room!"

More pounding on the door.

"I'm coming!" his father cried.

The front door flew back and slammed into the wall. Charlie jumped when it made impact. He crawled across the floor to try and listen.

"Noel Moore, this is a search warrant authorizing us to search the premises," a woman's voice explained.

# 52

Susan knew that pulling up in front of the Moore house at seven at night with a line of police cruisers and a forensics van behind her would be enough to cause a stir with the media that had been camped out across the street. It was just a matter of how many reporters were still on scene and how many had filed their story and gone for the night.

They turned the corner and coasted down Hillcrest Court. A few heads popped out of van windows, and doors slid open as a small cluster of reporters and cameramen scurried to get to their equipment. Susan drove up into the driveway and stopped. She looked at Liam, who was sitting next to her, his eyes fixed on the large house in front of them.

"You good?"

"Yup."

They climbed out of the car and waited for the others. A few reporters shouted to get their attention, but she ignored them. Her team got out of their cars and gathered in a circle. Two of the Lewisboro police cruisers stayed at the curb to help block the media and keep neighbors away.

"Everybody ready?"

Nods.

"Okay, we gotta make this quick. Knock, present the warrant, and enter. We know where we're going, so just get there. I'm the only person who speaks. Understand?"

More nods.

"Gloves on. Let's go."

Susan snapped on her gloves and jogged up the steps, hurrying to the door. Without stopping, she pounded three times and rang the doorbell.

"Police! Open up!"

The cameras behind her were starting to focus in on what was happening. She could suddenly see shadows around her, and everything in her periphery got brighter. They'd turned on their spotlights.

Showtime.

She pounded on the door again. Before she could ring the bell a second time, Noel Moore's voice boomed from inside.

"I'm coming!"

The door opened, and Susan pushed it until it hit the side wall near the coat closet. She stopped, expecting to see Noel, and instead found Father McCall standing before her.

"What're you doing here?" she asked.

Father McCall's cheeks blushed. "I'm sitting with Sidney and Noel. We're praying together. For Mindy."

"Well, it's time to go." She held up the warrant and yelled into the house. "Noel Moore, this is a search warrant authorizing us to search the premises." She pushed past the priest, and her team followed.

Susan heard Noel say something about calling his lawyer, but she wasn't really listening. Instead, she followed the hallway that led to the kitchen and tried to recall from Liam's grid map which door was the pantry and which door led to the basement.

"Second one," Liam whispered as if reading her mind.

Susan stopped and pointed to one of the officers who had come in with them. "I need you to stay with Mr. Moore in the family room. The woman and the priest leave. Mr. Moore sits on the couch and watches TV. Let his lawyer in when she gets here. That's it. No one moves from the family room until we're done."

"Yes, ma'am."

Footsteps on the stairs.

Susan looked up to see the boy, Charlie, coming down.

"Dad, what's going on?"

"Nothing," Noel replied. "Go back up to your room."

"No." Susan pointed to the officer again. "The boy goes with his dad. Family room. Now."

She turned and opened the second door, quickly making her descent into one of the most beautiful basements she'd ever been in. Wood-paneled walls, thick oak floors, a fireplace that sat under a seventy-inch flat screen. The bar was nicer than some five-star restaurants she'd been in, with all the high-end, top-shelf liquor one could have. Leather sofas, overstuffed suede recliners, mahogany tables, and antique wall sconces. The design was masterful, and it took a lot for her not to stop, spin around, and whistle with amazement.

"Keep going," Liam said. "Next door is the storage and gym."

The team crossed the basement until they reached a slightly more utilitarian section. The floors were concrete, the walls were plain drywall, and the ceiling was what they'd come for. The drop-ceiling design.

Liam walked past Susan through the small gym and stopped when he reached the storage section.

"This is it," he said and flipped on a light.

This area was basically the same as the gym but without the equipment. Plastic storage bins lined one wall, and a stack of black garbage bags, all of which had been searched on their first visit to the house, was piled against another. A few bikes were scattered on the floor from when the kids were younger and an old toy box pressed up against the side of the stairs. A locked gun cabinet was next to shelves that had hunting and fishing equipment on them. Three rifles were inside. The rest of the space was empty.

One of the forensic techs came in with a small stepladder. He unfolded it and climbed toward the ceiling. Gloved hands pushed gently on one of the tiles, and he maneuvered it until he was able to take it down. He handed it to another tech.

"Scrape that for a match sample," Liam said.

The tech on the ladder pulled a flashlight out of his back pocket, took one more step up, and his head disappeared into the ceiling.

"See anything?" Susan asked.

"Oh, yes," the tech replied. "About four feet to my left."

Susan counted roughly four feet and stopped. She looked up and noticed that a few of the tiles were discolored. "This spot matches your grid from the material forensics found?"

Liam nodded. "Pretty much."

"Hand me that bat in the corner there."

Liam retrieved the baseball bat that was leaning in the corner by a circuit panel and gave it to her. She reached up and poked at the tile with the fatter end.

"It won't budge."

"Something's probably on top," Liam said. "Won't let you lift the tile off."

Susan jammed harder, but without the ladder, she didn't have proper leverage. She pushed again, and the tile rocked up a bit. But not enough to see anything.

"Come on."

She put her shoulders into it and slammed the bat up hard. This time the barrel of the bat went straight through, and that was enough to make the entire section of ceiling crash down in chunks onto the floor. Everyone scattered as several tiles became dislodged and broke off the metal framing. As the pieces fell, the items being held in the space between the drop ceiling and the real ceiling fell too. It was over in a matter of seconds, but in those few seconds everything changed.

The basement was silent. Susan walked back over to where the ceiling had collapsed and looked down on the floor.

"You gotta be kidding me," she mumbled.

"What is it?" Liam asked.

She bent down and started picking things up, studying them. "Clothes. Towels. Washcloths. Sheets. All bloodstained. So much blood that it affected the integrity of the tiles. They were discolored and moist. That's why they gave way. We hit the mother lode. Case closed."

"I got a rolled-up rug to the right of where those tiles came out," the tech on the ladder said.

"The missing area rug," Liam said.

Susan nodded. "He didn't have time to properly dispose of any of this stuff. He knew we'd be scouring their property and their garbage, so he hid everything here."

The tech climbed down and brought the ladder over to where Susan and Liam were. "I got something sticking out of the fold in the rug," he said. "You should check it out."

He placed the ladder under the hole, and Susan climbed up. The tech handed her his flashlight, and she stuck her head into the ceiling.

"Do you see it?" he asked. "In the fold. Something metal."

"Yeah, I see it."

She reached over and gently pulled a carving knife from the folds of the area rug. "Looks like we got the murder weapon." She vanished into the ceiling and reached for the other item that was sticking out of the rug. When she reappeared, she was smiling.

"What is it?" Liam asked.

"A cell phone." Susan handed Liam the phone and climbed down the ladder. "Okay," she said. "Let's go get Noel. We'll take him out through the garage as quickly as we can. I don't need the press snapping pictures. They got enough of a show already."

# 53

Susan and Noel were back in the interrogation room at the Lewisboro headquarters. Charlotte Walsh was with him again, and the mood in the room was even more tense, given the way the last interview had concluded. Susan could only imagine the crowd of people huddled inside the observation room, watching the monitors and listening to the audio.

Susan cleared her throat. "Before we begin, I have to make you aware—"

"Yes, yes," Charlotte snapped. "We're aware of the cameras in the corners and the audio being recorded. And we're aware of the people watching somewhere around here. I hope they enjoy the show."

Susan looked at Noel. "Please acknowledge for the record."

"I acknowledge," Noel replied. His voice was soft.

"Thank you." She paused. "This is still file number three-three-six-Lewisboro PD. My name is Investigator Susan Adler of the New York State Police, Troop K. I'm here with Noel Moore, who is the father of the victim, Jennifer Moore, and Charlotte Walsh, Mr. Moore's attorney."

Charlotte wrote something on a piece of paper and slid it over to Noel. He read it and nodded.

"Anything you'd like to share?" Susan asked.

Charlotte shook her head. "No."

"Okay." She looked at her subject. "Mr. Moore, I'm not sure where to begin. I've asked you on more than one occasion about your involvement in Jennifer's death, and each time you told me you don't know what happened, and you recite this story about you and your wife waking up and not finding your daughter and your wife looking for her outside because you both thought she was jogging. You told me that story at least three times, each time with a straight face, I might add. And in every instance it was a lie. How about the truth this time? What really happened?"

Noel's chin hit his chest. He was silent.

Susan opened her file and placed pictures on the table. "Traces of material that make up your ceiling tiles were found on your basement floor when our forensics team did their initial sweep. That's how we narrowed down where to search. Look at these pictures. We found bloodstained clothes that look to be your wife's. We found six towels, seven washcloths, and thirteen rags, all with blood on them. We found a bag full of used paper towels, also blood soaked. We found the rug that used to be in your bedroom, and yes, there were pools of bloodstain on that as well. We found the Oxi cleaning material that you took from your housekeeper's supplies. And we found the murder weapon. A carving knife from a butcher block, but not from the butcher block in your kitchen. The knife also had trace amounts of dried blood on it. You didn't bother washing it very well because you never thought we'd find it. I understand. But the thing is, we analyzed the blood on everything that was hidden in that ceiling, and it all matches your daughter's blood type. We're working on the DNA, but you know that'll match too. We found everything. There's no more room for lies. Tell us the truth. This is your last chance."

"We need to talk about a deal," Charlotte said. Her tone was harsh. It was clear she didn't like being on the receiving end of a potential loss. "It's just as easy for me to sit here and instruct my client not to say anything, and we can be here all night. Or we can work together."

"There's no working together. Just cooperation. Big difference. We're charging him. He can't hide from this anymore. Not with silence or anything else."

"He wasn't even there that night."

"Mr. Moore talks now, or we charge him with accessory after the fact and obstruction, and everyone can move on with their night."

"*Or*," Charlotte continued, "we set the record straight with a few assurances."

Susan sat back. "What assurances do you have in mind?"

"No jail time."

A tiny burst of laughter slipped through. She couldn't help it. "I'm sorry, what?"

"My client didn't do anything to his daughter, but he will admit to covering up what happened and tell you everything you need to know. But I don't want any jail time, and I don't want an accessory after the fact charge. We can agree to obstruction of justice and probation. You give us that, we'll give you the truth."

Susan was stunned at the woman's audacity. "Miss Walsh, if your client did, in fact, cover up his own daughter's murder, then you know as well as I do that it doesn't matter if he actually took part in her death. What he did is a crime, and accessory after the fact is punishable with half the jail time applicable to the principal who did commit the crime. There's no way you're getting away with probation."

"We can get away with whatever the truth is worth to you."

Susan took a second to clear her head. "Look, I'm in no position to make a deal anyway. That's the DA's jurisdiction. Let's just talk, and we'll see where things go from there."

"No," Charlotte snapped, her head shaking violently. "Charge him with accessory after the fact, and he keeps his mouth shut. You want the truth about what happened, we get probation."

"If he keeps his mouth shut, I'll charge him with the murder itself. If he doesn't want the full murder change, he better start talking. Despite your best efforts here, you know we have the case that puts your client away. He either explains what happened, or he takes it all.

And if he really didn't kill Jennifer like you said, then that's one hell of a charge to take for nothing."

"He wasn't even home."

"He arrived home within the window of the victim's death. I'll charge him and it'll stick. You know I'm right."

Charlotte and Noel remained sitting, silent, the room crushing under the weight of the stress.

"Okay. I guess we charge him." Susan stood up from her seat. "Noel Moore, you are being charged with murder in the first degree. You have the right to remain silent. If you give up that right—"

"It was Mindy!" Noel cried.

"Not another word!" Charlotte shouted.

"No," Noel replied. He began to sob. "I can't. I can't hold this in anymore. And I sure as hell can't be charged for such a heinous crime that I didn't commit. I wasn't even there that night! I have to tell the truth."

"You'll go to jail."

"Maybe I deserve to after what I did."

"What about Charlie?"

Noel looked at his attorney. "I don't think we're even worthy of being his parents."

Susan knew she had to strike or she'd lose the momentum that Noel had given her. She sat back down and leaned over the table. "Mr. Moore, you have two seconds to start talking, or I press those charges. Go."

Noel wiped his eyes and sniffled. "I came home and checked in on everyone, but the only person in bed was Charlie. When I was in Jen's room, and I saw a flashlight in the back woods, so I went to see what was up. I thought maybe Jen was back there at a party, and Mindy was crashing it. I went into the woods toward the clearing, and I saw Mindy come out, covered in blood. She scared the hell out of me. She fell against me, mumbling and crying."

"What time was this?"

"About two, maybe?" He took a breath. "She was *drenched* in blood. I didn't know what was going on. At first I thought she was hurt. I started checking her to see where she was cut, but I couldn't find anything. Then Mindy told me that Jen was dead. That was the last thing my wife said before she started screaming. After that, the shock took over, and she really hasn't said anything since."

"You went to see Jennifer?" Susan asked.

Noel nodded. "Of course. I had to see what Mindy was talking about. I found Jen lying there all cut up and bloody. Mindy left the knife right next to her, so I knew I had to get rid of it. I ran back up to the house and started cleaning everything up. I put Mindy in the shower and got her cleaned. I washed the bedroom and bathroom where all the blood had splattered around. I couldn't clean the rug, so I rolled it up and got rid of it. But I also knew I had to call the police, so it's not like I could throw all that stuff out in the trash or toss it out back. We used to hide the Christmas gifts in that drop ceiling, so I knew there'd be plenty of room. I put everything up there and called 911. The rest is the rest."

Susan closed her eyes, her mind examining everything that she was hearing. "Did you ask your wife about what happened after you came back from the woods?"

"Yes, but I told you, she was already deep in shock. Other than a few mumbled words that didn't make any sense and the constant crying, she was pretty much mute. I asked her over and over. I *begged* her to talk to me, but she wouldn't."

"Mr. Moore, if what you're saying is true, then your wife killed your daughter in cold blood. Why did you feel the need to cover that up?"

"For Charlie," Noel replied quickly. "I swear to God, if Jen was our only child, I would've turned Mindy in right away. But I didn't want my son to lose his sister and know his mother did it. And I couldn't let him see her be put in jail as a killer. I figured we'd be suspects for a day or so, and then we'd be cleared. Since everything happened outside, I thought you'd concentrate on friends or boyfriends or a stranger. Something like that. And then you wouldn't find anyone, and we'd all move on. I didn't anticipate you'd connect the missing rug and the clean bathroom."

Susan took out another sheet of paper from the file and placed it on the table. "We also found a drop of blood in the foyer on the way up the stairs. It's Jennifer's. That's why I kept asking you if you had any blood on you when you came back in. And you kept saying no."

"Mindy," Noel mumbled. "She tracked it from the patio doors to our bedroom. If I had runners in the hall or on the stairs, I would've had to have gotten rid of those too. I did my best to clean everything, but I'm not surprised I missed a spot. I did the best I could."

"So your plan was to go on living as a family of three, and that was it? You were going to expose your son to the woman who'd already killed her daughter?"

"What else could I do? Charlie needs his mother. Once everything calmed down, I was going to find out from Mindy exactly what happened and get her the help she needs. But now it's all over. My family is destroyed. Maybe Charlie's better off without us."

Susan took a breath. "Did you know Jennifer had been sexually abused over the course of several years?"

Noel fell back from the table as if the question itself had pushed him away. "What?"

"She told Father McCall about it."

"Did she say who did it?"

"No. She never gave up the abuser, but I think the person who was abusing her was the father of Jennifer's baby. Jennifer refused to be intimate with anyone else. She was too scarred from the abuse."

Noel shook his head slowly, dazed. "My poor little girl."

"Were you abusing Jennifer, Mr. Moore?"

Noel snapped back to reality, and his face contorted. "How dare you! Of course not! That's insane!"

"As insane as killing your own child?"

Charlotte knocked on the top of the table "That's enough."

"Why do you think your wife killed Jennifer?" Susan asked, taking a different tack.

"I don't know."

"Maybe Mindy knows who the abuser is, and she didn't want her daughter running off to Duke telling tales of sexual assault. You do have a family name to protect."

Noel started crying, and Charlotte leaned forward to lower her voice to a growl.

"Tread easy, Investigator."

Susan moved her file and pushed an empty legal pad toward Noel. "I'm going to need you to write down everything you just told me. This will be your sworn statement. Miss Walsh can help you."

"I still want a deal," Charlotte said.

"I'll see what I can do. The DA's on his way."

She walked out of the interrogation room and turned the corner toward the dispatcher's office. Liam, Chief Haslet, and Sergeant Dunes poured out into the hall to meet her halfway.

"That was easier than I thought it'd be," Dunes said, smiling. "I thought Walsh's head was going to explode when he started talking. That was good to see."

"Sometimes the guilt gets too strong," Susan replied. "I've seen it before. All I needed to do was give him a little nudge."

"It was excellent work," Chief Haslet said. "At least now we know what happened."

"We know who killed Jennifer," Susan said. "We just don't know why, and we still don't know who was abusing her. I thought it might've been Noel, but I've been involved in abuse cases in the past. Sexual and physical. I've seen more than my fair share of victims, and arrested and interviewed the abusers. Actually ran a class on it at the academy a few years ago before the twins were born. Noel's reaction to me asking if it was him who was abusing Jenny was visceral. There was no hesitation in his denial, and he was upset at the question itself. Whenever I've interviewed abusers in the past, their reactions were fake. Staged. Noel's wasn't. I don't think he's our guy."

Liam leaned against the wall and placed his hands in his pockets. "We also have to consider that all of this could just be more BS. We have no idea if this is finally the truth. He's lied with a straight face before."

"If he's lying, he's going to jail," Dunes said. "And depending on what the DA says, he may be heading there anyway. Doesn't make sense to lie at this point. Not with his freedom at stake."

"He's got a great lawyer," Liam said. "And like Susan mentioned in there, if he's charged with accessory after the fact, his punishment is only half the jail time. Could be worth it if he was involved more than he's saying."

"You think he'd throw his wife under the bus like that?"

"I have no idea, but when you're facing the rest of your life in prison, people do desperate things."

A uniformed officer came down the hall and motioned toward Susan.

"We just got a call from Putnam Hospital," he said. "Mindy Moore is awake and talking. The doctor said you could see her."

Susan pulled Liam off the wall and headed back toward her desk. "I should really play the lotto tonight," she said with a smile. "Apparently, this is my lucky day."

# 54

Susan and Liam drove straight to Putnam Hospital. Dr. Fields met them on the third floor when they got off the elevator and escorted them to Mindy's room.

"Has anyone spoken to her about the case since she's been awake?" Susan asked.

Dr. Fields shook his head. "No. Our preliminary protocol is to go through her cognitive thinking, such as name, address, birth date. That kind of thing. Her recall was excellent, so once those initial hurdles were cleared, we called you. We didn't want to push her and cause any kind of relapse into the shock she'd been suffering."

"How is she, emotionally?" Liam asked.

"Still in a state of sadness and despair. As soon as she woke up, she knew what had happened."

Mindy Moore was sitting up in bed. Her IV was still connected, the monitors next to the bed measuring heart rate, blood pressure, and whatever else was on there that Susan didn't understand. Mindy herself looked a little different. There was more color in her cheeks, and her eyes were open a bit wider, but there was still a haunted look of hopelessness behind those eyes that Susan had seen since the day she met her in the family room of her home. Two white bandages worked their way up both of Mindy's arms, the remnants of her suicide attempt.

"Mindy," Dr. Fields began as he ushered them in, "this is Investigator Adler from the state police and her partner, Liam Dwyer. They need to talk to you."

Mindy looked at them. "I remember them. It's okay."

Tears came instantly. Mindy sniffled and grabbed a tissue from a small side table that also had water and a half-eaten peanut butter sandwich. Susan and Liam sat in the two chairs next to the bed, and Dr. Fields stood by the door.

"How are you feeling?" Susan asked.

Mindy leaned her head back on her pillow and looked up at the ceiling. "I can remember everything, and I wish I couldn't. I wish I could forget it all. That's why I did what I did. I know it was selfish, but I couldn't take the hurt anymore. I didn't want Charlie to have to grow up with a mother who did nothing but grieve. That's not fair for him." She held up her bandaged wrists. "But I'm still here. Go figure."

She began to sob, and Susan waited for a few moments.

"I can't imagine how hard this is, and we're very sorry for what happened, but I need you to take me through the night with Jennifer. I need you describe every detail you can remember. I'm going to record this so we don't miss anything. Is that okay?"

"You mean the morning. I found her in the morning."

Susan shook her head and offered a thin smile. "Noel told us what really happened. We know the story about finding her in the morning is a lie. He told us the truth. Now we need your version of it. Please." She placed her phone on her lap and began recording. "I also have to tell you that you can have an attorney present if you want. And you can stop talking whenever you feel you need to. You can also ask for an attorney at any point. Is that clear?"

"Yes," Mindy replied. "I understand, and I don't need an attorney. I have nothing to hide."

"Okay, then. Go ahead. Tell us what happened."

"Something woke me up. I don't know what it was. A feeling or an intuition or something. I felt like I needed to check on the kids, so I did."

"Where was your husband?"

"He hadn't come home yet. I was alone. I got up and checked in each room. Charlie was in his bed, but Jen wasn't. I thought she'd snuck out to go to a party or go meet a boy or something, and that was not okay."

"You were angry."

"Annoyed. I thought we were over these foolish sneaking-out-at-night games. I figured she was in the woods behind the house, so I went out there to catch her doing whatever she was doing. I know she was leaving for college in a few weeks, and was very aware that I wasn't going to be able to control her every move once she was gone, but I have standards, and as long as she was still here, I was going to make sure we upheld those standards. I thought if we built a solid foundation at home, she'd grow into a good woman. That's all I wanted for her. To be a decent woman with some self-dignity. A woman of the twenty-first century."

Susan had to keep herself from opining on Mindy's definition of what a good woman was. Jennifer was a teenager who wanted to have a little fun before leaving for college. She was like every other kid in America. But somehow Mindy deemed that wrong or immoral. If that was the case, Susan herself was a bad person and Beatrice was a bad mom. She bit her bottom lip to keep from disrupting the story.

"I got back into the woods and starting calling for her. I thought she was with a boy, and they were making out, or something worse."

"Did you hear anything when you were back there? Anyone running or movement or brush moving?"

"No. Nothing. All of a sudden I came to the clearing, and I saw her lying there. There was a full moon that night, and that's all the light I needed to see every detail. So much blood. She was covered in blood. I could see the knife wounds, but at the same time I couldn't believe what I was seeing. I fell on top of her and tried to cover the wounds to stop them from bleeding, but there was nothing I could do. I just cried and laid with her, and that's the last thing I remember before waking up here the first time. Everything else just comes and goes."

Susan took a moment as the room fell into an uncomfortable silence. She looked at Liam, who was looking at her.

"Mrs. Moore," she said quietly. "Are you saying Jennifer was already dead when you found her in the woods?"

"Yes. She was dead."

"We found the clothes you were wearing that night. They were covered in Jennifer's blood."

Mindy opened her eyes and lifted her head off the pillow to look at Susan. "I just told you I laid down on her. I was hugging her and crying. That's the last thing I remember."

"We also found the knife that was used to kill your daughter. Your fingerprints are on the handle."

"The knife was there when I saw her. I picked it up and tossed it aside. That's why my fingerprints were on it."

Susan paused for a moment, trying to collect her thoughts. "I have statements from friends and family saying that your relationship with Jennifer was tough. You rode her hard. Most of the people I talked to said you two had a very tenuous relationship, which is one of the reasons she picked Duke, even though she had offers from more local universities. She wanted to get away from you."

A new set of tears rolled down Mindy's cheeks. "I pushed because I knew she had such great potential. Jen could've been one of the great ones. It was in her, and it was my job to get it out, to show her what she could be. Yes, I pushed. And yes, I wouldn't accept anything less than high standards, but that was because I loved her so dearly. She made it almost impossible with the drugs and the drinking and the rebelling when she was younger, but all that changed. I guess she realized her mistakes and found God with my sister and Father McCall. She started volunteering and choosing new friends. I knew there was still some drinking and drugs, and I did my best to keep her away from them. Some might say my methods were harsh, but I was scared and desperate. I knew Jen was going to do great things." She sniffled and crossed her arms over her chest. "If you think I'd put in all that work over eighteen years just to kill her, then you don't know what being a mother is about."

"I am a mother," Susan snapped. "Twins."

"Then you know what true love is. You know. When you're a mother, you'd do anything for your child. I loved my baby with the kind of love that can't be described."

"And that's why you helped her with the abortion."

Mindy's eyes widened. "You know about that?"

"Yes. And we need to know who the father was."

"I don't know who the father is. I never asked. I didn't want to know. The entire episode was just so *dirty*."

"Do you have any theories?"

Mindy looked back and forth between Susan and Liam. "None."

Susan adjusted her phone, which was still on her lap. "Mrs. Moore, we have reason to believe Jennifer was sexually abused for a stretch of time dating back to when she was younger. We're thinking the abuser was the person who got Jennifer pregnant. Did she ever tell you about the abuse?"

Mindy froze, her gaze locked on Susan with such intensity Susan had to look away.

"Abused?"

"Yes, ma'am."

"I never knew. Jen just told me she was pregnant, and I figured it was her being irresponsible and stupid. I never pressed for specifics. I just wanted to get the entire episode behind us as soon as possible."

"Are you sure she never told you?"

"Of course I'm sure!" Mindy screamed. "Aren't you listening? Do you think I'd let someone get away with sexually assaulting my *daughter*? Never." She looked back up at the ceiling. "Oh my god."

Susan lowered her voice. "We also know Jennifer was adopted. When we did the swab of the family to rule out the DNA our forensics team found at your house, Jennifer didn't match. Your husband confirmed."

Mindy wiped her tears away with the back of her hand. "I don't care about DNA. That child was mine, and I loved her like she was mine. I would never hurt her."

"You have to make sure you're telling us the whole truth."

"I am."

"Things could get ugly for you if you're not."

Mindy huffed a laugh full of anger and hurt. "Have you been sitting there waiting for me to confess to killing my daughter? Trying to lower my guard with discoveries of adoption and sexual assault? Showing me your hand so I know I'm screwed if I don't cooperate?" She sat up in the bed. "Am I your main suspect? The tiger mom who pushed her daughter so hard she kills her? Is that your theory?"

Susan sighed and looked at her main suspect. "Your husband has already implicated you in Jennifer's murder. He's confessed to running into you in the woods covered in blood, mumbling about Jennifer being hurt, and slipping into shock. He's confessed to taking you into the house and washing you off, washing the house where you tracked blood in from the woods, and hiding the knife, your clothes, and everything he used to clean up. We found the items in the drop ceiling in your basement."

"Where we used to hide the Christmas presents?"

"He's been placed into custody and charged as an accessory after the fact. That particular charge carries a little less jail time than first-degree murder, and he agreed to the charge in exchange for implicating you in Jennifer's murder. He's told us everything. He suspects you confronted her about something in the woods, things escalated, and a crime of passion occurred. What happened out there? Tell us."

"I already told you. It's the truth."

"We're here to place you under arrest. You can remain in the hospital until Dr. Fields deems you healthy enough to leave, but there will be an officer outside the door, and you will not be allowed visitors. Do you understand?"

Mindy fell back on her pillows again. "I think I'll take that lawyer now."

# 55

Mindy called Charlotte Walsh, and Charlotte explained that although she couldn't represent both her and her husband since Noel was implicating Mindy in Jen's murder, she'd refer Mindy to another associate in the firm. Mindy agreed, and Susan and Liam waited until Trent Bosco arrived at the hospital in his well-fitted suit, skinny tie, pressed shirt, and impeccable haircut. Susan brought him up to speed on the charges the DA would be filing, and Trent dismissed both of them almost immediately as he walked into the room to begin building the case for his client's defense. Susan and Liam left soon after and were quiet for most of the ride, the weight of the day having finally taken its toll.

They swung into the Lewisboro police station's parking lot, and Susan pulled up next to Liam's car. Liam could hardly keep his eyes open but at the same time felt the rush of his mind working feverishly, trying to untangle the puzzle that was this case.

"I don't know how you do this for a living," he said, chuckling. "The ups and downs are hard to keep track of. I know we're filing charges, and that should feel like a victory, but something feels off."

"Something always feels off in an investigation like this," Susan replied. "You start piling up the unanswered questions, and then the lawyers get involved and stop their clients from shedding any light, and things feel unresolved."

Liam turned in his seat to face Susan. "Why would Mindy Moore spend Jennifer's entire life trying to make her into what she deems to be a proper woman, only to kill her days before she leaves for school? Why put in all the work and all the fighting for nothing?"

"Maybe she didn't realize it was for nothing until it was too late," Susan replied. "Maybe Mindy finally understood that Jennifer was a lost cause in her eyes and decided to kill her rather than let her go where she'd have no control over who she was with or what stories she told about her sexual assault or abortion or her upbringing. Jennifer's independence became too risky."

Liam nodded, his mind still swirling with unanswered questions.

"And you think Noel is telling the truth about him not being the one who was abusing Jennifer."

"Yeah, but not with one hundred percent certainty. Could've been him. Could've been a camp counselor or schoolteacher. Could've even been Mindy. We'll need to trace back someone who was in Jennifer's life since she was twelve. That'll create our list of suspects on the assault end of things. Until then, we need to concentrate on building the case on the homicide we're investigating. It's very possible one will feed the other."

Susan's phone started to ring, and she grabbed it from the cup holder.

"Who is it?" Liam asked.

"Donna Starr from channel twelve. She gave me her card, and I programmed her number so I'd know not to pick up by accident." She hit the red dot on her screen and refused the call. "No comment today, Miss Starr. Thank you."

"You have to deal with the press a lot during an investigation?"

"Not really. This is kind of high profile because the Moores are wealthy and the community is so beautiful and safe, but most cases have no press. Maybe one reporter we email a statement to. That's it."

"I never had to deal with the press on the forensics side. Then I became a fugitive murderer, and suddenly I was the front-page story. It was surreal. First they wanted to hang me, and then, when they found out I was innocent, they wanted to hail me as a hero. I spent months declining interviews. The media was voracious."

"They always are."

"We can't mess this case up. Not with the spotlight on us like it is."

Susan shrugged. "Then we won't. If we do everything by the book, we won't have to worry about blowback. Let's not give the press a reason to keep hounding us. We find our guy, close the case, and make them move on."

Liam smiled. "Sounds like a plan to me."

# 56

Susan kicked off her shoes inside her front door, hung her bag on the coatrack, and walked toward the kitchen. She closed her eyes, letting the day fall off her while at the same time allowing the sounds and smells to welcome her home. The kids were at the table talking about the picture in the puzzle they were working on. Dishes were clattering as her mother filled the dishwasher. No one had heard her come in. The lingering aroma of pork chops and grilled vegetables wafted through each of the rooms, her mother's familiar garlic rub tickling her nose. She'd missed dinner. Again.

"Hey, guys."

The twins looked up. Tim was holding a puzzle piece in his hand while Casey was examining the picture of four Labrador puppies, two Yorkies, and a beagle, all in a wicker basket. It was cute.

"Hi, Mommy!"

"Hi, Mommy."

"Hi, family."

"We didn't hear you come in," Beatrice said, shutting off the water.

Susan crossed the room and kissed her mother on the forehead, then made her way to the table.

"How're you feeling?" she asked Casey.

Casey's arm hung in a sling against her tiny chest. The pins and plate stuck out of the sling and looked like a spider crawling on her arm.

"I'm okay. Grandma helped us with the puzzle because we couldn't go outside with my arm hurt."

"It looks like you made some serious progress."

"We're almost done. Just one more piece." She pointed to the black Lab puppy. "I used to want a white puppy with brown spots, but this black one is so cute. I want this one for my birthday."

"You're not getting a dog."

"Not just for me. It'll be for me and Tim. We'll share it."

Susan looked at her son. "How're you doing, buddy?"

"I'm good," Tim replied. "I helped Casey get dressed, and me and Grandma helped her eat and drink with one hand. Grandma brushed Casey's teeth for her and got all wet. It was funny. And Grandma did pigtails for her hair because I didn't know how to do that."

"Thank you for helping out. It's nice to know you can count on each other. You guys are great helpers. The best team ever."

Tim held out the puzzle piece in his hand. "We saved this one for you. You can put the last piece in, and it'll be all done."

Susan took the piece and turned it over. Looking down at the puzzle, she could see the one space that remained. A small portion of one of the Yorkies' noses. All she had to do was slip it in, and the picture would be complete.

"You saved this for me?"

Both twins nodded.

"Thanks." Her eyes suddenly filled with tears. "That was really nice of you."

"It's not fair that we did the whole thing and you didn't do any of it," Casey explained. "This way we can say we did it all together!"

Susan choked back more tears that wanted to push their way out. She could feel her bottom lip quivering and bit it, breathing deeply to get herself under control. She didn't want to cry in front of the kids. They'd be confused and might think they did something wrong. They didn't quite understand happy tears yet, and Susan wasn't sure what kind of tears these were anyway.

"Okay, are you ready?"

"Yes!"

"Do it, Mom!"

Susan leaned over and placed the last piece of the puppy's nose. "Done!"

Everyone cheered and hugged and laughed, and it felt good.

"Okay," Beatrice said as she shut the dishwasher and got it running. "You guys go get ready for a bath, and I'll start laying the glue on this so we can frame it and hang it in the hall upstairs."

The twins scrambled off their chairs and ran out of the kitchen. Casey went down the hall while Tim went the long way to avoid the spot where the Bad Man had stood. Footsteps thumped up to the second floor.

"It's just a puzzle," Beatrice teased as she started wiping it down with a paper towel. "No need to cry. We'll get another one."

Susan laughed. "That was quite a gesture."

"I know."

"And maybe a few tears for the guilt of not being here to do it with them."

"I know that too."

Susan walked to the counter next to the stove and peeled away the foil that was over her plate. Pork chops, grilled zucchini, grilled onions, and sautéed red peppers, all with the garlic rub. "Looks good."

"You should warm that up."

"Too hungry."

She started eating while her mother dipped a small paintbrush into a jar of clear glue. Beatrice began gently painting the glue onto the puzzle, sealing the pieces together and creating a protective coating.

"How's the case going?" she asked.

"It's going. We think we have our killer, and we think we know what happened. Got some info tonight that could help us tie up a few loose ends that're still out there, so that's good."

"Are you getting any pressure to wrap things up since there's so much media attention on this one?"

"No. Not seeing a lot of political interference, either, which is a blessing in itself."

Beatrice finished painting the glue on, capped the bottle, and went to the sink to rinse the brush. "We're starting to get responses for the birthday party. So far, everyone who responded can make it. We got twelve confirmed and waiting on the last eight."

"That's fantastic."

"I also spoke to the petting zoo guy, and we picked out the animals he's going to bring. He has a reptile show that he does with snakes and lizards and stuff. I think the kids will get a kick out of that. He also has a bunny show, and he'll do something with our chickens too. And the pony rides will be in the front."

Susan finished her plate and put her knife and fork down. "Sounds like you got this all worked out."

"I told you I got your back, lady."

"Yes, you do." Susan pushed away from the counter and hugged her mother. "You're a huge help. You help too much as far as I'm concerned. I'm going to try and be around more. I'm not sure how yet, but I'm working on it."

"It's okay," Beatrice whispered in her ear. "We understand. You do what you do, and I'll cover for you. We got this."

"But you raised your kid. You did your duty. You should be living a nice retirement life right now."

Beatrice laughed. "Honey, I couldn't think of a better retirement life than the one I'm currently living. Those kids keep me young, and I love them so much. I'm good right here. As long as you'll have me."

"No, as long as *you'll* have *me*."

"Then I guess we'll be at this for a very long time."

Susan's phone rang, and she looked at the caller ID. It was Donna Starr calling again. She refused the call, put the phone on the table, and went upstairs to give her kids a bath.

# 57

Charlie's stomach was in knots as he waited in the prison's visitors' room for his father to be brought out. He'd left his phone at home, and his fingers itched to scroll through a feed or double tap on a picture or take a quick video of something funny that he could upload. But the phone, his most trusted companion in this world of digital content, had betrayed him. Now, instead of funny posts or texts with his friends, it only showed him stories about the worst mistake he'd made in his life. The news about him hiding Jennifer's bracelet in the woods had come out and was immediately picked up by all the major outlets as well as the cable news channels. People he didn't know and had never met were calling him a monster and accusing him of having a hand in his sister's murder. They were posting about him needing to die along with his sister or that he should've been the one out in the woods that night. They called him spoiled and entitled and immature and evil. Friends and classmates and kids he'd grown up with suddenly started unfriending him. And then his father had been arrested, and news spread of his parents' suspected involvement in Jen's murder. That's when he'd shut off the phone completely. He realized then that social media was as deadly as the knife used to kill his sister, and he couldn't stand the torture any longer.

The visitors' room was nothing more than a large concrete space with six sets of tables and chairs, everything bolted to the floor. One of the walls was full of bars and a door that remained locked from the other side. Another wall had two tiny windows up by the ceiling. He could see the morning sky, but nothing else. One guard stood outside the gate, and a second guard was inside with them. He, Aunt Sidney, and Artie were the only ones in the room.

A door opened somewhere he couldn't see, and the butterflies that were in his stomach began flapping harder. He watched as his father was escorted down the hall by two guards. He was dressed in a tan jumpsuit, and his hands were cuffed in front. This wasn't the confident man Charlie saw every morning dressed in an impeccable suit, always rushing to catch a train. There was no briefcase or shining black loafers or slicked-back hair or perfectly shaved face. This man was hunched over just a bit, his hair askew, stubble on his cheeks and chin, slippers instead of shoes. As soon as Charlie saw him, he wanted to cry, but he fought it back and clenched his hands into fists under the table, his fingernails cutting into the meaty part of his palms.

The gate was unlocked, and his father was escorted into the room by one guard. The guard sat him across the table from them, then took two steps back and waited near another table.

"My god," Aunt Sidney whispered. "What is happening, Noel? How are you still in here? I thought you had the kind of lawyer that could get you out of places like this."

"I do, but I can't get in front of a judge until later. They stuck me here overnight."

"What's going on?"

His father shook his head. "I can't explain everything right now. I'll be out on bail today, and we can talk then. Just take Charlie back to the house and stay with him. Don't let the reporters near you, and don't say anything to anyone."

"Can you at least give me the short version of what happened?" Sidney asked. Her voice was shaking. She was on the verge of crying. "I get a call to come for Charlie because you're being arrested, and now they won't let me see Mindy either. What's happening?"

His father gestured toward him. "Not in front of Charlie."

"Dad, it's fine," Charlie said. "You can tell us what's happening. We need to know. Seriously."

"I can't," his father replied. "I'm sorry, buddy. I'll explain everything later when I get home."

"But—"

"No buts. Everything we say and do in here is being recorded, so the less we talk specifics, the better." He turned his attention back to Aunt Sidney. "This will all be worked out one way or another, so for now I just need you to take care of Charlie."

Sidney threw up her hands and let them flop down onto her lap. "Mindy is my sister. Why won't they let me see her? She needs me right now, Noel. I can't imagine how scared she is."

His father looked at Charlie, then down at the table. "The police think we both have something to do with Jen's murder."

"Yeah, that's obvious," Sidney snapped. "But how come we can see you, and I can't see my sister?"

"I don't know. We're working it out."

Charlie was about to jump up and tell his father the truth about the Darth Vader pendant the police found in the woods. He wanted to pound the concrete table and explain how it was Bobby's favorite thing in the world and how Bobby freaked out when they were going to see the place in the woods where Jen was found. He wanted to say all that and save his family from being blamed for something they didn't do. He clenched his jaw and looked straight ahead, feeling his face grow hotter as he thought about how his friend was destroying everything. For the first time, with complete clarity, it hit Charlie how Bobby had been acting—how he'd panicked and refused to go to the crime scene—and the pictures he'd taken of Jen and the angles he'd taken them from and the places he'd been in the woods. All those things had been there floating in his mind as separate pieces, pushed away by the reality of what was happening to his family and his mother's suicide attempt. But now it was clearer than it had ever been. Bobby knew more than he was letting on. There was no doubt.

Charlie opened his mouth to declare his best friend the real suspect, then noticed the cameras on the wall filming them. He thought about how the guards would be listening and realized he couldn't say anything. Not in there. The people who ran the jail would just take the words on the recording and twist them around and make his father look even more guilty. His father had warned him earlier that they couldn't trust the police. He was right. The police had the wrong man, and they didn't care. He'd tell his dad everything when he got home. That was the safest place.

"How're things holding up at the office?" his father asked Artie.

Artie ran his hand through his hair and sighed. "Not good. We've been getting calls since this all broke. Most of the initial calls were condolences and offers of support. But since you and Mindy have become suspects, the calls we're getting are a bit more down to business. They want to pull their funds, Noel. I keep trying to reassure them that this is a big misunderstanding, but these are the kind of people who can't be tied to bad publicity. They want out."

"Did you talk to Uriah?"

Artie snorted a laugh. "Uriah was the first one who called. He's moving to Merrill. They're opening his accounts as we speak."

Charlie watched his father's head drop. "I'll call Uriah personally when I get out of here. Actually, make a list of who's asking out, and I'll call them all. They need to hear from me."

"It's going to be a long list."

"I'll call all night. I don't care." He turned away from Artie and focused on Charlie. His voice became low, almost inaudible. "How're you doing?"

"I'm okay," Charlie replied.

"You sure?"

"Yeah."

"I don't want you getting wrapped up in this. Don't talk to anyone. Not the press. No friends or their families. I'll work everything out."

"I got it."

"I love you. Mom does too."

"I know."

"I didn't kill your sister. The police are making a mistake."

"I know."

Charlie waited for his father to reassure him that his mother didn't kill Jen, either, but he straightened up and started talking to Aunt Sidney and Artie again. Not saying anything about his mom was really all his father had to say. Charlie would have to fix that. But not there. Not with *them* watching.

# 58

After Susan got out of the shower, she helped bring Casey downstairs and sat her in her seat while her mother made breakfast. She could tell the cast was getting heavy and the sling was cutting into the back of Casey's neck, so she rolled up a small dishtowel and placed it under the neck strap. She made a note on her phone to pick up a more comfortable pad at the pharmacy later.

When Susan was done with Casey, she helped Tim get dressed so he could go on his playdate with his friend from camp. The mother—Susan forgot her name—was supposed to pick him up right after breakfast and take them to the community pool and then to the park for lunch and swings. It was one of the first times Tim would be separated from his sister, and Susan couldn't tell if he was anxious or happy or worried or excited. She, on the other hand, was all those things. He hadn't been on many playdates, and she hoped it would go smoothly.

After the kids were set, Susan got changed, gave them hugs and kisses, left her mother with a small list of things they still needed for the party, and said her goodbyes. She stepped outside, only to be slammed by a wall of heat and humidity. The sky was bright blue, and the purest of white clouds hovered above, but there was no breeze to cool anyone. She knew the day would be one of the hottest of the summer.

She'd just shut the car door when her phone began to ring. She turned the ignition and blasted the air-conditioning before connecting the phone to the USB cord so she could talk hands-free.

"This is Susan Adler."

"Finally," an exasperated voice on the other end said. "It's Donna Starr."

Susan grimaced, cursing herself for not looking at the caller ID. "Donna, I have no comment about the case. As soon as I hear something, I'll let you know. I promise."

"I'm not calling for a comment," Donna shouted. "I've been leaving you voice mails all night. Haven't you been listening to them?"

"Yeah. They just said to call you."

"Then you didn't listen to the last one."

Susan grabbed her phone out of the cup holder and activated the screen. Donna had indeed called earlier that morning, but she must have been getting the kids ready. She put the phone back down and pulled out of the driveway.

"Sorry about that. I had kind of a hectic morning."

"Look." Donna's voice calmed down and grew quiet. "I'm not sure if there's anything here, and I never reveal my sources, so don't ask me who gave me this information, but there's something I've come across that I think needs your attention. This isn't about my job. It's about yours."

"Okay. Talk to me."

"Do you know who Bobby Teagan is?"

"No."

"He's Charlie Moore's best friend. The two of them have been friends for a while, and they've been inseparable since day one. Bobby is extremely close with the Moore family, just like Charlie is close with the Teagans. It appears Bobby had developed a rather unhealthy obsession with Jennifer."

"You mean like a crush?" Susan asked as she drove down the street. "He's like thirteen, right? How unhealthy could it have been?"

There was a pause on the other line. "Unhealthy enough that I think you need to check it out. I was given access to this diary/scrapbook/

notebook thing of Bobby's, and it's full of pictures of Jennifer. He used to follow her around and take the pictures without her knowing."

"And you're sure it's not the way kids these days have a crush? They're always taking pictures of everything. Maybe this is just the way he did his thing."

"No," Donna replied. "This is like that serial killer stuff you see in the movies where the police come into a room and the walls are covered in pictures of the victim. Like a macabre collage. This is scary. You need to check it out." She paused. "I don't want to jump to any conclusions, but I think a few of the pictures could be from the night Jennifer Moore was killed."

"Really?"

"I can't be one hundred percent sure. I'm just relaying what I was told. The pictures are looking into her room from the woods at night, but I can't confirm they're from that specific night."

Susan took the ramp onto Route 9. "Okay, I'll swing by and see what's what."

"I'm not done. There's more."

"Go."

"I found out that Bobby suffers from a mild case of intermittent explosive disorder. Do you know what that is?"

"Is it anything like your theory about Mindy Moore's excited catatonia?"

"That was a theory. This is fact."

"Go ahead."

"Intermittent explosive disorder is an impulse-control disorder where people have sudden episodes of anger for no reason. They have no control. It just happens without them being provoked. My source tells me he first got diagnosed when he was nine. The Teagans lived in Colorado at the time, and he beat another kid up so bad that they had to move away. Apparently that had been the last straw for the town he came from. He'd been lashing out at teachers and classmates, and no one knew why. When they landed here, his mother found a doctor who could treat him, and she keeps him on a tight regimen of drugs to keep the rage in check."

Susan tapped on the steering wheel, her mind thinking through next steps. "I know you can't reveal sources, but is the source trustworthy?"

"In my opinion, yes."

"Okay," she said. "I'll look into it. Thanks for the tip."

Donna didn't respond. The call disconnected, and Susan called Liam. He picked up on the second ring.

"Hey," he said.

"Hey. Where are you?"

"On my way to Lewisboro HQ."

"Good. I'll meet you there. We need to make a house call."

"You got a lead?"

"I don't know what I have, and I don't know if I can trust where it came from, but I wouldn't be doing my job if I didn't at least look into it. I'll pick you up in the parking lot and we'll take my car."

# 59

Bobby was waiting outside on the patio near the kitchen when Charlie and Aunt Sidney got home. Charlie had been crying in the car, and he knew his eyes were red and swollen. He sniffled as he opened the sliding door and tried to fake his way through with a smile.

"What's up?"

Bobby looked serious. Tight lips. Hardly any eye contact. "I need to talk to you."

"Why didn't you text me?"

"I did. Like a thousand times."

"Oh yeah. I left my phone here. How long you been waiting?"

Bobby shrugged.

"Did the press see you?"

"Nah. I came in through the woods."

"Okay."

Charlie stepped aside and let his friend walk into the house. Aunt Sidney was finished locking the front door and pulling the shades down in the living room. She walked into the kitchen and saw the boys.

"Hi, Bobby," she said.

"Hi, Sidney."

"You guys want something to eat or drink? I can fix you something."

"We're good," Charlie replied. "We're going up to my room."

She nodded, and the boys scrambled up the stairs to Charlie's room. Charlie noticed Bobby stop at the threshold and glance over his shoulder toward Jen's bedroom before coming in and shutting the door.

The butterflies Charlie'd had at the jail were nothing compared to what he was feeling with his friend in his room. He tried to think of how many times Bobby had come over and how often they'd ended up in that very spot. The number was countless. His house, Bobby's house. They were always together, and now, suddenly, things were so different. Jen was gone, and Charlie had questions that put his best friend at the scene of the murder. He wondered how any of it could be real, but at the same time he was so very aware of how real it was. His parents had been arrested, but Bobby could be guilty. The entire week had been like a dream.

Bobby walked over to Charlie's bed and sat, while Charlie sat in the chair at his desk. They both stared at each other for what seemed like forever. Bobby finally took a breath.

"I know you saw my scrapbook," he said, his voice barely louder than a whisper. "When you were waiting for me when I was at practice. That's the only time it could've been. I know you found it, and I know you looked through it."

"How?"

"I have a pencil mark on the wall that I put the edge of the book against so I'd know if anyone found it. Every time I take it out I make sure it's hitting the mark when I put it back, and every time I come into my room, I check it. I figured if anyone found it, it would be my mom, and she'd be a little freaked. Never thought it would be you."

"Maybe it was your mom."

Bobby shook his head. "Nah. I checked it right before I left for football practice that day. When I got home, you were in my room, and when you left, I checked again and saw that the scrapbook wasn't on the mark. I asked my mom if she was in my room, and she said no. Just that you were. That's how I know."

"Yeah, well, I know some things too." Charlie grabbed his phone from the top of his desk and held out a picture from his Instagram of Bobby wearing the Darth Vader pendant. "The police found your pendant in the woods near Jen. And I found those pictures in your book. Put it all together, and it can only mean one thing. You were there that night. You killed my sister."

Bobby shook his head as tears welled in his eyes. "I didn't."

"You did!"

Charlie couldn't control the fear and fury that came over him. One minute he was holding the phone, and the next, he was lunging across the room and tackling Bobby off the bed and onto the floor. It was like he was outside his body, watching the fight as an observer instead of a participant. He punched Bobby in the leg and then the stomach. He hit him again near the shoulder, and Bobby blocked his punch to the face.

"You killed her!"

"Get off!"

Bobby twisted his body until he was lying on his stomach and began throwing elbows behind him, connecting once on the side of Charlie's head and again on his left side near his ribs. He crawled to his hands and knees as Charlie fell off him, then both kids scrambled to their feet.

"You're my best friend!" Charlie yelled.

"I didn't do anything."

"Liar!"

Again, Charlie attacked with reckless abandon. He threw himself at Bobby and wrapped him in a bear hug as they both hit the floor. Charlie had a handful of hair and was pulling it while Bobby was squeezing Charlie's throat. Both boys were crying and sobbing, snot and tears flying with each punch thrown. Charlie could feel his face growing hotter, and it was getting difficult to breathe. He twisted the hair in his hand, but Bobby wouldn't let go of his throat. Charlie released Bobby's hair and pushed him in the chest as hard as he could. The two of them fell away from each other and again rushed to their feet.

"I loved Jen," Bobby said, panting and crying.

"You don't know anything about love."

"Maybe not, but whatever I felt for your sister was like nothing I ever felt for anyone else before."

"And she blew you off, so you killed her."

"No!"

Charlie made a move to attack again, but Bobby held up his hands.

"Just wait," he said. "Let me explain. I swear I didn't kill Jen. I'm serious. But you're right. I was there that night." He started to cry again. "I saw it all, man. I saw it all, and I was too scared to save her. I was too scared to help."

Bobby collapsed on the floor and put his face in his hands. Charlie waited.

"I know everyone thinks this is a stupid crush. You think I don't get that? But I'm telling you, I loved her. And I'm also not stupid enough to believe she could love me. She's going to college, and we're in eighth grade. I'm not an idiot. I just can't stop feeling what I feel for her. Love. Infatuation. Obsession. I don't know what it is, but I like to think it's love."

"It's not love. You're obsessed."

"Whatever. You're probably right. I was obsessed. I would run into the woods after school and watch Jen in her room before I'd ring your bell to hang out. And after I left, I'd be right back in the woods watching her. On the weekends and over the summer I'd sneak around and follow her and take pictures and pretend we were dating. I'd pretend she knew I was there or that we were meeting up at the CVS or the ice cream shop or the movies. She's all I thought about, and I'd take the pictures and put them in my scrapbook and I'd look through the pages every night just reliving the moment I took them and seeing what she was wearing and who she was with and the expression on her face. I loved her so much."

"You're sick," Charlie spat. "I knew you were crushing, but I had no idea it was this deep and this mental."

"I know." More tears. "I was in the woods that night like I was most nights in the summer. It's easy to sneak out of my house. My parents are asleep by ten, and I just hop out my window, climb down the trellis in the back, and jog through the backyards in the neighborhood until I meet up with the woods and follow a path I made. It leads away from the clearing in case anyone's there drinking or whatever. I plant myself in the same spot against this big elm tree, and I get a perfect view of Jen's room. I watch her until she goes to bed, and then I go home. I pretend we go to sleep together. That's why the police found my pendant. It fell off when I was running away after he killed your sister."

"Who? Who killed my sister?"

Bobby was distant as the memories came back. His voice grew softer as more tears slipped down his face.

"I was sitting there watching her room, and all of a sudden, she looks at her phone, then leaves. Next thing I know, she's walking out of the patio doors and comes into the woods. I just sat there, too scared to make a move. I thought she might've seen me or someone told her I was out there. I couldn't see where she went, so I crawled a little closer, and by the time I could see anything, he was kneeling over her, stabbing her, like three or four times. She didn't make a sound. Just the thumping noise every time he stabbed her."

"Are you sure it was a man?" Charlie asked.

Bobby nodded and wiped his eyes. "Not at first, but then I snuck out of there and ran down the path and out the back by the school. That's when I saw him come out on the far edge of the woods by the park. It was the priest. Jen's priest."

Charlie's mind was racing. "Father McCall?"

"Yeah." Bobby started crying harder. "I saw his uniform or whatever you call it. I saw his face. It was him."

"Why didn't you tell me or say something to an adult?"

"I was scared! I didn't want to get blamed for what happened to Jen. Who're the police going to believe? A man of God who's also an adult, or a perv Peeping Tom kid who sneaks out of his house because of his obsession with the girl who was killed?"

Charlie backed away. "So it wasn't my mom."

"No."

"Or my dad."

"It was the priest. Jen's friend. Your aunt's friend. I saw him."

Charlie leered at Bobby, his lips curling back to reveal his teeth. "You better be telling me the truth."

"I am. I swear."

Charlie took a few deep breaths and tried to steady himself. "Okay," he said. "We gotta tell my aunt. That's our only option. She'll know what to do. She'll call my dad's lawyer, and we'll tell them what happened."

"No!" Bobby cried. "I'll get in trouble with my parents for sneaking out, and the police will arrest me for spying on Jen. I've seen it in the movies. We can't trust the grown-ups."

"We have to. My aunt will make sure you don't get in trouble."

"You don't know that for sure. That priest is your aunt's friend. What if she takes his side over ours?"

"It'll be okay," Charlie said, trying to remain calm. "We'll talk to my aunt, and if she doesn't believe us, I'll call Donna Starr from the news. We're friends, and she'll help us. She won't let the police cover it up. We can trust her."

"Then let's just call her now."

"We gotta tell my aunt first. She's family, and she can call my dad's lawyer if she has to."

"She's going to think I'm a mental case."

"Not if you help catch the real killer and set my parents free. You'll be a hero, and no one will care that you're a stalker freak with stalker vibes and a stalker scrapbook. And neither will I."

Bobby laughed through his tears. "You sure?"

"I'm sure. We can trust her."

"Okay."

The boys ran out of the room, down the hall, and down the stairs.

"Aunt Sidney!"

"In the living room!"

Charlie sprinted down the hall with Bobby right behind him. He turned the corner and fell into the formal living room. "Aunt Sidney, you gotta hear what Bobby just told me. Mom and Dad had nothing to do with what happened to Jen. He saw the—"

He stopped, and Bobby almost ran right into him. Aunt Sidney wasn't alone.

Father McCall stood up from the couch and made his way toward them.

"Don't stop," he said. "Tell us what you wanted to say about your mom and dad. What happened? Who saw what?"

Charlie didn't have to turn toward Bobby when he heard Bobby make a noise. He knew exactly what the sound was. Bobby was so scared he was pissing himself.

The killer was in their house.

# 60

Susan and Liam climbed the stairs of a house that looked very much like the Moore residence. Large in both width and height, multiple roof angles and pitches, three chimneys, dozens of windows, cedar siding, everything done with impeccable taste. The porch was solid. There was no give in the wood whatsoever. She hung her shield around her neck, rang the bell, and waited. A part of her was certain she was chasing shadows and wasting her time, but she was also astute enough to know the doubt was more because the tip came from Donna Starr than that the tip was actually bogus. A kid who has a diagnosed rage disorder and an obsession with a homicide victim warrants a visit. Not to mention the fact that they'd found child-size footprints at the scene. They'd figured the prints to be Charlie Moore's since he'd confessed to being back there to bury the bracelet, but they weren't one hundred percent sure. Whether Donna was an annoying reporter or not, Susan had to admit that she'd done right by giving her a heads-up.

The massive oak door opened, and a frowning woman slipped onto the porch, shutting the door behind her. She looked at her visitors with pursed lips. Hands folded together as if in prayer.

"Mrs. Teagan?" Susan asked.

"That's right," the woman replied. "Monica Teagan."

"I'm Investigator Adler from the New York State Police."

"I know who you are. I've seen you on TV."

Susan smiled as politely as she could. "Of course. This is my partner, Liam Dwyer. He's assisting us on this case."

"What can I do for you?"

"We were hoping to speak to Bobby. Is he home?"

Upon hearing her son's name, Mrs. Teagan took a step back as if to block the entrance.

"What do you want with Bobby?"

"We just have a few questions for him. Of course, you're welcome to join us as his parent. Just need to follow up on a few things."

"About Jennifer?" Mrs. Teagan snapped. "What few things could you possibly need to follow up on with Bobby about Jennifer?"

Another smile. It was the best she could do at the moment. "I can explain everything. Perhaps we can step inside?"

Mrs. Teagan hesitated, then led them in. Everyone stopped in the foyer.

"Bobby's not home."

"Do you know where he is?"

"He went to Charlie's house. He asked if he could go, and I thought it would be good for Charlie to be with his friend since his parents are . . . away. I figured any kind of distraction or a chance to make things seem normal would be welcome."

"That's nice," Susan replied. "This must be hard on everyone in town."

"It's devastating."

The house had the same layout as the Moores'. They walked into the formal living room and sat on opposite couches. Susan took out her notepad.

"Do you mind if I cover something with you since he's not here?" she asked.

Mrs. Teagan shrugged. "I guess."

"We've come to learn that your son had a bit of an obsession regarding Jennifer. Did you know that?"

"Well, I wouldn't call a thirteen-year-old's crush an obsession. Obsession sounds like it's a bit more than it was."

"I think it was a bit more than a crush."

"It's not uncommon for a younger boy to start harping on about an older girl. It's all part of growing up and puberty and whatnot. Nothing the police need to be concerned with, that's for sure." Mrs. Teagan huffed out a laugh. "Do you think my son had something to do with what happened to Jennifer? That's ridiculous."

Susan's phone rang, and she glanced at the caller ID. It was John Chu. She let it roll to voice mail.

"Did you know about the notebook and pictures?"

Mrs. Teagan stopped chuckling. "What notebook and pictures?"

"We've come to understand that your son followed Jennifer around town taking pictures of her without her knowing. He even snuck out of the house and watched her at night through her bedroom window."

"My son is no *Peeping Tom*."

"I'm not saying that. I just want to talk to him and ask him if he saw anything while he was sneaking around that could help us."

Mrs. Teagan began chewing her bottom lip. She stared at the floor, then looked up at them. "He was sneaking out?"

"I'm just telling you what I heard. I have no proof."

Susan looked at Liam, and he nodded, both of them knowing the next step they'd have to take.

"Mrs. Teagan," Susan began. "We also know about your son's intermittent explosive disorder."

Mrs. Teagan closed her eyes. "So you think Bobby flew into a rage and killed her."

"I didn't say that either."

"You didn't have to."

"What kind of meds does he take for his condition?"

"He takes one antidepressant. Prozac. And one anticonvulsant—Dilantin. He's been on them for four years now, takes them once a day, and he's been fine. I can't remember the last outburst he's had. He didn't do anything to Jennifer. I don't care what you say, and you can't pin this on him."

"We're not pinning anything on anyone."

Mrs. Teagan got up from the couch. "I'm going to ask you to leave, and then I'm going to call my lawyer."

Susan's phone vibrated, and she looked at it as she rose to her feet. It was a text from John.

CALL ME ASAP

"Can I ask you what your son's cell phone number is?"

"No, you can't."

"Okay," Susan said. "Thank you for your time. We'll see ourselves out."

Susan and Liam walked out of the house and down the porch steps. The air was even heavier than when they first went inside.

"That went well," Liam said.

"You think?"

"We basically accused her child of stalking and murder, and all she did was ask us to leave. I'd consider that a win."

Susan put the phone on speaker and dialed John's number as they climbed inside her car.

"Hey, Susan." John's voice was crackling through the sedan's speakers. Reception was bad.

"Hey, John. Got your text."

"Remember that fabric we found torn in the woods right outside the scene where Jennifer Moore's body was?"

"Yeah. The black cloth."

"Right. We were able to analyze the fabric for any residues. We found traces of frankincense, benzoin, and myrrh."

"Okay."

"It's incense."

Susan was about to put the car in gear and pull out, but stopped. "Incense like from a church?"

"Exactly. The incense we found comes in brick forms like charcoal. It's mostly burned in high-end aromatherapy and church ceremonies."

Liam's eyes met Susan's. "Father McCall."

Susan looked down at the phone. "John, tell Crosby to call Yorktown PD and have them head over to Saint Mark's rectory. I want Father McCall brought in for questioning. If he's not there, have the unit stay put and pick him up when they see him."

"Understood."

"I'll follow up as soon as I can."

The phone disconnected.

"We heading to the rectory?" Liam asked.

"Yes, but first we need to stop at the Moore house. I have questions for Sidney Krittle about her priest, and if Bobby's there, maybe I'll see how he's doing too."

"Sounds like a plan."

Susan nodded. She could feel things getting close. "It does, doesn't it?"

# 61

Father McCall took another step closer, but Charlie couldn't move. He was frozen where he stood, his heart pounding in his chest, his breath quick and shallow. He was staring at the man who'd killed his sister in all the horrific ways he'd read about online. A priest. A man of God. A family friend. A priest had killed his sister and let his parents take the blame for it. A priest had killed his sister and made him believe his own mother and father could do such a thing to their child. That his best friend might be a monster.

"Charlie," Father McCall said softly. "What's the matter?"

Another step closer.

Charlie looked at him, but he couldn't get his mouth to work.

"What were you going to say?"

Another step.

"Charlie." It was Aunt Sidney on the couch behind them. "Honey, what's the matter? Talk to us. What's wrong?"

Charlie felt a hand on his arm, and he turned to see Bobby squeezing his sleeve. His eyes were begging Charlie to run. He motioned toward the patio doors.

Another step.

"Son, we can't help you unless you talk to us. It's okay. You're safe. No press is around. No police. What were you going to tell us?"

"Honey, talk to us. You're getting me upset. And Bobby, do you need to get cleaned up, hon?"

"You don't look good. Tell us."

"Please."

Another step.

Bobby tugged on his shirt, pulling him toward the patio doors. Charlie stumbled backward just as Father McCall reached them. The smell of urine was beginning to fill the house. Somehow that made everything seem real.

"Where are you going?" Father McCall asked. His expression changed just a bit. Charlie saw it. From care and concern to annoyance. To anger.

"Let's go!" Bobby finally screamed, breaking the calm that was teetering between the four of them.

"Come back here!" Aunt Sidney cried.

Charlie turned and followed his friend, both of them running through the rest of the house and bursting out the back patio doors. The humidity in the air hit them hard, but their adrenaline was too strong to quell their momentum.

"That's him," Bobby shouted as they ran, hopping over lawn chairs and thumping through a small flower bed next to the pool area. "He killed Jen!"

"Charlie!"

Aunt Sidney's voice echoed in the late morning air, but the boys ignored her. Charlie swiveled his head around to find Father McCall stepping out of the house.

"He's coming!" he cried.

"Get to the woods!" Bobby panted. "Split up and hide. Do you have your phone?"

"No. I left it in my room."

"Me too. Just run and hide and wait until dark, and we'll meet at the school in the smoking area around back. Then we'll go to the police."

"Okay. Go!"

Charlie ran into the first cut of brush and immediately turned right. He could hear Bobby behind him turn left, and his footsteps began to fade. Within minutes, he was alone, but he didn't stop running. He pushed through bushes, cutting himself on thorns and sharp branches. The pain was quick, but he ignored it, focusing on whatever was ahead, hoping he wasn't making too much noise. He hopped over tree roots and fallen birch, his arms pumping, his lungs burning. When he finally couldn't take it anymore, he slid under a holly bush and listened to see if he was being followed. His breath was loud and hard to control. He was gasping and wheezing, having trouble controlling it.

Leaves crunched on the ground.

A branch snapped.

Footsteps.

Charlie placed both of his hands over his mouth to try and keep himself quiet. He concentrated on breathing quietly through his nose. His heart was like a jackhammer in his skinny chest, and he wondered if he was old enough to have a heart attack.

"Charlie! Bobby! Where are you?"

Father McCall's voice echoed through the woods, and Charlie knew the priest was standing just inside the edge of the first tree line. He wasn't that far away, which meant Charlie had run too far to the right and not deep enough into the woods. He was exposed where he was lying.

"Boys! Where are you?"

Charlie carefully climbed to his feet and peeked over the holly bush. He couldn't see Father McCall through the thick brush. Hopefully the priest couldn't see him either. That was his chance.

"Come out! This is getting silly! I need to know what you want to tell us so we can help! Come on now. Let's go!"

Charlie duckwalked his way deeper into the woods, taking each step as carefully as he could while at the same time moving as quickly as possible. He was too scared to turn around for fear that he'd see the priest closing in. No, he had to keep moving. Get deep, hide, then meet Bobby after it got dark enough to move safely. That was the plan.

Footsteps began galloping through the first cut of brush, and Charlie knew Father McCall was running into the woods to find them. He had to keep going. He had to find a safe place to hide so he could get to Bobby and then to the police. It was the only way.

He was his parents' only hope.

# 62

Liam choked down the fear he didn't know was in him as Susan swung out of the Teagans' driveway and steered the sedan onto the road. Flashbacks of being chased through the streets of Philadelphia suddenly flooded his mind. The adrenaline he was feeling was reminiscent of what he'd felt when his brother—the brother he still couldn't believe was a killer—cornered him, and later, when his wife held him at gunpoint before eventually pulling the trigger. He absently rubbed the scars where the bullets had infiltrated his skin and tissue and ripped through his muscles and organs. Sweat began to form on his brow, and he wiped it away, cognizant that his breaths had become short and thin. He had no gun. He had no proper training. And they were closing in on their suspect.

They were only a few blocks from the Moore residence, and Susan stepped on the accelerator as she ended her call. "No sign of Father McCall at the church or rectory," she said. "Yorktown PD put a uniform outside both places. They'll grab him when they see him."

"Good."

*You need to tell her. Tell her how you're feeling. You can't let her think you have it under control when you don't. Tell her.*

"So we have a piece of clothing that traces back to a priest or a church," Susan said as she drove. "That's Father McCall. But we also have this Bobby Teagan kid who was stalking our victim and might even have pictures of her the night she was murdered. How does this add up?

Did the priest kill Jennifer? Did the kid kill her? Are the priest and the kid working together?"

*Tell her you're not okay. You're not ready for this. You're not trained for this. Tell her!*

Liam wiped more sweat from his face and noticed his hands shaking. "Maybe Bobby was in the woods doing his Peeping Tom thing and witnessed the murder. If Father McCall knows Bobby was there, then the kid becomes a liability. And that's one serious loose end hanging out there for him."

"So Father McCall keeps tabs on Bobby by offering to lend support to the Moore family through his relationship with Aunt Sidney and his friendship with Jennifer. He can't kill Bobby so soon after Jennifer, but he can't allow him to tell someone what he might've seen."

"Maybe."

*She needs to know you're not okay.*

"But where's the motive?" Susan asked. "What would make Father McCall want to kill Jennifer after growing so close to her over the last few years?"

"That's the thousand-dollar question right there."

Susan's phone rang, and she hit the button on her steering wheel to answer.

"This is Adler."

"It's John again."

"What's up?"

"Before, when you mentioned the name Father McCall, I remembered he was on our visitors' list from when we first entered the Moore property the day of the homicide. Frederick McCall, priest."

"Yeah, right. He was there."

"He was with Mr. and Mrs. Moore along with Mrs. Moore's sister and the son, Charlie. We took DNA swabs of everyone to eliminate them and find out if anyone else had been in the house."

They turned onto Route 123.

"What'd you find?"

"In DNA, the X chromosome that's passed from father to daughter is always the father's exact code for that generation. It doesn't change. You can draw a straight line of lineage."

"Okay."

"Susan, the DNA between the victim and the priest match. Father McCall is Jennifer Moore's biological father."

Silence hung in the car.

"Crime of passion," Liam whispered. "Just like we suspected all along. No premeditated motive. Something triggered in Father McCall, and he killed Jennifer."

"Thanks, John," Susan said. "You did good work. I'll call you later with an update."

"I'll be here."

Susan disconnected the call and stepped on the accelerator. Liam fell back in his seat and closed his eyes so he could concentrate. Focusing on the analysis calmed him, gave him back his sense of control.

"Father McCall knew he was Jennifer's biological father," he continued. "The coincidence is too improbable for him to be friends with the family and not know. Maybe he told her the truth, hoping to create some kind of relationship with her, but the shock of learning she was adopted in the first place, and then having to come to terms with who her father was might've been too much. Maybe she rejected him, and he couldn't handle it and he killed her."

Susan focused on the road ahead. "Which would make Noel Moore's story accurate. Mindy goes in the woods looking for Jennifer. She finds her dead and in her shock and anguish, she lies next to the body and gets herself bloody. Noel comes across her in the woods after seeing her flashlight and thinks she did it, so he helps protect his wife by covering the whole thing up."

"But how would Father McCall know Jennifer would be in the woods at that exact moment?" Liam asked. "And when did he tell her the truth about who he was?"

"I don't know," Susan replied. "But we need to get to the Moore house. Let's see what they know, and then have a talk with Father McCall. No more guessing. We need to find this guy and set things straight. It's time to figure out what really happened that night."

Liam nodded and kept his eyes closed, concentrating on his breathing, willing the wounds from his past not to surface once again.

*Tell her.*

# 63

Charlie had no idea if Father McCall was chasing him or if he was getting away. All he could hear was his breathing as he hurried through the woods, staying as low and hidden as possible. He couldn't move as fast as he wanted because he had to squat down, but he did the best he could, pushing his way through the brush and hoping he was being quiet enough to escape.

Sweat dripped into his eyes and blinded him. The saline burned, and he wiped it away with the back of an even sweatier arm. The air was thick and overbearing. The humidity was making it too hard to catch his breath as he continued forward.

He quickly hopped over a tree root, and when he put his foot back down to land, there was nothing more than a hole in the ground, camouflaged by a thin cover of moss. His sneaker sank into the hole, which was shin deep, and then, when his momentum was finally stopped, there were more roots underneath that bent his ankle in an awkward position with his toe pointing down and all his weight pulling away toward the right. The sudden drop into the hole made him lose his balance, and when he fell, he heard his ankle pop out of its socket. The sound came first, but the pain quickly followed. A wave of agony washed over him from the bottom of his body up to the top of his head. He'd never felt pain like that before. It was excruciating.

The blue sky dimmed for a moment as Charlie lay on his back and screamed without being able to stop himself. Somewhere in the back of his mind, he knew he was giving away his location and that Father

McCall would come for him, but he couldn't help it. Even when his inner voice was imploring him to shut up, he cried out, writhing in pain, his foot still caught under the ground at that impossible angle, his ankle swelling so quickly he couldn't untangle it from the roots and pull it back out. He was stuck.

Charlie bit his tongue to stop from screaming as hot tears streaked the sides of his face. Dead leaves and dirt stuck to him as he rolled from side to side, trying to figure out a way to free himself.

*He's coming. The priest is coming, and you can't move. You'll be easy pickings for him. He'll cut you up like he did Jen, and all you'll be able to do is close your eyes and wait for it. You're a mouse stuck in a trap. You're dead.*

"Help me!" Charlie cried, hoping someone else might hear him and come to investigate. "I'm in the woods! Help!"

*He'll definitely know where you are now. You're serving yourself up. Good luck with that. Even if someone else comes, they won't make it in time. The priest will get here and end you. You're making this easy for him.*

Charlie tried to move his leg again, and pain shot up through his entire body. He winced and began sobbing, knowing he couldn't get out.

"Help me. Someone."

He thought about his sister and the things he'd read about her online. The things Father McCall had done to her. Now the priest would do the same thing to him. There was no other way out, no other alternative than to wait and die.

Footsteps.

Charlie spun his head around and tried to see who was coming. He could hear leaves rustling and branches snapping. He knew it was Father McCall. He'd found him. This was it.

"Help!"

Charlie began tugging at his leg, every movement a flash of intense pain. He tried to fight through it and turn his foot so he could untangle himself from the roots, but nothing below his knee was working as it should have been.

The footsteps were coming closer now. Running. Charlie closed his eyes and waited. There was nothing else he could do.

"Charlie," a voice whispered. "What happened?"

Charlie opened his eyes to find Bobby at his side. Relief washed over him for a moment, then panic.

"I fell in this hole and I broke my ankle or something. I can't get it out. I'm stuck. And even if I get it out, I can't walk or run."

"Let me help."

"No. Just get to the police. Forget about waiting until tonight. Get some help. Go to a neighbor or get your mom to call 911 or something. They need to know what Father McCall did."

Bobby started to cry. "I can't leave you. He'll find you."

"I don't think we have a choice. You have to go."

"I can't."

"Go!"

Bobby stood up and spun around to run back into the woods. As soon as he took his first step, Father McCall emerged from a cluster of wild honeysuckles and grabbed him by the back of the shirt.

"Stop running!" he yelled. "Enough!"

Bobby was frozen with fear. Charlie looked on as the world around him dimmed again. He was going to pass out from the pain. That's the only thing he could think of. He took a deep breath, and before he closed his eyes, began calling for help as loud and as frantically as he could. The voice in the back of his mind laughed.

*None of this matters now. You're both dead.*

# 64

Susan pulled onto Hillcrest Court and immediately saw the cluster of news vans across the street from the Moore residence. She sped past them and into the driveway. In her peripheral vision, she could see reporters and camera operators scrambling to get another shot of her and Liam walking into the house, and she wondered how much B roll they really needed. All she was going to do was ring the bell and enter. She wasn't sure why that needed to be filmed.

"Father McCall is here," Liam said, pointing to a maroon Lincoln sedan parked in the space next to Sidney's Kia. "I recognize it from when we were at the rectory."

"Okay." She shut off the ignition and sat in the hot car. "I guess bringing everyone to the station until we find the priest is no longer relevant." She thought for a moment. "I can bring Father McCall in for questioning with the torn piece of cloth we found and the DNA match with Jennifer, but there's no way we can charge him if that's all we have. I think we should keep everyone here, split them up, and get individual statements. Maybe he'll get spooked and do something stupid like flee. Then we'll know we got him. But when we get inside, I plan to be blunt about everything so we can figure out the truth."

"Sounds good."

They got out of the car, and Susan approached the state trooper who was sitting in his cruiser in front of the barrier that kept the news vans at a distance. He rolled down his window as she approached.

"How long you been here?" she asked.

"Since eight this morning," the trooper replied. "Our barracks are rotating with Lewisboro PD. I got the day shift."

"You see the priest go in?"

"Yes, ma'am. The aunt and the boy came back about an hour ago. The priest arrived maybe twenty minutes after that. Noel Moore arrived about ten minutes ago."

Susan looked back at the house. "Noel Moore is in there?"

"Posted bail this morning. Taxi dropped him off about ten minutes ago."

Susan bent down closer toward the car. "Do me a favor. Call for some backup. Nothing crazy. Just a few guys in case things get heated in there. We think the priest might have something to do with what happened to the girl, and I don't know who's connected at this point. I'm going to start asking some pretty pointed questions once I'm inside, so in case things go sideways, I'd like a few more hands on deck."

"Yes, ma'am."

"And tell them to come in quiet. I don't want to alert the press that something might be going down. Just come in, park, and be ready."

"Roger that."

She walked back across the street while reporters shouted questions at her and the cameras kept rolling. Liam met her at the edge of the driveway, and as they approached the house, she noticed Liam stumbling more than walking. His hands were clenched into fists, and his face was red.

"Are you okay?" she asked.

Liam nodded. "I'm good."

"You don't look good."

"It's just this heat and humidity. I'm fine."

They walked along the flagstone path, up the steps to the porch, and stopped at the front door. Susan rang the doorbell and waited.

No one came.

She rang again, then knocked.

"Hello? State police. Can you open up, please?"

Nothing.

"I don't hear anything," Liam said. He had his ear pressed up against the side window, which was covered with a thin curtain. "No TV or talking or moving around. There's nothing coming from inside." He began to walk down the length of the porch, looking in the windows.

Susan knocked again.

"You see anything?"

"All the windows have curtains on them."

"Hello! State police!"

Liam stopped and cupped his hands against his head and stared through the windows farthest from the door. "I think we have a body down inside, but I can't see clearly."

Susan unclipped her holster and pulled her Beretta out. She kicked at the door, and on the third kick, the frame shattered and the door fell open.

"This is the state police!" she cried as she held her weapon out in front of her and entered the house. "Who's here? Sound off now!"

Silence.

She made her way down the hall and turned right into the family room. She could feel Liam behind her, and she was very much aware that he was unarmed. The situation was dangerous for both of them.

Sidney was lying facedown on the floor against the couch, a pool of blood surrounding her head like a halo. Liam rushed to her and felt for a pulse. "She's alive." He turned her slowly to try and get a better look. "Looks like a blow to the base of the skull."

Susan worked her way toward the kitchen and saw that the patio door was open.

"They're in the woods," she shouted over her shoulder. "Call for backup and have them come in from the northern end of the woods. Let them know I'm in there, and so are two kids. I don't want anyone getting shot by accident."

"You got it."

"Tell the trooper outside what's happening, and get an ambulance here for Sidney. If you guys see anyone come out from the back, grab them. I don't know what's what at this point."

Before Liam could answer, Susan marched out of the house, across the stone patio, past the pool area, and into the woods. As soon as she crossed the first line of trees, she heard a scream.

"Help me! I'm in the woods!"

She waited to try and determine which direction the voice was coming from. Luckily there was no wind, but she didn't know about the topography or how the sounds played there. She closed her eyes and waited, her grip tightening on her gun.

"Help!"

East. He was east. Susan turned right and ran as fast as she could, crashing through the bushes and vines that had spread in the late summer months. Staggering over branches and roots and shrubs and fallen dead trees, Susan concentrated on where the boy's cry was coming from, hoping there was still time.

"Help!"

Charlie's voice cut through the thick and humid air, and Susan tweaked the direction in which she was running just a bit north. He was deeper than she'd originally thought, but just how deep and how far she had no idea. The woods weren't massive, but they were large enough to get lost in if you didn't know where you were going. She could recall the map Sergeant Dunes had up on the wall in her workstation and the vast acres of nothingness beyond the small section of cul-de-sacs and gated communities where the Moore house stood. It would be an easy escape should one choose to keep moving northeast.

"Stop running! Enough!"

Susan dropped to her knees when she heard Father McCall's voice, deep and angry. They were only a few yards to her left. She could hear both of the boys crying and whimpering.

"You need to tell me what's going on," Father McCall said.

Susan crept closer, staying low and out of sight. She positioned herself between the trunk of an elm tree and a cluster of ferns. Hardly the cover she needed, but the priest was preoccupied with the boys and wasn't looking around.

Father McCall had Bobby by a fistful of his shirt. He'd pulled the boy close to him, but was glaring at Charlie, who appeared to be stuck in a hole at the base of a tree. She took a deep, quiet breath, held her Beretta out in front of her, and jumped up from her position.

"State police!" she yelled, cutting through the crying and the whimpering, aiming her weapon at the priest. "Let the boy go."

Father McCall turned and looked at her, focusing on who was standing before them, on the gun in her hand. He immediately let go as Bobby fell back and scrambled next to Charlie.

"He killed Jen!" Charlie cried. "Bobby saw it. He was there! He killed my sister!"

Father McCall turned toward the boys. "What are you talking about? I did no such thing. Is that why you were running from me? You thought I hurt Jennifer?"

Susan cleared her throat. "Father McCall, I need you to turn back around and face me. Put your hands on top of your head and get down on your knees."

The priest turned as he was told, but he remained standing, his hands at his sides. "Investigator Adler, there's clearly been some kind of mistake."

"Adler! Susan, where are you?"

Voices from the backup officers filled the air.

"Back here! Northeast!" she cried.

Father McCall took a small step forward. "I assure you, I—"

"Get your hands on your head and kneel on the ground!"

Father McCall began talking quickly. Panic was setting in. "Wait. Wait. Just wait a second. I need to tell you something. Something you should know." He took a quick breath. "I'm Jennifer's biological father. I'm her father. Me."

"We already know that."

"Then why would I hurt her?"

"All things we can discuss afterward. Right now I need you to get on your knees and put your hands on top of your head. Don't make this any harder than it has to be."

A shot exploded in the quiet woods, and before Susan could register what was happening, Father McCall was thrown backward off his feet, landing hard on the ground below. As soon as he landed, he stopped moving. Susan hit the dirt and crawled toward the priest.

"Hold your fire!"

Voices from her backup echoed as they got closer.

"Shots fired!"

"We have shots fired at our location!"

She got to Father McCall, but there was no sense in trying to examine him. The wound in his chest was massive and gaping. His heart had been torn apart. He'd most likely been dead before his body hit the ground. She knew that the caliber of weapon used was too large for the officers backing her up to have.

Someone else was in the woods.

Noel.

Before Susan could take a position, Noel came forward with his hands raised in the air. He knelt next to Charlie and Bobby and interlaced his fingers before placing them on his head.

"My rifle's straight back there about fifty feet," he said. "I'm done. I surrender. Do what you have to do."

Susan stood up and aimed the Beretta at him until her backup arrived.

"What was that?" she asked.

"That was me protecting my family," Noel replied. "And avenging my daughter's death. It's what any father would do." He looked up at her. "And now it's done."

# 65

She didn't want to draw further attention to what had already blown up into a chaotic scene around the property, so Susan decided to stick to her original plan and quarantine each witness in a separate room of the house rather than march them out in front of a press gathering that was turning more frenzied by the minute. She put Bobby in the dining room, Charlie on the couch in the formal living room with an EMT looking after his ankle, and Noel in the study. Sidney was taken to an area hospital to be treated for a severe concussion. She was conscious when she'd been lifted into the ambulance and stated that she didn't see Father McCall hit her. One minute she saw the boys running out of the house, and the next she was on the floor with EMTs tending to her.

A state trooper was placed with each person to ensure no one came in or out of the rooms at any time. It was important to keep them separated and their stories their own. Any cross contamination could muddle things and make an already incredible tale impossible to dissect. The story from the two boys had been simple enough. Bobby confessed to his slightly unnatural obsession for Jennifer. He talked about how he used to follow her around and take pictures for his scrapbook and was embarrassed to admit that his fantasies had evolved from innocent things like getting married and having a family together to the kinds of fantasies all boys his age eventually graduated into. When asked about his reluctance to go to the police after he witnessed Jennifer being killed by the priest, he explained that he was scared he'd get in trouble for sneaking out of his house to spy on her and was even more frightened at the thought of Father McCall getting out on bail to come after him. He also didn't think any adults would believe his word over a priest's. He confessed to everything with his mother sitting at his side, shock and sorrow having overtaken a woman who was used to quiet neighborhoods, safe spaces, and the tranquility of a white-collar town where violence was reserved for other places. Bobby wrote his statement, and they left without another word.

Charlie confirmed he was the source for Donna Starr. After what had happened between the police and both of his parents, he was too scared to accuse his best friend of murder until he was able to find more proof. He explained everything from finding out about the Darth Vader pendant in the woods, to Bobby's scrapbook, to the fight they had, to Bobby's eventual confession to having witnessed who killed his sister. He walked Susan through the chase in the woods and how he fell into the hole next to the tree and how Father McCall had tracked them down. A social worker was with him during the interview. When he was done, he was loaded into an ambulance that would take him to the hospital so a doctor could make sure he was okay.

Susan made her way into the family room and sat across from Noel, who was staring out the wall of windows that looked out onto his backyard just as his wife had done several days earlier, overcome by the vision of her daughter dead in the woods.

"They're out there again," he mumbled. "Police, medical, CSI folks, the press, the neighbors. Just like that morning."

"You created another crime scene when you pulled your trigger," Susan replied. "Now we have to process everything. Just like before."

"Yeah, I get it."

"I want you to walk me through what happened today."

Noel sighed and let his head fall back against the couch. He rubbed his temples. "My bail hearing was set for nine. Charlotte got me in and out, posted bail, and I took a cab home. I'd scheduled a call with Mindy's attorney for later this afternoon to start working on getting her released, and I was in the middle of sending Mindy a text when I walked in the house and saw Sidney on the floor. I started calling for Charlie, and I saw the patio door was open. I didn't really know what was happening, so I ran downstairs, got one of my rifles from my safe, and ran into the woods."

"Why didn't you go outside to the trooper who was across the street? Or call 911?"

"To be honest, I forgot that guy was even out there. I've become so accustomed to not looking toward the news vans. As for 911, you're right. I should've called. But at that point I was just reacting."

"What happened when you were in the woods?"

"I was walking, trying to see if I could find any tracks or anything, and then I heard my boy cry for help. I just beelined toward the direction the cry came from. Heard him a few more times as I got closer, then got into position behind a tree. I saw you there, so I thought everything was under control, so I was just watching. Then I saw him make a move, and I fired."

"He wasn't making a move."

"Looked like it from where I was standing."

"You killed that man in cold blood."

Noel lifted his head off the couch and looked at her. "I saw him making a move, and I thought you were in trouble. I shot him. I'll admit, maybe that felt better than it should because now I know I can bury my little girl with her killer having been brought to justice, but I saw what I saw. I thought he was making a move. I did it for my daughter."

Susan paused for a moment. "Jennifer was Father McCall's biological daughter," she said.

Noel blinked a few times, letting the sentence penetrate. "Are you sure?"

"Yes. We got a DNA match."

"So he killed her to keep his secret? She found out and he silenced her?"

Susan shrugged. "We'll never know. You killed him before he could tell us anything."

Noel took a deep breath and steadied his chin. "Then I guess it's case closed," he said. "One way or another."

---

Susan met Liam out by the pool area. The crowd of responding personnel was beginning to dissipate. Things were wrapping up.

"Find anything I need to know about?" she asked.

Liam nodded. "We found a large rock in a tote bag in the trunk of Father McCall's car. Looks like it has dried blood on it. Maybe a few hairs. I'm thinking that's probably the rock that caused the bruising on the back of Jennifer's head. John never found it at the crime scene. We also retrieved Noel's rifle where he said it would be. We're taking it in for further analysis, but the rifle was still warm from being fired. That's our murder weapon."

"I got a team heading to the rectory to go through McCall's things. I'd like you to go with them."

"Sure. No problem."

Susan looked up and saw Liam staring at her. His eyes were soft, kind. "What?"

"I get that it's a little late for coming clean, but I wanted to let you know that I wasn't okay back there. I don't know why it came over me as quickly as it did, but when we pulled out of the Teagans' driveway, I felt like we were getting close to ending this thing."

"We were."

"Yeah, but that brought on a pretty serious panic attack. All these things started running through my head about what happened with my brother and my wife and all the people who got hurt and everyone thinking I was guilty. It brought me right back to my dining room when I almost died myself. I was scared, Susan. I was scared, and I wasn't in the right mind to assist you when we went into the Moore house. I'm sorry."

Susan leaned in and rubbed Liam's arm. "Nothing to be sorry about. I didn't know we were walking into what we were walking into, or I would've had more sufficient backup. You're not armed, and I didn't realize I might be putting you in harm's way. That's on me. As for you panicking as we were closing in, I feel like that would be a normal reaction with what you've been through. No need to apologize. We're fine."

"Thanks."

"Go find me something in Father McCall's room."

Liam smiled, and he relaxed as if a weight had been lifted. "Copy that."

# 66

Word spread around town, and with the help of the major news outlets continuing to cover the story, Jennifer Moore's funeral was standing room only at Saint Patrick's Church. The ceremony was beautiful and heart wrenching all at the same time, as Susan figured funerals were meant to be. When it was over, scores of mourners followed the procession to South Salem Cemetery, where final blessings were cast and the family said their last goodbyes.

Susan and Liam hung back by a large marble statue of an angel, waiting until everyone walked back up the small hill to their cars and drove away. Noel, Mindy, and Charlie stayed at the grave a bit longer, Mindy resting her head on her husband's shoulder and hugging him close to her. She'd been a mess most of the day, breaking down twice and collapsing into Noel's arms. Now it was just the three of them, quiet, contemplative, all of them probably wondering how it could have come to that. When the last few cars left, the surviving Moore family stepped away from Jennifer's grave and made their way to the idling limousine.

"She still there?" Liam whispered as he scanned the cemetery, trying to see.

"Yeah," Susan replied, pointing. "She's heading over now."

They waited until the nurse pushed the woman's wheelchair down the concrete path and stopped at Jennifer's plot. Susan had first seen her outside the church, sitting across the street. She never came inside but was in the same spot when the funeral was over and everyone came out. Liam found her at the cemetery, hanging back by a small gathering of mausoleums, almost hiding while the last few prayers were offered. Now the cemetery was empty, and she'd emerged. Her head was bowed, and she was praying.

"Hello, Sister."

Sister Ann Michael slowly craned her neck as Susan stepped in front of her. The woman was thin, her habit framing her long face, showing nothing but skin and blue sunken eyes. Strands of brown hair peeked through, flickering in the wind. Her lips were thin and chapped, colorless. Despite the time of year, a thick blanket covered her from the waist down. She'd been beautiful once, but the cancer had eaten away at everything, leaving only remnants of life that would soon be snuffed out.

Susan showed the nun her shield, then put her hands up. "We just want a quick word, if that's okay."

Sister Ann Michael tapped the nurse on her wrist, and the nurse stepped away to give them privacy. Liam caught up, and he stood at the head of the grave next to Susan.

"It was a beautiful ceremony," Susan said. "You should've come inside. You'd have been welcome."

"I didn't want everyone looking at me, wondering who I was."

"Must've been hard to get up and out in your condition. Come all the way from New Jersey. I'm sure Jennifer would've been thankful."

Sister Ann Michael nodded.

Susan took a step closer. "These past few days had to have been rough for you. Father McCall and Jennifer. The two people who shaped your life the most dying within a couple of weeks of one another."

The nun closed her eyes. "You know."

"We do," Susan said quietly. "Father McCall was Jennifer's biological father. You were her mother."

The revelation hung in the air between them. Neither said a word.

"As part of our investigation, we had to go through Father McCall's belongings at the rectory," Liam explained. "We came across a file hidden in the back of his closet under a piece of rug he'd dislodged from the floor. The file contained photocopied documents of Jennifer's original birth certificate before the adoption was sealed. It listed him as the father and you as the mother. We also found correspondence he'd written to you explaining how he'd found Jennifer and his desire to make contact."

"He was a fool," Sister Ann Michael whispered. "To think he could try and reconnect with that child after all this time. It was crazy, and he was going against the church's orders to stay away and never speak of what we'd done." A thin smile appeared. "But I guess his bravery is one of the things that made me fall for him in the first place. His bravery and his inherent righteousness."

"Tell us about it."

A sigh. "I was thirty when Father McCall came to our church in Riverhead on Long Island. He was twenty-five, fresh out of seminary, and on his first real assignment as a priest. I taught at a Catholic school there, and he was one of our priests. Also doubled as a gym teacher. We became friends quickly, and though I won't turn this into a romance novel with seedy details, I will say there was a mutual attraction neither of us could deny but both of us knew was wrong. He began having doubts about remaining in the church, and as I tried to counsel him, our friendship became something more. We were together a few times, and I got pregnant. Confessing that to the pastor and my reverend mother was the hardest thing I ever had to do. Father McCall was sent to a parish in Montana to get him as far away from me as possible, and I was transferred to Sisters of Christian Charity in Mendham, where you came looking for me. I was hidden away in that convent until I gave birth. After Jennifer was adopted, they had me work at Helping Hands, where I remained. I never gave that episode in my life a second thought, and I worked every day for forgiveness, which I was finally granted by the archbishop. Everything was fine until one day I got a letter from Father McCall, telling me he was back in the area. That letter was followed by a phone call and then a visit. By then, no one around me knew what had happened. It had been almost twenty years, and the elder nuns from that time had passed on or moved away, so they just thought I had a priest coming to pay me a visit, which wasn't unusual."

"What did he say?" Susan asked.

Sister Ann Michael looked up at the sky. "Too much. He explained that he'd been working over the past twenty years to increase his status in the church in order to find Jennifer. He'd purposefully transferred over and over so when he did find her and requested a transfer to be near her, the church wouldn't deem the request unusual. He found her living in Lewisboro, I'm not sure exactly how, and he transferred to Yorktown. He befriended Jennifer's aunt as a way of gaining access. He told me he was going to tell his daughter the truth."

"Did Father McCall want you to meet Jennifer too?"

"Yes, but I refused. He kept sending me letters, giving me progress reports. I didn't want anything to do with it. I'd been forgiven, and I was happy where I was. After a while, I just sent the letters back, unopened. Next thing I know, you showed up at the convent, and I read the rest in the newspapers."

"Did he ever tell you anything about Jennifer that we should know before you started sending his letters back? Anything at all?"

"Just that she had been the one to seek him out and that he saw that as a sign from God. He said she was troubled and was beginning to open up to him. She was telling him things she felt she couldn't tell anyone else. In one of the last letters I read, he seemed torn between wanting to tell her the truth and keeping the secret because he felt like their friendship was growing into something more. He was afraid telling her his truth would ruin that. I didn't want to know anything else."

"And you started to send the letters back."

Sister Ann Michael nodded. She looked back and forth between Susan and Liam. "I realize I hadn't seen Father McCall in almost twenty years, and I readily admit that a person can change at any point in their life, but I just can't put my arms around him doing what I read he did. All that violence? Father McCall was a kind and gentle man. I know he wanted to have a relationship with Jennifer because he wanted to love her the way a parent is supposed to love his child. And the fact that he was contemplating keeping his secret because he knew he could help her more as her priest and friend flies in the face of someone doing something so selfish and horrific. He didn't do it. I'm sure of it."

Susan turned into a breeze that swept across the cemetery and let her hair blow back from her face. "I wish I could assure you that you're right," she said. "But the facts are the facts. We have an eyewitness."

The nun sighed, sadness washing over her. "I know. Sometimes people make mistakes."

"You mean Father McCall."

"I mean your eyewitness."

# 67

Susan and Liam left the cemetery and went straight back to the Lewisboro station house. The spare office they'd been using was full of boxes that held the remnants of their investigation. Susan had lifted a few of the boxes off the desk and set up her laptop. About an hour had passed, and she found herself scrolling through the initial crime scene pictures John Chu had taken upon first arriving at the Moore house the morning Jennifer's body was discovered. She landed on the photograph of Noel Moore's luggage that had been left just inside the front door. She'd looked at that picture about half a dozen times, and something about it had always made her stop and examine it, but nothing had ever clicked. This time she saw it, only she wasn't sure exactly what she was seeing.

"Son of a bitch," she mumbled.

Susan clicked to enlarge the photo, then did it again, and waited for the pixels to right themselves and come into focus. The luggage tags on Noel Moore's bags were from a different flight. He was supposed to have been on flight 725, and she remembered the flight number because that was Lieutenant Carter's old badge number, but the tags on the luggage in the crime scene photo read flight 226. The date stamped was a full day early too.

"Noel Moore was home a day before anyone knew he was here," she murmured to herself. "And he lied to us about it throughout the entire investigation."

Liam suddenly ran into the office and placed on her desk the bracelet Charlie had buried. "I found something," he said. "This bracelet isn't a regular piece of jewelry. It's a recording device. I was going over all of our evidence to tag and inventory, and I found a tiny microchip that was placed behind one of the fake diamonds. I started examining it a little closer and also found a speaker. It's hidden in one of these star charms. The chip gets fed into a USB adapter to upload the recording onto a computer. I didn't know that was a thing, but I looked it up, and apparently they make watches and necklaces and rings that all do the same thing."

Susan picked up the bracelet and placed it in her palm to study it. "What's on it?"

"I don't know," Liam replied. "But I pulled the chip. Let's have a listen."

# 68

***Five Months Earlier***

*Jennifer walked into her father's study and carefully closed the door behind her. Her father was sitting behind the oversized oak desk he'd found at an antique shop in New Hampshire two ski vacations ago, head down, writing something in a notebook. His computer was on, and the combination of the weird light coming from the monitor and the bifocals he was wearing made him seem ten years older than he was. He'd been so focused he hadn't even heard her come in. She held her stomach and tugged on the edge of her sweater, pulling the arms up to ensure the bracelet she was wearing wouldn't be hidden. She couldn't believe she was going to record her confession, but she knew she needed evidence in case the conversation turned into a "he said, she said" kind of thing. She just wanted proof that she'd at least come forward before telling anyone else outside the family.*

*"Dad?"*

*He looked up, startled, quickly pulling the glasses away from his face. A smile appeared. "Jen, you scared me. I didn't hear you come in."*

*"Can I talk to you a second?"*

*"Sure. Just let me finish logging these current valuations. Sit down."*

*Jennifer sat on the leather sofa opposite a giant bookshelf and watched her father finish writing. She was three months away from graduating high school and so ready to move on. Ready to start a new life. Ready to run away from the current one.*

*Her father typed something in the computer, then tossed his glasses on the desk and rocked back in his seat. "What's up?" he asked, his smile never wavering.*

*Jennifer's stomach lurched again, and she thought she was going to throw up right then and there. She was so nervous. Her hands shook as she struggled to take steady breaths.*

*"I have to tell you something."*

*"Okay."*

*"I don't want you to get mad, and you need to understand that I tried to solve this problem on my own. But I think I'm going to need your help. I've been trying to keep this my secret, and I didn't want to involve anybody else, but I can't make it stop. No matter what I do or what I say or where I go, I can't make it stop. I need you."*

*She started to cry, and her father got up from his chair and walked over to the couch. He sat beside her, pushing her hair out of her face, his smile fading as his concern grew.*

*"You can tell me," he whispered. "Is it the drugs again?"*

*"No."*

*"Are you in trouble?"*

*"Yes, but not how you think."*

*"Whatever it is. Tell me."*

*"I'm afraid you're going to get mad."*

*"I'll try not to. I promise."*

*"I wanted to solve this myself. I'm just not strong enough."*

*"Tell me."*

*The tears came harder now. Her head swam with images of him touching her, yelling at her, commanding her to do things. It all felt like a dream. A nightmare.*

*"It's Uncle Artie."*

*Her father slid closer. "What about him, honey?"*

*"He's not who you think he is."*

*"What do you mean?"*

*More crying. "This is so hard."*

*"Tell me."*

*She looked at her father as tears blurred his image and her voice shook in her throat. "He . . . he keeps touching me. He won't stop." More tears that poured forth. "Artie was the guy who got me pregnant. He's been molesting me for the last six years."*

*Her father was frozen for a moment, then recoiled, slowly easing himself away from her to the opposite end of the couch. He stared at her, his mouth open, his brow furrowing.*

*"Artie?"*

*"It started when I was twelve. He'd come over when you were out and sneak up to my room. He'd babysit for you and Mom. He told me we were playing a special game that only special people are allowed to play. After the first few times, I knew it was wrong. It didn't feel right. I told him I didn't want to play anymore, but he said I had to. He said that if I didn't play the game with him, he'd tell you and Mom, and you'd send me away to live in a foster home with strangers and adults who beat children and starved them. Obviously, I believed him at that age. But then, when I got older, his threats became more real. He'd pick me up from school or meet me when I was walking home from hanging with my friends. He threatened to kill you and Mom if I said anything. He threatened to kill Charlie. He told me that he was a pillar in his community, and I was a drug addict slut who no one would believe. So I kept letting him do it. And the more I let him do it, the more drugs I took and more alcohol I drank. I tried to numb myself."*

*Each word became easier, and Jennifer didn't want to stop her momentum. She kept talking, letting everything spill out, pushing herself forward.*

*"Even after he got me pregnant, he didn't stop. Two days after Mom brought me home from the clinic, he made me . . . perform on him. He's sick, Dad. He's sick, and I can't take it anymore. I'm leaving for school in a few months, and I wanted you to know in case he tries anything before I leave. I can tell he's getting nervous about me keeping the secret. I already threatened him that I'd tell someone at Duke once I was safely away from him, but then*

*he just threatened to kill you guys again. I don't want anything to happen to you or Mom or Charlie. I almost told Father McCall, but I can't tell if Artie's threats are real or not, and I don't know if he's connected enough to make something happen to us even if he's in jail. Then I started thinking. If I tell you and we go to the police together, he can't hurt you or the family. Please, Dad. I need you to help me."*

*She waited for her father to leap up from the couch and throw something across the room. She waited to see the anger and outrage. She was expecting to have to calm him down and keep him from getting in the car and driving over to Artie's house to kick his ass. Instead, he calmly closed his eyes and dropped his head between his knees.*

*"This can't be happening," he muttered.*

*"It is. It has been. We have to go to the police."*

*"No. We can't tell anyone. We can't."*

*Jennifer wasn't sure how to respond. "What? Why?"*

*Her father lifted his head and looked at her. "I need him. The firm needs him. This is bigger than you."*

*Jennifer couldn't believe what she was hearing. "Dad, Uncle Artie is a child molester. I might not be his only victim. We have to tell someone."*

*"There's nothing we can do." Her father climbed off the couch and stood in front of her, hands shooting around the room in a panicked fashion. "Everything you see around you—this house, our cars, your clothes, your college—it's all because of the partnership I have with Artie. He has the network of clients we need to be successful. He brings them in, and I land them. That's how it's always been. He can't close without me, and I can't get the opportunities with those people without him. We're codependent when it comes to our success, and, honey, we're extremely successful."*

*Jennifer stood up, the tears coming again. "I'm standing here telling you your best friend has been molesting me since I was twelve years old, and you're telling me to shut up about it?"*

*"For the good of the family, yes. You don't understand. You always had this level of success in your life. But I came from nothing. I worked hard*

*to provide for you all, and I'm not going to let anyone take that away from us. We keep this secret, and we keep living how we've become accustomed to living. I'll handle Artie, and I'll make sure he never touches you again. But you need to bury this secret. You don't tell anyone else. This is between you, me, and Artie, and it'll end now. I promise."*

*"Dad," Jennifer choked through her sobs. "You can get other clients. You don't need him."*

*"I do. We do. This family does. Just like his family needs me. That's the way it is."*

*Tears were turning into rage. "I want him to go to jail. I want him to pay for what he did to me. He got me pregnant. Maybe I need to call the clinic back and fix my paperwork. Maybe I need to identify who the father is. Maybe I need to make a confession to my priest."*

*"That would be catastrophically stupid."*

*"He can't get away with this."*

*"Yes, he can. I know that's not what you want, but sometimes in life the bad guy gets away with it. The faster you learn that, the faster you'll understand how the real world works. I'm sorry, but this is how it has to be."*

*"I can't believe what I'm hearing. I need you to be my dad right now. I need you to be my protector."*

*"I am protecting you. I'm protecting our entire family. If he goes down, we lose our firm. And if that happens, we're ruined. We lose everything. I can't have that. I'm sorry."*

*Jennifer felt like she was going to throw up. She ran toward the office door to try and make it to the bathroom, and as she passed her father, he grabbed her by the arm, stopping her momentum and swinging her back so they were face-to-face.*

*"I love you," he said as his eyes glassed over. She could smell his stale breath when he spoke. "I'm sorry this happened to you, and I will put an end to it, but the secret gets buried right here. Right now. Do you understand?"*

*"Yes."*

*"Are you sure?"*

*"I'm sure."*

*He let her go, and Jennifer bolted from the office and into the first-floor bathroom. She knelt over the toilet, waiting to throw up, but the nausea passed. After a few minutes, she stood up and looked at her reflection in the mirror over the sink. A still-shaking hand reached up and touched the bracelet on her wrist. It wasn't the proof she was expecting, but it was proof of something.*

*It was proof that she was on her own.*

# 69

Susan and Liam took the elevator up to the seventh floor of what was soon to be the Hudson Tiers condos on the west side of Manhattan. When the doors opened, all she saw were the mountains of New Jersey across the way and the Hudson River below. The wind was strong as it blew through the half-built structure, whipping down empty spaces and narrow corridors that would one day be marble hallways leading to luxury homes for the elite.

Noel Moore and Artie Breen were standing next to each other, looking out across the river, when the elevator doors opened. They turned around with smiles on their faces, but those smiles faded when they saw Susan, Liam, and four NYPD police officers step off.

"Investigator Adler," Noel said as he approached the group. "I'm sorry—I didn't know you were coming. I was about to have a meeting."

"Yes, I know," Susan replied. "With Uriah Sitchel. I'm afraid he can't make it. We met him at the airport when his jet landed. He's back at the station giving a statement about you leaving his house on Sanibel Island a day earlier than you told us."

Noel held up a hand. "I'm sorry, I—"

"Don't bother," Susan said. "One of the photos from the crime scene shows the bags you came home with and left by the front door. The luggage tags from the airline show a different flight number and date. Uriah simply confirmed the information we already had and told us you'd asked him to lie and say you left the following day. He thought you might've been seeing another woman, so he agreed. Even after you were arrested, he never believed you were capable of murdering your own daughter. Airport security footage did the rest."

Artie pulled away from the edge of the building and joined his friend. "What's going on here?" he asked.

"We're done with Jennifer's case," Susan replied calmly. "We know what happened."

"Yeah, no shit. That priest killed her."

"Actually, Father McCall is innocent. I'm here today to set the record straight."

Artie shook his head. "Seriously, what are you talking about?"

"We already knew Noel killed Father McCall. I was an eyewitness. But, as impossible as it sounds, we also know Noel killed Jennifer."

Noel staggered back, away from them. "I'm sorry—I did what?"

"And we know about Arthur molesting Jennifer since she was twelve years old. We know she was threatening to tell others about the sexual assault, which made her a serious liability that needed to be dealt with."

Artie huffed a laugh, but his eyes betrayed him. He was scared. "You can't be serious."

Susan walked past both of the men and looked out the windowless frame. The sky was so blue, and the sun was out. She could see boats on the river below. Such a perfect day.

"Listen," she said. "I don't want to turn this into a *Columbo* episode where the three of us have to play a game of cat and mouse and I hint at some evidence I have, and you play dumb, and we go back and forth wasting everyone's time. I don't have the patience."

Noel chuckled as his voice cracked. "Okay, but I swear I don't know what you're talking about."

Susan dug into her pocket and came away with a thin gold bracelet. She laid it out across her palm, turned away from the building's edge, and showed him. "Does this look familiar?"

Noel examined it and shook his head. Artie did the same.

"This was one of Jennifer's bracelets. In fact, this was the bracelet Charlie buried as a prank that got Jennifer out in the woods that night in the first place. That's why we have it. We had to keep it as evidence. Looks like a normal piece of jewelry, but it's actually a recording device."

Liam hit a button on his phone and held it up.

*"Please, Dad. I need you to help me."*

*"This can't be happening."*

*"It is. It has been. We have to go to the police."*

*"No. We can't tell anyone. We can't."*

*"What? Why?"*

*"I need him. The firm needs him. This is bigger than you."*

*"Dad, Uncle Artie is a child molester. I might not be his only victim. We have to tell someone."*

Noel's face went pale.

"That's not true," Artie snapped. "I never touched her."

"It doesn't matter what you say at this point," Susan replied. "We have proof. Wouldn't be here if we didn't." She walked back from the open window, her heels clicking on the concrete. "We executed a warrant at your house this morning, Arthur. The knife used to stab Jennifer is from an old butcher block set you keep with your tools in your garage."

"I told you, I was home with my family the night Jen was killed."

"Yeah, I know. But your partner was here in New York. In the woods behind his house, as a matter of fact, when everyone else thought he was in Florida. You gave him the knife because you guys knew he couldn't use one of his own. Once he called 911, he'd be a suspect until he was cleared. Needed to have that full set of knives in the kitchen, and no one could be caught on a store security camera buying a knife. That wouldn't be smart."

Artie's eyes narrowed. "Shut up."

"Jennifer's confession to her father changed everything. As soon as she told him what was happening, she became a liability to your very wealthy company. She threatened to tell Father McCall, and she was also about to travel six hundred miles away, where there was no way you guys could keep her in check. Not at that distance. Jennifer was a maturing woman who was becoming self-confident and already showed the courage to tell her father what happened. If she could tell him, you knew she could tell others, and you weren't about to risk the firm and the money and your freedom. She had to be silenced, so Noel took care of it, thinking he had the most solid alibi a guy could have."

All the color had run out of Noel's face. He took a step back. "I didn't . . ." But his voice trailed off.

"How did you know she was going to be out in the woods that night?" Susan asked Noel. "What were the odds of her being out there and you being home early that night?"

"It was supposed to be a home invasion."

Artie's eyes widened with horror. "Noel, shut your mouth!"

Noel shook his head as he began to talk through his tears. His voice was distant, as if he was in a trance. "We weren't sure if Jen had already told the priest, but we also knew we couldn't take any chances. Not with her going all the way to Duke with this on her mind. I'd put a stop to it, but Jen wouldn't let it go. She kept begging me to go to the police, and when I'd refuse, she'd get angry and threaten to go herself. She said she didn't need my permission. She just wanted my support. I wouldn't give it to her. No matter how hard I tried to convince her it was over, she wanted to see Artie behind bars."

"So you came home to fake a break-in."

"Stop talking!"

Noel nodded. "We knew Father McCall visited one of his parishioners every week to have dinner and sit with her to pray until eleven o'clock. Rosa Clarkson. Father McCall had mentioned that he visits her each Wednesday to keep her company after her husband died. She lived on the other side of the park, and we knew Father McCall took a shortcut through the park to see her. He told us he liked the walk in the summer. We figured if we killed Jen and left a piece of cloth that tied Father McCall to the scene, someone might see him in the park or Rosa could confirm he was in the area that night, and the case would be open and shut. Artie got into the sanctuary of the church one night when we knew Father McCall was out with Sidney and stole one of the robes."

"And you were going to stage the home invasion, kill Jen, and leave that piece of cloth we found in the woods somewhere in the house."

Another nod. Noel was crying now. "I was waiting that night until all the lights went out, and then, out of the blue, Jen came running through the backyard and into the woods. I followed her to the clearing and took advantage of the situation. I killed her outside the house, which was like a gift all in itself. Mindy didn't have to see it. Charlie didn't have to see it."

Susan took a step closer. "But Mindy did see it. You didn't anticipate Mindy getting up in the middle of the night and walking back there."

"This is crazy!" Artie screamed. "I can't hear any more of this bullshit! Father McCall is the killer."

Susan looked at Artie. "Come on, Mr. Breen. We're past that at this point. It was a good try, though. I'll give you that. You were the one who suggested we look into the priest the night I met you at the train station. You knew we would find that bit of cloth at the murder scene and the rock in his trunk, and between that and him being in the vicinity, he'd be charged. Only thing is, when we were at your house this morning, we found the cassock that you stole. A piece of it was missing. About the size of the piece we found in the woods. It's over. We have all we need."

Artie looked at her, his eyes blazing.

She turned back to Noel. "As soon as you found Mindy in the woods with Jennifer's blood all over her, you knew your plan was in chaos. You had to bring her back inside, but in doing so, you contaminated the entire house, which meant you had to get everything clean before calling 911. But you also had to keep Mindy quiet. She couldn't tell the police what happened because things would get too complicated, so you kept feeding her a slight overdose of the Valium she'd already been taking. You got her into an almost constant state of unconsciousness, and when she tried to commit suicide, you knew she'd be deemed mentally unstable, so whatever she said would be dismissed anyway. She stayed quiet, you controlled the narrative, and everything was working until we found the items in the drop ceiling. At that point, you had to play victim yourself, and you turned your wife in. Your innocent wife. Another person you were willing to send away for the good of your fortune. What a guy."

Noel looked at Artie, and his expression changed. No more confusion or anguish or pain from such loss. His face was stone. His eyes were cold.

"You did this," he said to his partner. "All of it. And I can't stand the lying anymore. You made me kill my daughter. For what? Money? Success? We don't deserve any of it. Not after what we've done. I can't do it anymore, Artie. I can't live with it."

Artie approached Noel as the NYPD officers moved in.

"You're a coward," he said. His face was tense, the veins in his forehead popping. "She wasn't even really your daughter. She was nothing."

Both men were placed in handcuffs.

Artie laughed aloud. "You don't have anything that'll stick," he said. "Even Noel's so-called confession is a bunch of garbage. With the lawyers I can afford, they'll shred your case. Jennifer's dead, so all you have is that tape, which means nothing. It's her word against mine. And that stuff you found at the house won't even make it to court. My lawyers will get that thrown out. You don't have anything on me. I wasn't even there that night."

"Maybe," Susan replied. "But even if you beat this, do you think any of your clients are going to come back to you? You'll eat up your money on your high-powered attorneys, and if you beat the rap, you'll have nothing left. Clients were already starting to leave when Noel got arrested. What do you think they'll do when they hear about what the other partner was doing to his buddy's daughter?"

Artie opened his mouth to say something, then shut it again. Susan gently pushed him onto the elevator and waited until the officers escorted Noel on as well. She hit the down button and watched as the car began its descent, leaving her and Liam alone on the seventh floor.

"Nice job," Liam said. "I think we shook them good."

"I hope so," Susan replied. "I hate to admit it, but Arthur's right. He and Noel are both rich enough to get away with what they've done. Their lawyers will be a team of Charlotte Walshes."

Liam smiled and put his arm around her shoulder, hugging her close to him. "Have faith, Investigator Adler. We're the good guys, and it's our turn to win. For Jennifer."

"Yes." Susan hugged him back. "For Jennifer."

# 70

Charges were filed against Noel Moore and Arthur Breen, and what had once been regional media interest in a small community quickly ballooned into an international, jaw-dropping news story. When Artie's sexual assault allegations became public, another victim came forward—the twenty-year-old daughter of a friend from his old neighborhood who said he'd molested her on three separate occasions when she was twelve and Artie was visiting his parents. Artie eventually confessed under the weight of the evidence that had been stacked against him. His cooperation, along with the power his attorneys wielded, would lead to some kind of a deal. Noel hadn't been so lucky. He'd confessed from the start of his arrest, and although his cooperation was appreciated, he was afforded no accommodations when it came to the list of felonies he was being charged with. In the end, deal or not, Susan and Liam had found Jennifer Moore's killer, and their case was finally closed.

Susan stood over the kitchen table pushing candles into the sheet cake she'd gotten for the twins' birthday party. They'd decided to have the picture from the puppy puzzle printed on the cake, and it had turned out better than expected. She could hear the kids playing outside, screaming with excitement, running, climbing, laughing. Everything had gone off without a hitch.

All the kids who'd been invited came. The petting zoo staff was spectacular. They'd set up a station in the side yard with the reptile exhibit. Goats, sheep, and rabbits had been put in a pen for the kids to walk into and pet. And the pony was in the front giving rides. The kids went from station to station and back around as many times as their little feet could carry them, playing with the animals, learning about life on a farm, squealing when the lizards and tarantulas came out, and hopping on the pony. Beatrice was in charge of the chickens and let the kids come into the coop, where she showed them the place she collected the eggs in the morning and the beds where the chickens slept at night. Everyone was having such a great time. It couldn't have gone any better.

There was a knock on the sliding door, and Susan spun around to find Eric standing outside. She waved her ex-husband in and turned back to the cake, placing each candle on the outer perimeter of the picture, spacing them as evenly as she could.

The door slid open, then closed again.

"Hey," he said.

"Hey."

Footsteps brought him farther into the kitchen.

"Great party. You did a fantastic job. Everyone looks like they're having fun. And the twins are thrilled."

"It did turn out okay, right?"

Eric gently touched her arm, and she looked up at him.

"Look," he said. "I know with everything that's happened with Tim and now with Casey breaking her wrist, you're questioning things. The whole work-life-balance stuff."

"Can you blame me?"

"You're a good cop, Susan. I read about the Jennifer Moore case in the paper. The fact that you can solve that case and still be standing here putting candles on a cake is astounding to me. You're one hell of a woman."

"Thanks."

"I'm serious. When I take the kids on the weekends, I can see how much you're influencing them. Their manners and kindness and love. That's all because of you. That's the household you built, and I'm so proud to be their father." He took her by the shoulders. "Don't stop being the person you are. You're an excellent cop and the absolute best mother. All at the same time. Truth be told, I wish I could be more like you. You're amazing. Don't forget that."

Susan looked past Eric and saw Casey running across the yard grasping a handful of balloons, laughing and skipping along, her sling bouncing along with her. Pride suddenly overtook her. Yes, she did have a good family. One of the best.

They hugged, and Susan was grateful to have Eric in her life, despite the divorce and him leaving her for another woman. She didn't want them to be the couple who were always fighting. He was Casey and Tim's father as much as she was their mother. They were a team. That's how it would have to be.

A car horn began to blow outside, and Susan pushed Eric away, smiling.

"It's time," she said.

"For what?"

"You'll see."

She took him by the hand and walked back outside into the yard.

"Okay, everyone!" she called. "We have one more animal for the petting zoo party. Casey and Tim, are you ready?"

The twins bounced up and down. They could hardly contain their excitement.

"We're ready!"

"What is it?"

She winked at her kids. "Okay, Liam!"

The black-and-white puppy made it around the side of the house before Liam did, its wiggling little body pulling on its leash, tail wagging, desperate to lick faces and join in the fun.

"It's a puppy!" Casey screamed.

"Just like we wanted!" Tim screamed.

"Happy birthday!" Susan laughed. "Meet Ollie."

All the kids ran over to the puppy and knelt beside him, petting and hugging and kissing him simultaneously. Ollie couldn't get enough as he flipped and squirmed and jumped, licking as many children as he could.

"A dog, huh?" Eric said with a giant grin plastered on his face. "You're even braver than I thought."

"Brave or dumb," Susan replied. "I haven't decided yet."

Liam handed the leash to Tim and made his way over to Susan and Eric. The two men shook hands, and the three of them watched as the twins gushed over the newest member of their family, leading Ollie around the yard as the other kids screamed with delight.

"The perfect gift for a petting zoo party," Liam said.

"Thanks for picking him up for me."

"Sure, no problem. Team Adler, right?"

She laughed and rubbed his arm, then, before she could talk herself out of it, took his hand in hers and interlaced their fingers. It felt like she thought it might. It felt right. She squeezed his hand as she looked at the kids. He squeezed back.

"Amazing party and an amazing gift," Eric said. "Thanks for inviting me."

"You never need an invite," Susan replied. "We're family. Always."

Eric broke away and joined the kids as they ran around to the back of the house with Ollie chasing them. Susan watched them go, then looked at Liam.

"I need you to do me one more favor," she said.

"Getting dog hair all over my car wasn't enough?"

"No. Sorry."

"Okay, what it is?"

She pulled him toward her. "I don't want you to think I'm crazy or weird or jumping the gun or making things more difficult than they have to be."

Liam laughed. "What's the favor? The suspense is too much!"

She took a breath. "I want you to kiss me."

Liam stopped laughing and looked into her eyes. "Right here? At a kids' birthday party? In front of everyone?"

"What better place?"

He bent down, and she closed her eyes as his lips gently touched hers. Time slowed as she leaned into him. It felt like forever before he pulled away, and she took a moment to savor something she hadn't felt in a long time.

"I've been wanting to do that for a while," she whispered. "Truth be told."

"Funny," Liam replied. "I've been wanting you to want me to do that for a while. Truth be told."

"See how things like that work out?"

"Like it's meant to be."

"Like it's right."

The kids came back around to the front of the house, Ollie running alongside them, jumping and wagging his tail, loving every minute of this new game. They screamed and laughed and hopped and ran, enjoying what had turned out to be the perfect party. Beatrice walked up to Susan, and when Liam wasn't looking, motioned at the two of them holding hands. She winked, and Susan winked back. There was no need for words. Susan knew that in that moment, she didn't have to find the balance between being a cop and a mom and a daughter and a lover and a friend. She already had. It was this. And it was perfect.

# THE END

## ACKNOWLEDGMENTS

So this is the place where I usually thank the people involved in the creation of this book, and I'll do that in a minute, but first I want to talk about writing a thriller novel filled with villains and murder and sorrow and fury during a worldwide pandemic. In a word, it's been surreal. I write for entertainment. I write to allow my readers an escape from real life, even for a quick chapter or two. I take great pride in pulling my readers away from the stresses of their days and giving them access to a made-up world where the action doesn't stop and the whodunit aspect of the story always keeps them guessing. During this pandemic, the act of writing this book did for me what I hope reading it does for you. I hope I've distracted and entertained you, because if I was able to help someone escape for even just a moment from all the carnage the world has known this past year, then I feel I've done my job. I hope I've helped with my past books, and I hope I help with this one. I am forever in debt to my fans and readers. I do this for you. Always.

Okay, let's thank some people . . .

To my agent, Curtis Russell of PS Literary Agency. You continue to advocate for my work and career. Thank you so much for your feedback and advice. I appreciate you more than you know.

To my editors, Megha Parekh and Caitlin Alexander. You see things in my stories that I never do, and when you coax them out of me, a much better book is born. Thank you for your feedback and encouragement. You guys are truly the best.

To Sarah Shaw and the entire Thomas & Mercer team. Thank you for everything you do out in the marketplace on behalf of my books.

Again, a special shout-out to the line editors and copyeditors who keep things in order so the story is one cohesive (and readable) thing. What you do is special, and I'm truly thankful for your help and suggestions.

To Crystal Patriarche and the BookSparks team. Thank you for helping spread the word about my books to the farthest reaches of the book-reading community.

To Melvin Padilla Jr, chief of police, Bedford Police Department. Thank you for the tour of your department and for answering my questions about certain procedures that aided in my story. I appreciate your help.

To Investigator Brian Martin of the New York State Police, Manhattan, and Sergeant Peter Deak, NYPD. You guys have become my law enforcement go-to team for any and all police-related questions. Thank you for sharing your insights on the inner workings of the police departments you work for and for responding to my texts about murder, protocols, and random procedural questions. If I got anything wrong, that's on me.

To my family and friends, who continue to support me. I love you all and thank you from the bottom of my heart.

To my wife, Cathy. Here's book number four, babe. Can you believe it? I love you, and I love sharing every step in this journey with you.

To my two daughters, Mackenzie and Jillian. You're growing into young women now, and I'm so proud of the people you're becoming. I love you both so much.

To my father, Marty. Stay strong. I love you, and I'm here any time you need me. Day or night. The family will get through this. We all have your back.

Finally, I'd like to take a moment to acknowledge my mother, Mary Farrell, who lost her battle with cancer on May 1, 2020. She's been my number one fan since I was writing short stories in grade school and my biggest advocate once my books were out in the marketplace. Even on the morning she passed, she was telling one of her nurses about my books and showing them the links where they could buy copies. I miss her very much. We all do. I know she's looking down on us and blessing us with her love as she did when she was with us. I love you, Mom. Always and forever.

Happy reading, all.

MF